JOURNEY

✦ To ✦

SUNYATA

Mountains,
Monsoons,
and
Magic

A NOVEL

Other Titles by

DENISE MIHALIK

Albums

Light of Compassion

JOURNEY

to

SUNYATA

Mountains, Monsoons, and Magic

DENISE MIHALIK

New Jersey

For information about this title or to order other books and/or electronic media, contact the publisher:

Sound Awakenings LLC
denise@soundawakenings.com

Cover and interior design by The Book Cover Whisperer:
OpenBookDesign.biz

979-8-218390-78-5 Paperback
979-8-218390-79-2 eBook

Printed in the United States of America

FIRST EDITION

CONTENTS

Based on a True Story . . .

Prologue

Nepal

Allie wasn't able to pay much attention to the opening ceremony. Although she heard the chanting and drumming, saw the movements of the shaman, and smelled the incense, her mind was elsewhere. *Spin on the skull?* One part of her felt ready—*I came all this way . . . I **have** to do this*—but another part was terrified. *What if nothing happens? What if I don't spin? And why do all these people have to watch?* Fear and negativity rose again to dominate her internal dialogue. Allie gulped a full, smoke-filled, stale breath and coughed through her tight throat. *I'm an adventurer now. I'm not going to stay in this chair because of fear.*

"Allieji, you are next!"

She saw her teacher's mouth move with the invitation, but her pounding heart drowned out his words. Allie rose tentatively, as if the curtain were rising on a performance she had forgotten to prepare for. *This is Indiana Jones stepping into the unknown cavern, the black abyss, the pit of awakening . . .* Her mind raced, as fear tried to drown her.

Soaked from both rain and sweat, all eyes followed her, and she hoped it didn't look like she'd wet her pants.

Babaji took her hand and instructed, "Step careful. Slow. Feet together, bend knees." Whispering and coughing rattled in the background.

The grains of rice felt both comforting and painful on the soles of her feet, which barely fit into the large "skull," a giant tortoise shell that represented the highest incarnation of the shaman's teacher. It felt brittle, and she was concerned that her weight would crack it.

She tucked into a deep, awkward squat, but couldn't find her balance. *This is impossible!*

"Breathe, Allieji, is okay." Babaji knelt next to her, offering support. His fingers tapped her shoulders gently at various times to help her remain upright. She was an apple floating in a wild river current, destination unknown.

The shaman's penetrating gaze hooked her, and, although she had no idea what was about to happen, she knew that an intention was needed.

Purification. She forced a smile.

Silence. Not even a mosquito dared to buzz by.

As if the shaman sensed her intention and readiness, he began to intone a deep, guttural chant in an unfamiliar language. The primordial, soothing groans put Allie at ease. A conch sounded loudly, then a rattle and a drum. Suddenly, pressure pushed into her forehead, like a tug from some radiant force above. Not uncomfortable or frightening, just new, strange. She began to spin—slowly at first, as if this new energy were testing the waters.

"Oh my God, I'm spin . . . ," words died as she simultaneously felt tension in her forehead and steadiness through her feet.

The spinning accelerated and thinking-Allie disappeared. There was no other place to be. No body, arms frozen around her knees. She could feel Babaji tapping her occasionally to keep her upright. The room, a blurry, spinning vortex of energy, she went 'round and 'round, and time ceased. No control, nor did she know who or what was making her spin.

"Oh, my God! Oh, my God!" whispered Babaji.

At the sound of his voice, a thought moved through her in slow motion: *What - is - happening*? She hadn't been scared, but his reactions were not comforting.

The faster she spun, the more quickly and loudly he repeated, "Oh my God!"

CHAPTER 1

The Adventure

New Jersey, Six Years Earlier

Allie was not an adventurer. In her 34 years on the planet, the most she'd explored was stepping onto the opera stage to perform in front of thousands of people. But she didn't consider that adventure. It was her well-practiced art. As she'd don her costume, makeup, and wig, already sweating from the heavy fabric, her excitement would rise along with her fears. She juggled not only a well-rehearsed opera character, but also the untamed characters of her mind—masters of manipulation, all singing a competing aria: *You're not prepared enough. What if you blank out in front of everyone? Run out of breath? Miss the high note in the third act? Could be a disaster.* The "what ifs" were endless.

With the audience rustling in the background, and her mind rattling front and center, the curtain would begin its slow ascent. There was no turning back. Allie's heart raced and her butt cheeks trembled. She both loved and hated that moment as she stepped onto the stage and into the mouth of the wolf. *In bocca al lupo.* But that wasn't adventure. That was blatant stage fright trying to suffocate her love of singing.

Allie's "unadventurous" life took a sharp turn a few years later, when her husband proclaimed his love for his mentor and invited her to live with them. The trio would work it out, he proudly rationalized. Forced to take a final bow from the man she loved, Allie couldn't leave fast enough and temporarily moved in with her mother. But that certainly wasn't adventure. That was heartbreaking survival.

The building crescendo of sudden change knew no mercy for Allie's planned, "safe" life. Her father's alcololism, that had been bubbling in the background for much of Allie's childhood, rose like a river in a torrential downpour and began to drown them both. The loving father-daughter duet she once knew had now shifted into a devastating trio and the alcholol knew no mercy. Sucking her dry, the leech that was once her father cried for help, only to refuse it. As much as she tried, she couldn't save him; it was all she could do to save herself. That wasn't adventure either. That was suffocating despair.

In just a matter of months, the tornado of life rumbled over her and crushed the natural twinkle in her clear blue eyes, stole her trusting smile, and hardened her heart. Deflated, she could no longer sing an opera aria. Her mental chatter, however, bellowed a strong and long lament. Incessantly.

It's no wonder Allie was drawn to Babaji's radiant

confidence and steady presence. His smile, a monsoon of compassion, could pulverize boulders and create pathways for seeds of love to sprout. He simply played a singing bowl, chanted a soothing tone, and invited her to breathe. He called this Sunyata. Emptiness. But this, too, was not adventure. This was a return home. A remembrance.

So how could she *not* go to Nepal, when Babaji called with an invitation six years after their first meeting? The image of a peaceful pilgrimage in the serene Nepali mountains watered inner seeds of renewal. The curtain had fallen hard on her life, but now it was time for it to rise again. This indeed promised to be an adventure, and she hoped it would be the adventure of a lifetime.

ALLIE FIRST ENCOUNTERED BABAJI in her home state of New Jersey shortly after losing her father. One might call it fate or coincidence that her favorite yoga studio was the first on the east coast to host Babaji's sound healing concert. Intrigued, she couldn't sign up fast enough. She had been exploring meditation as a coping mechanism, and, as a result, purchased a small singing bowl. Compared to the complexities of an opera aria, it was simple. She'd sit and rub the edge of the bowl with its wooden mallet and sing "OM," steady, operatic, and vibrant—striving for the perfect tone that was long programmed into her psyche. Yet when she sang with the singing bowl, her body relaxed and her mind settled.

Sometimes while singing the "OM," she could hear a second voice groaning from deep within her throat, as if there were a shaman trying to voice himself, sharing an ethereal duet from within. His rough, imperfect OM reached from a depth that seemed to come from another dimension. She could almost see him: a bare-footed mountain man, slight in height with dark, wrinkled, sunbaked skin and short black hair. Something was trying to express itself, but . . . *Nah, it's just a play of harmonics and my vivid imagination.*

ON THE DAY OF Babaji's sound healing concert, Allie arrived early, tingling with nervousness but not understanding why. Low lights glistened on forty or more singing bowls that were thoughtfully arranged, fanning out in a triangular pattern from smallest to largest. *What an orchestra!* She chose her spot in front of the largest bowl and was tempted to sit in it.

Lavender-scented candles invited relaxation as the last rays of the setting sun warmed the room. Content to be close to the mother of all bowls, Allie couldn't help but lie back and close her eyes as the room began to fill. The shuffle of people with their soft chatter lulled her into a light sleep.

"Welcome, dear friends. Rest, please, on mat. Find comfort." A velvety baritone wafted over her, startling her awake as it filled the now packed room.

In a thick Nepali accent and sweet English, he continued,

"Taking a few deep breaths together—inhale full, exhale complete."

"*Bonnnnnnnngggggggg!*" He sounded a large bowl. "*Bonnnnnnnngggggggg!*" and then another, "*Bonnnnnnnngggggggg!*" and another. Their vibrations traveled through the wood floor, transforming Allie's yoga mat into a magic carpet.

"As if you float on a cloud of sound, relax, listen, let go," the smiling Babaji continued.

"*Bong, bong, bong.*" Several smaller bowls sounded, and Allie felt well-patterned tensions begin to melt. "We practice Sunyata, empty of all thoughts. Let go of everything. Take full inhale, and slow exhale."

He began to chant softly; a deep, guttural sound in an unfamiliar language. *Beautiful.* Her mind began to quiet. Words relaxed and disappeared . . . she was being taken away by the sound . . . *How?* And suddenly she was asleep . . . or was she?

A deep voice, speaking louder now: "Rub hands together, cup eyes, take long, full breath."

Too relaxed to keep up, Allie hesitantly came back to the space, to the concert. An hour had passed. *Wow!!! It's over already? Where was I?*

Although she could hear the bowls and the sound of Babaji's voice, Allie had been floating in a timeless place that was light and free. Free of everything. Free.

I really feel healed. Of what, she didn't know.

"You look so peaceful."

Allie opened her eyes to see a small woman standing over her. She leaned heavily on a tall, curved cane, and, although her skin showed signs of age, the stranger sparkled like diamond dust, seemingly ageless. Her soft peach dress danced in the breeze. But, there was no breeze.

"I've never seen such peace in someone's eyes," the radiant stranger delighted.

Allie could only smile back, unable to find words. A numinous love surrounded her, and she closed her eyes to revel in the sensation. *Peace.* She had long forgotten the feeling, and her body welcomed the once-familiar ease, warmth, and contentment.

Allie opened her eyes to say goodbye to the stranger, but she was already gone.

In this unusual mental quiet, Allie was embraced by inexplicable recognition of returning home; as if her lifetime of musical studies were meant to lead her to this very moment.

Allie was in the unfamiliar but lucid space of the heart, free from the judge, critic, worrier, and other chattering characters of her mind. She had clarity but no details. And that was ok. *Whatever just happened, whatever this is, I need to learn more.* Taking a deep breath, she tried to memorize this precious space, because she knew from experience that, once those chattering characters became involved, they would spin like a pinwheel in a hurricane, sabotaging her with doubt and fear.

Leaving the concert to drive to her mother's house for Sunday dinner, Allie basked in what Babaji referred to as

Sunyata. Emptiness. Her mind quiet. Blissful. A sensation she had experienced as a child, sitting barefoot high in a tree on an endless summer day. For the first time in a long while, she knew she was going to be ok. *Thank you, thank you, thank you.*

"SORRY I'M LATE, MOM," she called out, reentering the world of bustle and sameness.

"Glad you're here, Al. Can you mash the potatoes?" Her mom didn't mean to be terse, but life weighed heavily on her, and habitual worry pursed her lips.

"Happily." The steam from the potatoes felt fresh and alive.

"Where were you?"

"Oh mom, I just attended the most beautiful and unique sound healing concert at my yoga studio."

Her mother froze. "A healing concert? What do you need to heal?"

Allie mindlessly dropped the masher, and time stopped. *What do I need to heal? . . .* Her thoughts screamed but her voice remained silent. *Well, I'm grieving the loss of my husband and father. I can't talk about it, because we always pretend everything is okay. I feel like a complete failure, because I left my father to die alone. Oh, and my husband cheated on me, and I don't have a career because I haven't been able to keep up with everything. I'm working four jobs to barely pay my rent. What do I have to heal? What **don't** I have to heal?*

In that brief, timeless moment, Allie realized that her

mom didn't know how broken she felt. Or maybe she did, but she didn't know how to deal with it. Allie was always her shining light, the positive only child who saw the best in people and situations. But now that light was covered by a shadow, and no one, including Allie, knew how to cope with it. Everyone put up a front of happiness, but for Allie, it was a shell about to shatter.

Continuing the masquerade, Allie responded, "I don't know. I guess it just felt good to relax. Is Aunt Lillian coming tonight?"

One month later, Allie's mom died from a hidden, fast-moving cancer, a loss that even the most tragic opera aria couldn't express.

What do you need to heal? Her mother's words reverberated. *Grief. Too much loss. Too soon. I'm drowning in grief.*

CHAPTER 2

The Invitation

Until Allie met Babaji, she knew nothing about Nepal. An east coast girl, through and through, she was in love with the Atlantic Ocean and had no desire to travel further east. She'd had to look on a world map to learn that Nepal bordered China and India.

"Nepal is magic," Babaji told Allie as she began her studies with him. About 5'4" and all smiles, his sincere presence lit up even the darkest place–including the void within Allie's heart. "There is no mountains like our mountains. The land speaks to you. It heals you."

Healing. That word was not a part of her vocabulary. Allie associated it with the Bible, miracles, or radical recovery, not everyday life. Healing didn't happen to someone like her. And it certainly didn't happen for her parents. She called out for it, even begged for it, but healing passed them by. As far as she was concerned, it had its chance, and failed.

It wasn't until she met Babaji that "healing" slipped into her vocabulary and started to reveal its potential.

"Pay attention to breath." Babaji gazed into Allie's eyes, into her soul. "Anyone can ring singing bowl, but not everyone pays attention to breath." On this particular day, Babaji dove deep.

"Healing is happening in this moment. For you. Do you feel? Is magic."

Allie didn't feel. She was numb to her own numbness.

"You can't make happen. You become it. Don't do. Be the breath."

Tears filled her eyes.

"Breath is gateway to healing. You feel it now?"

Flashes. Faces. Memories tucked deeply behind a locked door. It was too much. She didn't want to unlock it.

Babaji sensed her struggles. "Physical body needs breath. But emotions and many thoughts changes breath, steals breath. Suffocates body. You need to notice your breath, Allieji. This is the key to healing. Is gateway. Precious gift. When we don't have breath, we don't have life."

Allie knew breath. She'd developed the control and capacity to sing a three hour opera, but here, looking into Babaji's warm eyes, she struggled.

He sounded a small bowl. "Follow sound and empty mind of thoughts."

She listened.

"Sunyata. You are not your thoughts. You are more than that."

"But, when I try to empty my mind . . ."

"Don't try. Just be."

Allie didn't understand, but she tried not to try.

ALLIE DROPPED HER OPERA career to focus on learning Babaji's methods and traditions. Friends feared she had joined some crazy cult. She didn't care. Ringing the bowls helped soften the shards of glass in her heart, and that was reason enough to sit with ten very expensive metal bowls and several soft mallets. It was also reason enough to jump for joy when her beloved teacher called late one night with a special invitation.

"Allieji," Babaji beamed over the phone, adding the customary "ji" out of respect, "I have big surprise! You need take a deep breath."

Allie obeyed. "Okay, breath taken. What is it, Babaji?"

"Is time for Nepal trip. Are you ready to go?"

"Really?" She leapt out of her seat. "Yes. Yes! I'm beyond ready to go!" Allie hadn't expected to ever hear those precious words. "When?" Even if it were tomorrow, she would make it happen.

"October best. Weather perfect." His excitement enhanced his accent and he spoke his next words slowly. "I ask, since you are one of my first student, can you be organizer of trip?"

Flushed and humbled by his trust, she stammered, "I-it would be my honor?" mistakenly ending her response as a question.

Allie wanted to assert, *Sure! I'm up for anything. Bring it on.* But, just making a grocery list was adventure enough these days. Organizing a group's travel arrangements to Nepal was not on her wishlist.

Babaji must have sensed her hesitance. "Is okay, Allieji, I have cousins in Nepal who is organize tours. We need work with them. You organize from U.S., and they organize in Nepal. Is perfect." His trusting confidence always made things sound simple.

Allie's butt cheeks began their familiar tremble. *Pathetic! Breathe Allie. Just trust.*

"And I have friend who is travel agent. He is happy to help with flights," Babaji sparkled.

Perhaps it was his kind, gentle manner, or boundless energy. Or maybe it was simply his welcoming smile. Whatever it was, Allie was enchanted the moment she met him, and now she was finally being given the opportunity to realize a dream that only moments ago she began to embrace.

Taking a deep breath, she tried to match Babaji's confidence but instead squeaked, "It would indeed be my honor, Babaji."

THE PLANS FOR THE October trip fell into place smoothly and

easily, making Allie feel foolish for ever doubting herself or Babaji. But as soon as she started to relax, as if on cue, the phone rang late one evening.

"Allieji, is new development." Babaji's confident, smiling tone was stifled with insecurity.

Her stomach jumped.

"I learn Gai Jathra Festival is August and . . . ," he paused, his discomfort palpable. "Is sometimes September but this year is August and is most auspicious festival of year. Most sacred." He dwelled on the *M* in a most endearing way. "Is to honor my mother."

She knew his mother had passed away a few months ago.

"My family is blessing her new journey during festival. All village comes together." He paused again. "I need to go in August and is too long for me to stay until October. I'm not sure how to make both trips."

Allie's heart dropped to her toes.

Last-minute changes were typical of Babaji. He juggled many different commitments and lived so much in the present moment that practical details frequently slipped past him. Change was his only constant.

"I hesitate to ask you and others to join me," he continued.

"Why?" A moment of hope.

"Is monsoon season and travel is *very* difficult."

Silence.

"How difficult do you think the travel will be?"

In his thick accent, he boomed, "Indiana Jones difficult!"

She could sense his wide smile as he yelled through his laughter, "Roads are very muddy and travel is dangerous. Indiana Jones would have fun time!"

Allie couldn't help but join Babaji's contagious laughter, but . . . *How serious is he?* Quick flashes: Indiana Jones outrunning falling boulders, flying spirits, snakes. Lots of snakes. Then: dense jungles, monsoon rains, and mudslides. Her heart fluttered, and the tone of her laughter shifted to include something else . . . fear. She swallowed hard. "Oh."

Laughter died down, and a heavy silence floated in the air.

You've always wanted to be an adventurer! I have? Don't do it. There might not be another opportunity. How bad could it be? You want adventure, not a monsoon. Allie's mental chatter enjoyed the familiar debate. "Well . . ." *Don't do it.* "If we're going to Nepal . . ." *Are you crazy?* "We might as well have an adventure!" *Yup, crazy* "I think we should ask the others!"

"Oh, yes, Allieji, I am so happy!" Relief washed over Babaji. He didn't like to disappoint anyone. "Yes, ask others. See what they say! It will be grand adventure!"

Within a few days, all nine pilgrims, including Allie, were on board. Monsoon rains were not going to stop them from supporting Babaji at his time of loss, and they embraced the "Indiana Jones Adventure" as the motto of the trip. In addition to the mosquito netting, water purifiers, bug spray, backpacks, Pepto-Bismol, and other supplies, Allie also decided to buy the hat!

CHAPTER 3

The Flight

As one of the organizers of the trip, Allie did her best to actually be organized and had been packing, rearranging, and repacking for months. But as much as she tried, on the day of departure, she couldn't find anything. The one exception was her most treasured and necessary resource for traveling halfway across the world: her trusty snack bag. Anyone who traveled with tall, lean Allie knew that her appetite was insatiable, and she always had to have a snack on hand, just in case. She packed a wide variety of dry goods: instant oatmeal, peanut butter packets, graham crackers, pretzels, power bars, nuts, dark chocolate, raisins, gum, and ginger candies. If she were going to outrun snakes and mudslides, she would need the extra nourishment.

Allie met another of Babaji's students, Kate, at Newark Airport to begin the long journey that was estimated at a mere 36 hours. Even without the snakes and mudslides, Allie might devour her snacks well before landing in Nepal. With first class a dream for another lifetime, Allie and Kate squeezed next to each other at the back of the plane and filled their space with travel pillows, snacks, and a selection of carefully chosen books—none of which were ever read.

Allie hugged her knees into her chest and tried not to anticipate the next 14 hours in the air. "What brings you on this grand adventure, Kate? Any special intentions?"

"Oh, I'm just . . ." Kate paused as she usually did. The wheels turning slowly in her mind. "You know . . . ready to be a sponge. To absorb. All that I can." She smiled and gazed into the distant future. "I feel like I've waited all my life for this trip but I have no idea why." She took another long pause. Allie rested her head back, waiting patiently. "Nepal, this tradition, the singing bowls . . . they were never on my radar, but after meeting Babaji, everything shifted, like puzzle pieces coming together." Kate's eyes glistened.

"You know, I feel the exact same way . . . Nepal was never on my radar. I didn't even know where it was! But there **is** something that's calling me, for sure. It's like, I had NO choice. I **needed** to go on this trip."

"Right?" Kate chimed in, "It's like destiny, or something."

"Destiny, for sure, and I hope destiny has a plan, because I have grand expectations for this trip.

"Oh yeah? What are you hoping for?"

"Not much really, just complete healing and peace."

"Gotcha. I suspect destiny can help you out with that!" Kate added playfully. "What are you hoping to heal?"

Suddenly Allie's seat felt way too small. *That question again. Should I? Do I really want to go there?*

Kate nodded as if she heard Allie's thoughts. "We've got all the time in the world. And if you want to heal it, it'd probably help to name it."

"I've . . . got . . . tons of forgiving to do. My parents' deaths, my divorce, anger, betrayal, loss. You name it. And as much as I work through it, it just keeps coming up. Over and over again, like simmering lava from some void or endless pit. I don't think I'll ever truly be free from it."

Allie mindlessly hugged herself. "I miss me. I miss who I used to be––light, positive, hopeful. Trusting. It's gone. I didn't know I could lose it. But, it's gone." She sat for several breaths with her flashing memories. "Actually, I feel free when I sit with the singing bowls. I put the bowl on my chest and all I hear is the sound. I feel the vibrations, and they shake away the stress and shatter the swirling thoughts. For a few moments the uninvited characters in my head take a break. I think that's the precious *Sunyata* Babaji references."

"Yes, Sunyata. Emptiness. Just being," Kate added. "That quiet for me is so rare. I think you know, I'm a cancer survivor and sometimes that fear comes in, the 'what ifs,' you know? And as soon as I can, I get one of my bowls and sit with it. It's so peaceful. And it's healing." Kate took another long pause. "I'm sorry but I didn't know about your parents. Did they die in an accident?"

"No. It's . . ." Allie sighed, "wow, uh, well . . . My mom died very quickly from cancer. Esophageal cancer. By the time they diagnosed her, it was already too late. She was gone within a month. My dad . . ." She exhaled slowly and steadily, letting go of her plan not to bring up any of her baggage during the trip. "He died alone. We were estranged at the time." Allie stared into the distance at nothing. "It's beyond complicated, but now I know how people become homeless, even when they have families. He was an amazing person. I loved him so much. But he lost himself to alcoholism, definitely fed by mental illness. I had a few distant family members berate me, they called me a deserter, but what they couldn't see or maybe chose **not** to see, was that he was killing both of us." She glanced toward Kate, still not seeing. "The man who was my father became lost in the shell of his body. I wouldn't wish that on my worst enemy. To experience it or to observe it." She was trembling as she always did when she talked about it. "I never stopped loving him, but I couldn't help him, and he died from it. Alone." Allie swallowed tears. "I'm trying to forgive myself for not being able to help either of my parents . . . and I honestly don't know how I can go back to my life as it is."

So much for leaving it behind. Allie shivered. "So, when I found this tradition and the peace that it immediately brought me, the healing, it was a great gift." Allie met Kate's glistening eyes. "There ya go. How about THAT for light conversation to pass the time?" Allie laughed nervously, putting her Pollyanna persona back on, digging into her purse for a tissue.

Kate took her hand. "Friend." Allie waited patiently for the next words, "It's an honor that you shared with me. Thank you. You're on this trip to heal it. I know it!"

"Thank you for listening and thanks for being my travel buddy." Allie perked up, momentarily forgetting her heavy baggage. "I can't believe this is finally happening! This . . . 'pilgrimage' . . . I know, I just KNOW there's going to be healing in the land; the beauty, the magic, AND . . . the Indiana Jones holy grail . . . Sunyata!"

They raised their hands to offer up an air toast, "Here's to the grand adventure!"

And then, within minutes, Kate was snoring lightly.

Allie pulled out a power bar and let her mind drift back to her most recent session with Babaji...

"Healing is many things, Allieji. Many wanting physical healing. Relief. But it goes deeper. Through breath, we go beyond our experiences, our story and remember who we truly are."

Allie was attached to her story. She couldn't put it out of her mind.

"In this moment, where are you, Allieji? Are you really here or are you in your past?"

"You caught me, Babaji. Both."

"This is why universe brings us together now." His smile

warmed her. "Reliving stories, we pretend we can change things. Make it better. Right? But, we only miss present moment." His eyes teared up. "You have breath, Allieji. Do you not see this gift?"

"I know it's a gift. I want to live twice as hard in honor of everyone who's no longer here, Babaji, but . . ." she paused, afraid to voice it. "I don't deserve it. Okay? I feel . . . failure. There, I said it. I failed. My marriage, my parents, my struggling career. And it feels like two concrete weights, pulling me to the bottom of the ocean."

Babaji knew. He could feel the weight of failure. See it, like she was covered in oil. But he knew she was more than that.

"Where do you feel this in your body?"

"My heart, my gut, throat." *Every cell.*

"Lie here, on floor, Allieji." He placed a bowl on her chest and began to play it, chanting softly.

Her tensions immediately softened.

"This is not your burden to carry."

She wasn't ready to believe him.

"Feel bowl vibrations and follow sound."

The vibrations tickled her toes and fingers.

"This sound, you can't hold on to it, even if you try. It needs to pass through. Right?"

Allie nodded, eyes closed, already in a relaxed state.

"Life experiences pass through each of us, some good, some bad, some horrible, some amazing. And we have choices." He continued to sound the bowl.

"You try to hold onto story and stay in failing of past. But you are here now. You are alive, beautiful, and have breath to live this life. You have more to share, Allieji. More than concrete. You are love and you are loved."

Somewhere deep in her being she knew this was true.

WHEN THE PLANE LANDED in New Delhi, India, it had been twenty-four hours since leaving her home, and it showed. Smudged eye makeup, unbrushed greasy hair, and a loud grumbling stomach had her craving a hot bath and a real meal. She fortified herself with the knowledge that there was just one more short flight––to Kathmandu. Only an eight-hour layover to go.

After mazing their way through customs, Allie and Kate optimistically handed their tickets to a second security agent, whose frown would have melted Frosty on the spot. With piercing eyes he barked, "Go to counter."

The two friends followed the guard's gesture to a small, deserted seating area next to an abandoned counter. It was close to midnight, and there was no agent of mercy to be found there or, apparently, anywhere.

"There's no one there. What do we need? We've already been through customs and security."

"Stamp. Must have stamp." And with that declaration, he firmly waved them away.

With the path forward temporarily blocked, the two

weary women gathered their luggage and obediently sat on the cold, metal chairs in the deserted waiting area.

All was quiet with only a few random travelers passing by. Fresh exhaustion settled in, and Allie sat back in the hard chair and closed her eyes.

On the edge of sleep, the radiant stranger from Allie's first sound healing concert long ago appeared before her closed eyes. She was smiling and leaning on the tall cane. *"You look so peaceful. I've never seen such peace in someone's eyes."* The clear, soothing voice echoed gently and pulsed in Allie's mind's eye like a heartbeat, moving further and further away until . . . it was gone. In her semi-sleep Allie resolved, *I'm going to find that peace again.*

CHAPTER 4

The Connection

"Hah!" Kate's gasp jostled Allie awake. "It looks like there might be some action soon," Other transfer passengers, mostly local men, filled the area around them. "Have you noticed that we're the only foreign females? Actually the only women here. "

"Yes . . . I wonder . . . Oh, there's someone at the counter." Two uniformed men appeared, fussing busily around the computers. Kate rushed forward. "Let's go!"

The ladies, anxious to get closer to their connection and the last leg of the trip, rushed to the counter, first in line . . . or so they thought. The other travelers confidently followed suit and clustered around them. With the men continuing to push forward and past them, they realized an organized line was not anyone's priority, let alone personal space. The two lone American women stood in the crowd of men, tickets in hand, patiently waiting for the necessary stamp that would let them pass through to the final gate. Allie, with her blonde hair and height of 5'9", towered over everyone, yet both women remained invisible to the agents as they waited on the men.

Impatiently, Kate shoved up to the counter and, standing inches from the agent's face, yelled, "Excuse me?" Nothing. "Excuse me!" No response. "This is ridiculous." Mimicking the men's technique of pushing into the line, she grabbed Allie's arm. "We need to be more aggressive. Come on."

Kate plowed through the crowd with Allie grasping Kate's sleeve, in an attempt to stay connected.

"Excuse me. Oops, Sorry. Excuse me," Allie muttered as she burrowed into the crowd, steamrolling her suitcase over someone's foot. "We just—sorry about that."

"We got this," Kate thundered over her shoulder.

Finally reaching the other agent, they parked themselves side by side, extended their elbows out, like twin cormorants drying their wings, and protected their space. Together they thrust their tickets onto the counter.

No more messing around.

The agent regarded them blankly and robotically stamped their tickets. The two women turned to each other triumphantly. Kate winked. "Mission accomplished."

"And so it begins," Allie answered.

CULTURAL LESSON #1
Orderly lines are irrelevant.
Do not fail to be aggressive, especially in crowds
of men, and use elbows when necessary.

With stamped tickets in hand, they marched back to the security gate. The scrutinizing guard watched as they placed their luggage onto the belt. Grumbling an order, another guard rushed over and hovered over Allie's backpack, glaring at her.

Oh, come on. After three check points, what on earth's left to be found? Allie's stomach turned over at the sight of armed guards, who looked ready to fire. Vague stories of people being unnecessarily detained in third-world countries flooded her. Had she done something wrong? Still rattled from the aggressiveness at the counter, she was on high alert.

"Open," the guard commanded Allie, pointing at her bag.

Allie's nervous fingers fumbled open the bag and the challengers dove in, searching as if for treasure. Kate watched patiently while the flood of men passed through security without any challenges.

The guards rummaged through Allie's snacks, probing every nook and cranny until they found her stash of batteries for the cameras, digital voice recorder, and water purifier.

"Too many." They unceremoniously removed all of the batteries and put them to the side, not in the garbage as they do in the States.

"No, no, no, you can't have my batteries!" Allie looked over at Kate. *Are you kidding me?*

"I **need** those batteries!" She showed them her camera and water purifier. "PLEASE. please," she implored, knowing that good lithium batteries would be impossible to find in Nepal.

Her head tingled, and she wanted to scream and cry at the

same time. "I need those batteries." She held up her recorder again. "Please." The first guard huffed away; his work was done. The remaining guard hesitated and glanced around. With no one looking, he slipped one pack back into her bag. Afraid to say anything, Allie smiled a thank you. The guard's eyes shifted to something resembling compassion as he turned and shuffled off.

"Absolutely ridiculous!" she squeaked to Kate. "I did everything right and they robbed me! What am I supposed to do? Did they even check any of the men's bags?" It all seemed so simple when Babaji playfully mentioned an Indiana Jones adventure. So far, this was proving to be Indiana Jones exasperation.

"I'm sorry, girlfriend. But, for some reason, my batteries got through. I've got you covered!" Kate smiled mischievously. "Sometimes it pays to be short and average.

The two weary travelers puttered along, dragging the baggage that seemed to be growing in size and weight. Allie's high-tech backpack with no wheels was NOT helping. *How do the backpackers do it?* In all her careful planning, she could have made a better choice.

Then, in the distance, they saw an oasis: hard, metal, empty lounge chairs. Was it a mirage? Could they get there before someone else did? As if water had just appeared in front of them in a dry, hot desert, Kate rushed ahead.

"Hurry," she sputtered.

Laughing in spite of herself, Allie chugged along.

They settled into the inflexible chairs, molded to the shape of somebody else's body, set an alarm, and gathered their luggage around them with a limb touching each piece of their belongings. Too afraid to oversleep and miss their flight, Allie listened to Kate's instant snoring and pondered which snack she should have. She was grateful to be one step closer to boarding the small plane to Kathmandu.

CHAPTER 5

The Arrival

Giggling with excitement, Allie and Kate, the only westerners on the flight, finally boarded the puddle jumper for the last leg of the trip.

Seasoned tourists probably know better than to travel to Nepal during monsoon season. But. . . Allie defended herself, *we aren't visiting just as tourists. We're traveling as honored guests of Babaji . . . Indiana Jones hat and all.*

Shortly before landing, the pilot announced in both Nepali and English, "Look to your left and you'll see Mount Everest."

Allie gazed in awe as the mighty Himalayas rose above the soft, cotton-ball clouds. The sharp white slopes shimmered like diamond dust, while sunlight danced on their white peaks.

"*Welcome home.*" Mount Everest's glowing snow-covered, majestic outline whispered to her from above the clouds. Encased in these silent words was a strange familiarity from somewhere deep within, as if she were indeed returning home. Unexpected tears welled up in her eyes. *Am I crying because I'm delusional with exhaustion or am I really coming home to something? What is it?* Unanswered questions rattled through her mind, as all too soon, she watched Everest disappear behind the clouds, and the plane began its final descent.

FORTY-EIGHT HOURS AFTER LEAVING their New Jersey homes, Allie and Kate touched down in Nepal. An oppressive wall of heat and humidity with a tickle of dust greeted the friends as they took their first steps in the magical and foreign land. They'd made it! They followed their fellow passengers across the jetway into a tiny structure bustling with people—some international business travelers, some backpackers, and many locals. The mental fog of jetlag, hunger, exhaustion, and endless travel left Allie feeling like she was walking in a dream.

"Allieji, Kateji!" Babaji's glowing smile and shiny bald head rushed over to welcome them. He placed a freshly made garland of marigolds around each of their necks. "You made it! Welcome! You are first to arrive! Come! Here is water for you."

"Babaji! Your hair?" Allie burst out.

"Yes, Allieji, is custom for men in mourning to shave head for a year. Do you like new look?" He rubbed his head. "Is good for Indiana Jones adventure, yes?" He laughed. "Come, meet Sunita!" He ushered them toward the parking lot where Babaji's cousin stood quietly next to a dusty white car.

"Meet Sunita. She is lead organizer of our tour here!" Babaji presented his cousin, a short, rotund woman with long, dark hair pulled into a loose ponytail. She smiled shyly at the strangers.

"Sunita! So nice to meet you!" Allie had heard so much about her while planning the trip with Babaji.

"Sunita doesn't speak any English. Is no worry, I will translate!" Babaji explained.

"Oh, Namaste!" Allie said confidently.

"Namaste," Sunita looked happily surprised that Allie offered the traditional greeting.

"Come, take photo!" Babaji ushered the ladies into formation in the middle of the lot. The warm morning sun was already tanning Allie, with a sunburn following close behind.

Towering over everyone, Allie hunched over, trying not to look like the blonde giraffe from America. *Nothing like capturing the grunge of travel,* she thought as she took a long drink of water and wiped the sweat from her brow. She smiled amiably toward the camera, sweat, smeared makeup, dust, and all.

"Good, good! Now off to hotel. I wait here for others. They will soon arrive."

Before they could get further details from Babaji, Sunita ushered the two guests into the back seat of the waiting car and then hopped into the front passenger seat. As they drove away, Babaji yelled after them, "Purify water before you drink! See you at hotel later!"

Allie noticed her half empty bottle. *Crap.* In the excitement of everything, she had forgotten to purify it. Leading up to the trip, Babaji had warned that even bottled water could not be trusted in Nepal. There was actually a market for counterfeit spring water. "You must purify everything, or you get very active tummy!" he repeated during the planning meetings.

Great start, Allie! She scolded herself with true concern of getting the "hydraulic kaboots" already.

In preparation, she had packed antibiotics, Pepto-Bismol, grapefruit seed extract, Imodium, DiaResQ, EmergenC, electrolytes, charcoal tablets, and probiotics. Those, combined with the three-week's-worth of snacks and her one pack of batteries, was contributing to her peace of mind as well as her sore, weary back.

"I forgot to purify this water. Did you? And with all of my prep, I can't even find the water purifier! It's got to be in here somewhere," Allie grumbled to Kate.

"Here, give me your water," Kate zapped both bottles with her magical purifier. "We'll be fine, don't worry." She smiled. Allie was enjoying the confident and quick-acting Kate. She didn't know she had it in her, and it was fun to see.

The distance in kilometers to the hotel wasn't far, but the traffic in the city was formidable. Having grown up near New York City, both Allie and Kate thought they knew traffic, but this—this was beyond even their wildest rush-hour Metropolitan experience. Buses, motorcycles, scooters, tuk-tuks, and cars all rushed up to the many red traffic lights, creating more lanes than the road accommodated. The crush of traffic was reminiscent of their experience at the ticket counter earlier: overwhelming and chaotic. To add to the mix, chickens, goats, dogs, and cows wove their way in and out of the traffic. Some simply stopped and spontaneously napped in the middle of the road.

The driver was hoping to oblige the western visitors by offering the comfort of air conditioning, but as they sat in the unmoving traffic jam, the tiny system lost the battle against the beating sun, car exhaust, and increasing body heat. The sound of the whirring compressor was promising, but they felt nothing. Sandwiched amidst their luggage, Allie rested her feet on a suitcase with her long legs tucked to her chest. Trickles of perspiration crept down her chest, pooling at her belly button and eventually soaking her underwear. A blend of sweat, engine exhaust, and stale breath heightened the stench in the vehicle. *Why didn't I think to brush my teeth during the layover?*

Allie was certainly stepping out of her comfort zone and yet, surprisingly, she remained calm. At home, she would have freaked out, screamed for gum, cooler air, open windows. But somehow here, in a land so foreign to her, it was easier to tolerate discomfort and simply relinquish control and go with the flow. The adventure was unfolding in real time, and, just like stepping onto the stage as the curtain was rising, there was no going back. She was realizing her dream of pilgrimaging to Nepal and **this** was part of the adventure––smells, discomfort, and all.

Allie drew in a shallow, warm, smelly breath and gave

in to the crowded car and the congested streets as the questionable bottled water rolled around in her stomach deciding what it would do next.

CULTURAL LESSON #2
If you can't change it, don't fight it.
Go with the flow.
Brush your teeth after a long flight.

CHAPTER 6

The Gift

A few miles and an hour later, the driver turned onto a dreary alleyway that surprisingly opened up to reveal the hotel complex, lined with burgeoning bougainvilleas, succulents, and a two-tiered fountain flocked with pigeons. The bustling activity of the main drag immediately muffled in the distance, as the wide-eyed guests took in their accommodations for both the start and end of their trip.

"Cool!" Kate said in a slow drawl.

"Ooh, I didn't expect this," Allie exclaimed. She knew that Babaji selected this four-star hotel because their lodgings outside of Kathmandu would be simple and less accommodating to western ideals. He wanted his friends to begin and end the trip comfortably with hot water, air conditioning, and a beautiful in-ground pool. Upon seeing the hotel in person, they realized Babaji outdid himself to make them feel welcome and at ease.

The Nepali language was very different from the familiar

romance languages Allie had learned in her opera career, and her understanding was limited to: thank you, bathroom, my name is, hello and goodbye. Silently, Sunita handed them their room keys.

"Your friend," the fluent receptionist explained, referring to Sunita, "has arranged for you to have a massage. They will arrive in fifteen minutes. It's included."

Allie was hesitant.

"A massage! That's wonderful. I'll do it if you do it," Kate chirped.

"I-I don't know." She didn't come to Nepal to get a massage. And, she had heard stories. . .

Kate's eyes widened in desperation. "Please?"

"Do you think it's legit?" Allie was trying to talk herself into it for Kate's sake.

"Of course! Sunita set it up. It'll be fine. Let's do it!" Kate implored.

I'm an adventurer now, right? It's just a massage.Get over yourself. "Okay."

"It'll be great!" Kate said with wholehearted reassurance. "Just a little self-care in preparation for our big adventure."

Now bonded after two days of travel, Kate and Allie hauled their luggage to their single rooms that were, gratefully, adjacent to each other. They agreed to yell loudly if either of them needed assistance during the massage.

A few moments later, Allie heard a firm knock on her door as well as Kate's.

Here's hoping. Allie opened it to see a stunning, tall, fair-skinned woman with long, bleached blond hair sporting a very serious expression.

Unsmiling, she entered the room, looked at Allie and said, "Open."

Allie looked around. *Open?* She wondered. *Open what?*

The massage therapist mimed undressing and stood waiting and watching. Allie began to remove her shirt.

"Yes, open." She walked to the air conditioning unit and turned it on to cool the stuffy room, anticipating that this American would want to be cool and comfortable. As she pulled the pristine white covers down on the bed, Allie, ever modest, went to the bathroom and undressed to her bra and underwear. When she returned, her hostess, with her deadpan face, looked at the remaining clothing.

"Open." She pointed to it impatiently.

Really? Allie hesitated. Standing naked in front of a stranger didn't conform with her upbringing. Allie's wide eyes glanced toward Kate's room hoping for X-ray vision.

"Open, open!" Arms flailed with impatience.

Allie listened for Kate yelling or complaining. Nothing. *What's the big deal, anyway?*

A moment later, buck-naked, but donning an imaginary Indiana Jones hat on her head, she lay on the bed as her serious hostess prepared the oil. Cool air moved through the stuffy room, and Allie's fatigue helped her melt into the comfort of the soft bed. Abruptly, icy hands and cold oil shocked her arm . . . really cold oil.

Interesting. Not . . . really . . . relaxing, she stiffened. Her arms were being rubbed with firm intensity.

"Hard?' the massage therapist asked, unsmiling and unyielding.

"Yes," Allie replied. Her fatigue blocked her words and she couldn't think of the simple opposite. Eventually, she squeaked. "No! Hard. Uh, no hard, soft?"

The massage therapist softened the pressure slightly but continued to rub with vigor. Testing the power of positive thinking, Allie pretended that it was better and tried to convince herself that it was relaxing.

I hope she knows what she's doing! A special Nepali technique? I'm just too sensitive. Trust, Allie, relax.

"You relax?"

"Sure?"

Having become accustomed to a heated massage table and a cozy blanket, Allie shivered in the open air. She'd never experienced this technique: cold oil, totally exposed, hard rubbing as if her skin were being scraped off. Bits of oily, dead skin dotted the white sheets.

Gross. Oh, Allie, just chill, will you? Chill IS the word, it's cold in here!

Allie's goose-bumped arms and legs and perky, naked breasts screamed to be covered. At her prickly legs, the therapist looked up.

"You new mother?" she asked, referring to her towering nipples.

"Huh?"

"New mother?" she repeated strongly indicating Allie's breasts.

Oh God, Allie thought, her freezing cheeks at both ends flushing.

"No! Cold!!" Allie was mortified, chilled, and rigid. *When will this be over? KATE!*

An hour later, with no old skin left and her sheets littered with dirty remnants and oil stains, Allie took a blissfully warm shower and headed downstairs to meet the others for dinner. Her heavy eyes could barely stay open.

Well, that aggressive technique might have worked. I'm finally relaxed. She saw Kate. "How was your massage?" Allie tried valiantly for casualness with a twinkle in her eye.

"Different," Kate responded with wide eyes.

Too tired to share details, they tossed it off as another bonding experience.

CULTURAL LESSON #3
Avoid massages.

CHAPTER 7

The Pilgrims

At dinner, as the other pilgrims trickled in, Allie quickly learned who the talkers were. She met Doug and Gloria from Texas. Congenial and humble over email, but in person, overbearing and boisterous. Doug, a retired dentist with a wide smile and an in-your-face personality, leaned into Allie as he spoke, making it known that he needed to be the center of attention. His freckled face paled in contrast to the jet-black hair that shot from his scalp in all directions like frozen fireworks. With stunning blue eyes that shifted in color along with his mood, he commanded attention as he made it known to anyone listening that he and Gloria flew first class and were close friends of Babaji.

Close friends, huh? Allie knew that Doug and Gloria were only recent acquaintances of Babaji. *This is not what I anticipated.* Her head tingled. Doug reminded her of her ex-husband, and she was already triggered.

Gloria matched her husband's height but doubled his

weight. Her sharp stance pierced the space as if to say, "Don't mess with me." And Allie didn't plan on it. Thinning red hair helmeted her round face, and sharp bangs matched her precise, piercing words that contracted every muscle in her face like a ticking time bomb. She sensed that Gloria was carrying the emotional weight of her work and needed this trip to decompress. They were a well-practiced unit, and Allie hoped they were a good match for the trip, trying not to doubt Babaji's choices.

Then there was Jane from Arizona, who'd coerced her comfort-loving husband, John, to join the Indiana Jones adventure. Having been on a local retreat with both of them the year before, Allie knew that they were also strong personalities with strong opinions. Jane was born in Portugal and walked with an elegance and confidence that enhanced her natural beauty. She was an expert at micro-managing and left no stone unturned for others to complete. And yet she was also generous to a fault. Allie was hopeful that Jane had left her scrutinous eye at home. John, originally from North Carolina, had weathered his seventy-five years well. He was a few inches shorter than Jane, and his salt and pepper ponytail enhanced his firm, square jaw and cutting brown eyes. With a hint of a southern drawl, he communicated confidently as if he were an expert on every topic. And, indeed, he believed he was, which also made Allie's head tingle. Jane suspected that this would be their only trip to Nepal, due to their age and recent health concerns, so she insisted that John join her.

Both retired from successful careers in the corporate world, Jane was now dedicated to Babaji's sound healing methods, and John was a dedicated self-pronounced master chef.

Allie observed the energy of the two couples as they met, the men each trying to talk over the other as if this moment would determine who would be the alpha couple of the trip. They danced around like two peacocks displaying their vibrant colors and huge plumes. Doug with his puffed-up chest and John with his jutting chin and piercing eyes, they each commanded, *"Look at me!" "No, look at me!"*

As one of the coordinators watching the dynamics unfold, Allie was already feeling responsible for the well-being of everyone. *Interesting power play. I guess they didn't get the twenty emails explaining that this is a spiritual journey.* Her sarcasm was lighting up. This journey might be a challenge for some. In fact, that was probably the understatement of the moment. With beers in hand, Doug and Gloria beautifully exhibited their prowess and dominance over the conversation while John and Jane seemed to acquiesce, at least for now.

Kurt, the gentle giant, was the quiet one of the group. He was easily the tallest at 6' 4", handsome and fit. A distinguished philosophy scholar, he oozed professorship with his perfectly trimmed brown beard and mustache and wire-framed bifocals. Identifying as the invisible observer, he rarely spoke, but when he did, it was in a whisper. A master herbalist as well, he'd traveled to Nepal from Nevada with an extra suitcase full of supplies to support the trip. His permanently furrowed brow displayed sincere concern for everyone's well-being, particularly as they all coped with jetlag. Allie liked him instantly.

Marianna arrived from Upstate New York, and, although she managed an interior design business in New York as her full-time gig, she was also a yoga instructor. Her warm, husky alto enhanced her natural elegance with her flowing silky brown hair and golden eyes. And her smile . . . her smile was transporting. She radiated kindness with her simple actions and consideration of others and was an immediate soul sister to Allie.

Then there was Pearl, who was Allie's chosen roommate for the pilgrimage. They had met a year ago at one of Babaji's classes and immediately hit it off. Sisters at heart, Pearl and Allie were ready for the journey together. Hailing from Oregon, Pearl was an adventurer who loved extreme sports. She was tall, thin, and muscled with long, fine brown hair. Her wide shoulders revealed the strength of the triathlete she was, and she was ready to trek through the Himalayas, if only she could. This being her first trip to Nepal, she would forgo the trek to stay with Babaji. Pearl was vibrant, stunning, strong, and, most importantly, comfortable with silence.

All of the pilgrims, with the exception of Doug, Gloria, and John, had been trained at the advanced level by Babaji. They worked long and hard to learn his special methods and to meet the necessary requirements to represent Babaji as practitioners of the tradition. Allie had thought the trip was going to be for his students only, but, as the guest list grew, she tried not to question Babaji's special invitations. *He must have his reasons.*

"Friends! Namaste! Hello, hello!" Babaji made his entrance along with Sunita and several other cousins. "How is hotel, is okay?"

"It's perfect!" Doug raised his beer and made his presence known.

"Good, good! Welcome to my home country, Nepal! Is great honor that you make great effort to join me on our sacred adventure!" he said. "Not just sacred adventure but Indiana Jones adventure!" he exclaimed playfully. "Did you each bring hat?" Everyone joined in his laughter. "We will begin journey tomorrow, so eat and get good sleep. Tomorrow is big day!"

The entourage enjoyed a welcome dinner that satisfied Allie's raging hunger. The pilgrimage would officially begin tomorrow, and the day promised to be a full one in Kathmandu.

How can I be so exhausted and also so wide awake?

Allie gave in to her restlessness and sat up in bed. It was dinner time the day before in New Jersey, and, even through her bone-tired fatigue, her confused internal clock wouldn't allow her to sleep. The air conditioner chugged noisily, now barely cooling the stuffy room, a drastic change from the earlier nipple episode. Allie suspected that the full hotel was conserving its energy.

   With a heavy head and a rumbling stomach that anticipated dinnertime halfway across the world, she fumbled for her phone and typed in the code from the wi-fi instruction card. No connection. She tried several more times with different access options. Room number, last name, first name. *Frustrating.* And then again and again and again. Bingo. Sixth time was the charm. *Gotcha. The code only works if the stars are aligned.* Allie typed a brief message to her aunt saying that she had arrived safely and then turned her phone off for the rest of the trip. She pulled out her journal and pen.

⚘

Journal

After incredibly long travel, we all arrived safely.

I knew that on paper it would take about 36 hours to

get here, but in reality, it took almost 48 door to door

and actually felt like 80. I'm pretty wiped but also

wildly excited. Our group is much more complex than

they all appeared over email. There are some strong

personalities, which is disappointing. I feel bad writing

this, but there's something about Doug that rubs me the wrong way. Without saying a word, he makes my head tingle, which is never a good sign. I'll leave it at that and hope it all just gets better. I was really hoping for a quiet and deeply spiritual trip with people who would elevate me, not pull me down. Doug seems like a puller, not an elevator. But, we'll see.

So far, the food has been delicious and safe. We've been warned to eat only stews and cooked food. No fresh veggies or unpeeled fruit that may have been washed in the water. Hopefully, nobody'll get sick. Babaji warned us that we'd all have to stay behind until they recovered if that happened. Our tour's jam-packed and I don't want to miss any bit of it! We have Kathmandu, Babaji's village, a couple of shaman adventures, and Chitwan.

I'm not sure what the shamans will offer to us. The only experience I have with a shaman is the one that I envision within myself! That deep, guttural sound that I sometimes feel inside me singing along with my chanting. Maybe I'm here to meet my shaman!

With only a couple of the cousins speaking any English, the smile is the universal language. We share, 'Namaste' which means hello and goodbye and also 'The light in me honors the light in you.' That's a good start.

Long ago, Babaji asked us to set our intention for the pilgrimage. Mine is purification. I'm ready to release all of my baggage and be free to trust and love again. I really miss my connection to God, Spirit, the Universe ... I don't even know what to call it anymore. I pray for clarity. And direction ... I'm already dreading going home. Part of me doesn't even want to go back. Not that life there is bad. I love what I do, but it feels so empty. Empty. Babaji speaks of that, 'Sunyata.' But this isn't the empty he speaks of. His empty is full, I suspect with Love and Light. My empty is dark and heavy.

I'm ready to lighten up and find a new me.

That's all for now. That's plenty.

She put down the journal and easily fell asleep.

CHAPTER 8

Day 1

A soft glow hinted at the rising sun as Allie's alarm chimed. With her hunger leading the way, she washed up and dressed in a modest shirt, white flowing pants, and a white scarf, just in case she needed to cover her head at the temple later. She knew Babaji loved white and was hoping to dress appropriately for this new culture.

Allie was the first to arrive at the buffet: a surprising assortment of local food such as dal, rice, and potatoes along with dry cereal, oatmeal, and eggs to order as a gesture to the tourists. Not to mention the fresh fruit: peeled ripe papaya and pineapple. She ordered a black coffee, which, upon first disappointing sip, was Nescafe instant, made with milk. Trying not to be the coffee snob that she was, Allie moved on to chai, which, by default, became her go-to comfort drink.

The air conditioning blew at full speed and was freezing. Shivering, she wrapped her scarf around her shoulders. "They must think we Americans are only comfortable with the AC blasting all of the time," Allie said to Kate and Marianna, as they sat down to join her.

"Us spoiled? Americans wanting to be comfortable! Never!" Marianna joked.

Having no way of knowing if the water was filtered, Allie pulled out her water purifier, feeling a bit embarrassed by the gesture of penetrating each glass with the large infrared light. She didn't want to seem too "foreign," but it was too late for that. Here she sat, with her blonde hair, tall height, thin frame, and Jersey accent, holding a light-saber water purifier, modestly thanking the server, "Dhawnyavawd," as she zapped each glass.

The server giggled, "Welcome," in an equally thick Nepali accent as she walked away.

"Why did she laugh? Isn't that Nepali for thank you?" Allie questioned.

"Not sure, you'll have to try again!" yawned Marianna. "Did everyone sleep?" Her smile embraced her new friends.

"Like a log," Kate replied.

"Not really." Allie caught Marianna's yawn. "But I suspect the activities of the day will keep us awake."

The server brought them more chai. *Here I go!* "Dhan-ya-vad," Allie said confidently, pronouncing each syllable.

The server giggled again. "Welcome, ma'am."

"Isn't that right?" Allie asked. "Dhan-ya-vad?"

"Thunyuvud." The server tossed it off quickly as if it were just one syllable.

"Dawnyuhvawd," repeated Allie with some Jersey slipping in.

"Yes ma'am, welcome!" The server slipped away, laughing.

"You just can't take the Jersey out of a Jersey girl!" Marianna chimed. "Good try, though!"

THE HEAVY AIR PROMISED a hot day, as a blurred orange ball, reminiscent of the sun, rose into the dense smog, whispering, "I'm here, in the distance."

Allie stood alone at the hotel entrance for the 10:00 a.m. departure: no cousins, no Babaji, no one. *Really? Where is everyone? I guess we're on Nepal time now.* She had heard that time moved at its own pace in Nepal. Perhaps it was due to traffic or a casual commitment to getting somewhere promptly or a general appreciation for the present moment. Whatever the reason, Allie was not on Nepal time yet, and it took a great deal of flexibility to wait patiently.

Okay. As usual, I'm the first to arrive. Hurry up and wait. But as an organizer, it's my job to be prompt, right? Still, it's rude for everyone to be late. The familiar characters in her head were having a great conversation. *Take a breath, Allie. What's the rush? You're in the middle of Nepal. Just look around. Be in the moment, will you?*

So there she stood, tucked into the courtyard of the hotel, protected by a canopy of ficus, succulents, and sweet-smelling bougainvilleas. Although she didn't need to don her pollution mask yet, Allie knew the exhaust and dust waited just beyond the alleyway. She noted that her white pants were destined to be a different color by the end of the day. *Definitely not the best choice.*

SELF LESSON
Don't wear white in Kathmandu.
Let go of your expectations of others.

"Gee, I thought I was late!" Pearl rushed up behind Allie.

"Apparently, we're on time. But no else is." Allie referred to the two couples casually finishing breakfast, seemingly oblivious to the time.

As if on cue, a small van rushed to the entrance and screeched to a halt. Sunita and a new face hopped out, wearing beaming smiles of greeting. In perfect English, Rajesh introduced himself.

"Hello, nice to meet you. I'm Rajesh. I'll be with you for the entire trip." His resonant bass voice had Allie-the-opera-singer swooning. *Wow, I'd love to hear him sing.*

Taking charge, they eventually gathered the tardy pilgrims and ushered them into the hot van. The packed vehicle of excited travelers rushed onto the main road, only to be halted by the thick, noisy Kathmandu traffic. Exhaust fumes spilled in through the open windows, and Allie fumbled for her mask.

Rushing to the front of the van, Babaji yelled. "We close windows. Too much pollution here. Everyone have mask?"

Babaji continued in Nepali to the driver, and Allie felt a pinch of tepid air drift through the vents. He turned back to the group. "Friends, we begin trip at Pashupatinath Temple. Is most sacred Shiva temple and is very auspicious to visit. We will have special welcome ceremony. We cannot enter Temple but instead visit Temple city that is built around temple. You will see."

"Baba," Doug boomed so all could hear him, perhaps knowingly leaving out the respectful 'ji' from his friend's name. "I brought my flute!"

"Hahaha, wonderful. We all make music together in my home village!"

"Wait until you hear," Doug continued, "I've been taking lessons, and I have it mastered,"

"Ah, is very good! Flute is sacred instrument! I did bring my double flute. We will play. Did you know that Allieji is opera singer? We will have small band on trip!"

Allie smiled at Doug and she noticed his face flush.

"He sings too," his supportive wife, Gloria, chimed in. "He's very good, and he sings opera as well."

"Really? Where did you study opera?" Allie encouraged. The opera world was small, and she was sure that they would have several acquaintances in common.

"Oh, I've studied with many famous teachers," he said as he turned away to talk privately with Babaji.

All right then. The proud peacock has disengaged from me. So much for that conversation. I tried, but I'm not here to compete.

She'd had enough of that in her career. She was here to decompress, learn, and absorb the new culture. In the process, she also hoped to heal old wounds, not create new ones.

"We love opera," Jane said from behind her. "Who's your favorite composer?"

"Ah, that's a tough one, there are so many." Allie searched her mental database . . . "To sing, definitely, Rossini. But to listen to, I would say, Puccini's at the top. How about you?"

"I'm a fan of Wagner," John butted in, "but Jane prefers Bach. So, we jump time periods often."

"Nice, I'm looking forward to learning more about the music here. I know some Sanskrit chants but don't know much about this culture." Allie was excited at the prospect.

"Same here. I'm a master of Kundalini chants, so I'm sure there're some similarities," John boasted loudly enough for Doug to hear.

"We just enjoy chanting." Jane tried to soften the rising arrogance.

"Glad to hear. Hopefully we'll have opportunity to chant together." Allie settled back into her seat, happy to retreat from the "master" competition. She hadn't expected to bring her ex-husband on the pilgrimage with her, but here they were: two boasters representing a relationship that broke her heart. *You can only run so far, until it smacks you in the face to heal it. You asked for it, Allie, with your intention of purification. Be careful what you wish for.*

As the van inched forward, she shifted from the awkward

small talk of the van to the streets of Kathmandu. Focusing more fully on the scenes around her, she began to notice a sort of order amidst the chaos. What appeared to be a disorganized mash of cars, motorcycles, buses, and scooters was actually an improvisational dance of merging, inching, and squeezing into two narrow lanes through the communication of horns, eye contact, and a flick of the hand. The drivers all moved with perfect fluidity in the dense traffic. The rhythmic honking was different from the aggressive, impatient New Jersey horn blast. Instead, it appeared to be a language within itself. There was the short honk to move forward; the series of honks to get into the lane; the long honk to signal passing; the honk to let someone in, and many others. The constant noise was more of an orchestral car symphony but one that was not yet music to Allie's ears.

CULTURAL LESSON #4
Driving in Kathmandu: Don't.
But for fun, learn the language of the horns.
Traffic lights appear to be optional.

One hour later and just a few miles further, they finally reached the temple gates. Already glistening from the weighted humidity, the relieved pilgrims ejected themselves from the van and onto the streets of Kathmandu. No movie, book, nor research could have prepared them for the full attack on their senses: the ever-present babble of traffic; the

acrid smells of dirt, garbage, body odor, and living animals;
the ageless appearance of poverty, barefoot children in cloth
diapers and sun-cracked elders; the tumbled buildings left
in heaps of stone from the recent earthquake; the relentless
swirling dust and the open hands and mouths of beggars,
both genuine and professional, reaching out from the lined
streets and alleyways; the taste of smoke from the wood fires
that filled their mouths; the soot and ashes that burned their
already-dry eyes. Welcome to Kathmandu.

And yet, there was also intense beauty: the curious smiles
and sincere warmth of the locals; the numerous children
covered in dust, playing joyfully; the feel of community and
hospitality; the vivid colors of the clothing; the immense
splendor of the ancient architecture with its equally ancient
history; the massive green and snow-peaked mountains in
the distance. The remarkable duality left Allie awestruck.

A female stranger, slight in height and wearing a peach
sari, leaned on a tall crooked cane and freely offered Babaji
and the group a handful of dry food, quite possibly the only
food she had for that day, in order to welcome the pilgrims
to the temple city.

"Ah, we have a special offering for us! Prasadam. Is safe
to eat, and is given with love. Please accept. In our culture,
we give what we have to welcome you." Babaji instructed the
overwhelmed pilgrims to hold out their right palm to receive
the mixture of rice and grains.

How can this be repaid? Allie wondered as she carefully

nibbled on the offering. It was sweet, bursting with unfamiliar spices. The stranger disappeared into the crowds before Allie could offer her gratitude.

CULTURAL LESSON #5
What appears to be poverty is full of riches—an unmeasurable wealth of love and generosity.

NOTICE
ALL THE FOREIGN VISITORS ARE
KINDLY REQUESTED TO PURCHASE
ENTRANCE TICKET TO ENTER

A small sign greeted them at the gate. Sunita silently ran off to purchase their entrance tickets, while Allie and Kurt peered in through the gates.

"It's a precious gift to experience a new culture," Allie whispered in reverence and respect. Her mind was trying to catch up to *actually* being on the streets of Nepal.

"It sure is," Kurt marveled and snapped some photos.

The opening gate was made of simple clay bricks topped by copper roofing and gold pointed tips. It was sandwiched by two little street shops the walls of which were covered with large painted Pepsi logos. Visitors would never know that this unassuming gate led to one of the most sacred temples in all of Nepal.

"Pepsi seems to be very popular here," Allie remarked.

Kurt chuckled, "Yes! It sure does! I don't drink Pepsi, but

I could go for one now. It's damn hot." Kurt gasped. "Can I say damn here?"

"Sure. But behave yourself once we get on the temple grounds," Allie teased.

Sunita rushed back waving the tickets with a wide smile. Allie, with her blonde hair and dusty white outfit and Kurt with his shorts, sneakers, long white socks, and Indiana Jones hat led the way through the gate. They didn't go unnoticed. If the white socks and the hat weren't a dead giveaway of an American tourist, then the camera around each of their necks was the kicker. The peddlers immediately rushed them, as they made their way down the long road to the temple.

"One dollah." The short peddler's smile revealed his few remaining teeth. Holding his hand up to Kurt's face, he dangled necklace-sized malas made of wood, gems, and seeds of all colors.

"No, thank you," Kurt said politely as he waved his hand.

"One dollah, for you. You take," persisted the peddler, trying to place a mala in Kurt's hand.

"No, thank you," Kurt repeated.

"For you! Good price!" insisted the peddler, pushing the mala into Kurt's face. Other peddlers gathered around the group hoping to get in on the action.

"No," Kurt whispered intensely through a clenched jaw and flushed face.

Allie thought the gentle giant might bite the tiny peddler.

Babaji noticed the situation, the first of what would be

many, and rushed to save Kurt by saying something in Nepali to the gathered peddlers. They backed off just enough to allow the group to walk freely but followed close behind.

Laughing, Babaji exclaimed, "'No' means 'maybe' here!"

CHAPTER 9

Temple City

The cobblestoned road inside the Temple city was closed to motorized vehicles, so the traffic and street noise began to fade into the distance. As the group walked further into the complex, the bustle of daily life spread out before them with new sounds, sights, and scents. One man carried ten stacked plastic chairs on his back; another, a large sheet packed full of laundry. Women balanced baskets on their heads, and stray cows and dogs hovered around piles of trash. A strong smell of smoke hung in the air. Individuals, families, communities, and silent monks went about their day as Allie and her group took a step back in time, merging into a complex culture that could only be described as Nepal.

The parched land beckoned for rain, but the cloudless, shining day showed no signs of relief. Sunita, Rajesh, and several other cousins led the already melting group to the entrance of the Shiva Temple. The intricately carved wooden pagoda reflected care and respect for the sacred space.

Golden yellow and light blue exterior walls were adorned with different deities, including a carved Shiva, front and center, holding a trident.

"You see Shiva here," Babaji explained simply. "Shiva is Destroyer. In destruction, there can rise balance and contentment. Shiva energy frees us . . . frees us from ego, anger, limits, fears and opens wise thinking, immortality, bliss. Let us look inside from here." They inched toward the wide entrance that was protected by an armed guard. "See giant gold bull?"

Only the back portion of the statue was visible to the peeking pilgrims. Its immense size appeared to dominate the small square.

Babaji continued, "This is Nandi, sacred transport and door-keeper for Shiva. Removes . . . how do you say . . . snares . . . obstacles on path. Clears doubt. Is tradition to whisper in Nandi's ear your deepest wish or prayer." Babaji looked again toward the entrance. "Since we can't do inside, instead we can do from this distance. Please take this moment, picture whispering in Nandi's ear your intention for your trip. Your greatest hearts-desire."

Allie imagined walking up to this giant Nandi and effortlessly getting close to its ear. She whispered, *I ask for purification. Please, free me from my failures and pain, and let me experience love.*

After a few moments, Babaji added, "Everybody whisper to Nandi?" He met everyone's eyes with the exception of Gloria and Doug, who had wandered off to take photos of the structure. Babaji was unfazed. "Your intention is heard. This is such a very special trip already! Now, let us go to river. Is very holy to die here. People come from all over. Is very important to be cremated on banks of Bagmati River. Come, we continue to river. Come!"

Before moving on, Allie and Pearl inched closer toward the entrance for one last glance. Aside from the glowing gold back of Nandi, they couldn't see much; just groups of people milling about. Turning to leave, Allie noticed that a cow and stray dog had joined them. They, too, were peering into the temple courtyard, standing side by side. It was as if they knew they were on sacred land but, just like the visiting pilgrims, were not welcome to enter.

"They look like they really want to go into the temple," Pearl told Allie.

"They're just pilgrims in another body, drawn to the sacred, just like us." Allie snapped a photo of the scene. "We appear to be different, and yet, here we stand together feeling something special, wanting to enter . . ." She sighed. "But man-made rules won't let us go in."

CULTURAL LESSON #6
Intentions matter and prayers are heard,
whether or not one is allowed into the
"sacred" structure.

CHAPTER 10

The River

Allie and Pearl walked on, eventually catching up to the group. In the distance, the Bagmati River appeared before them. Its banks were built up with clay bricks to provide structure for the many funeral pyres that spread out before them.

Now high in the sky, the sun warmed everything but didn't slow the bustle of the temple city. A group of women dressed all in orange sat under small umbrellas as they prepared garlands to sell for offerings at the temple. Their nimble fingers moved quickly as they expertly threaded the freshly picked flowers. Everywhere sadhus, or renunciates, with long, matted hair and equally long, uncut beards, milled about, begging or praying. Most were dressed simply in only a wrap around their groins; their bodies coated with ash to signify death to worldly life, their faces painted specifically to honor their God. Many were willing to take a photo for a dollar, and some also offered a blessing.

Along the banks of the river lay numerous funeral pyres.

The smell in the air, Allie realized, was not just wood burning but also burning bodies. And yet, it wasn't a smell that this westerner would expect. It was almost pleasant, due to the herbs used to prepare the bodies for cremation.

Babaji gazed downstream, and everyone followed his direction. "You see here women washing clothes?"

Okay, now that's gross. In all of the remains? Allie tried to accept that she was inhaling human ashes.

Babaji continued, "The linen comes very clean here. They think animal fat from remains in water was first soap. Very easy to wash here." He grinned.

The group came upon a cremation that was just beginning across the way, and Sunita and Rajesh ushered them to sit on the cement stairs to observe. The deceased was laid atop the pyre at the edge of the bank, while the loved ones, one-by-one, walked down to say their final goodbyes. The wife bellowed in grief from the top of the stairs as family members tried to pull her down to the unlit pyre to pay her last respects. Resisting, she collapsed onto the cement steps, her fingers grasping the pavement while her whole body convulsed in despair. They pried the distressed widow from the ground and carried her down the stairs while the rising emotion built to a family bellow. This was SO different from Allie's experience with death and funerals. Her family did not cry in front of each other, let alone wail loudly.

"I feel like we're intruding. This is too personal," murmured Kate.

"It's heart-wrenching," Marianna groaned.

Yet the group stayed, following the lead of Sunita and Rajesh. Not knowing what else to do, Allie prayed silently: *Please help this family. Offer them loving support and healing. Let the deceased find rest and peace.*

Finally, too exhausted to resist, the wife fell onto the body of her husband. She held on screaming, unwilling to let him go. Allie's heart couldn't handle any more.

"Why are we here?" she uttered to no one as she glanced at the others in the group.

Aside from Gloria snapping photos quietly, all sat in silence. Allie had wanted to experience the culture, but this? This wasn't what she had expected.

Welcome to Nepal! Let's watch a body burn!

Two men started the fire as the wife was pulled away. It is said that the ancient tradition required the living widow to throw herself onto the pyre to die along with her husband. Although the tradition is long altered, this woman's anguish almost engulfed her as well. As they watched the pyre ignite, the body and their grief were merged within the dancing flames.

Allie couldn't help but think about her own parents. She'd had the gift of being with her mom when she took her last breath. But her dad had died alone and wasn't found for days. Allie certainly grieved and cried hard, but only in the privacy of her home, car, or closet. She'd kept the sorrow to herself as best she could. This communal expression, as heart-wrenching as it was to watch, was refreshing: *Perhaps my suppressed emotions are the very catalyst for my fiery anxiety, continuously stoking the hardened, unburnable cement wall of grief. Perhaps this is what I'm here to extinguish.*

Sunita and Rajesh stood, indicating that it was time to move on. The solemn group followed their guides up several stairways to a secluded area that overlooked the periphery of the temple city. Here, they would experience the special, private welcome ceremony.

CULTURAL LESSON #7
Bellow when you need to bellow.

CHAPTER 11

The Ceremony

"Please," Rajesh gestured to the ground, "sit." He held tiny pieces of paper and asked everyone to choose one. Allie selected hers and opened it: "1."

Wonder what this means? Allie loved surprises. Marianna had "6" and Pearl, "8."

Four long throw rugs were laid in a rectangle under a large Banyan tree that provided much welcome shade for the ceremony. The priest was set up on one side, while the pilgrims sat cross-legged on the remaining rugs around him. The thin rugs provided only a small cushion from the firm, dry earth, and Allie's white pants didn't stand a chance.

In English Babaji described the actions of the hired priest. "We have all elements here: water, fire, air, earth, ether." The priest drew a symbol in the sand. "This represents seat of Divine. Inviting Divine to sit here, be present. Food and water is offered to Divine energy, and fire is offered to burn away negative energy, to clear path for safe journey. Water is life and cleansing."

All the while, the priest chanted in an unfamiliar language that pulsed through and around Allie like a warm, sonic embrace. This was a welcome respite from the morning's activities and she was enjoying the quiet, private space. *I'm in Nepal. Wow! I'm IN Nepal.* She was trying to process it all, and emotion bubbled up within her. *Don't think, just listen.* The ceremony helped her to relax, take some deep, smoke-filled breaths, and sit in gratitude for the group, Babaji, and her guides.

"We place water in right hand, and you place on forehead," Babaji said, "wash away impurities."

Allie gladly brought her cupped palm to her head to cool her forehead and wet her hair.

Next, Babaji put herbed rice in everyone's right hand, and they offered it at the seat of the Divine. He prayed, "Please bless trip. Bless each person here. Bless loved ones who support trip for us here."

One by one, each participant was invited to receive a blessing from the priest as he placed a smudge of red-colored powder on their foreheads. Babaji translated, "Is to remember True Self. Third eye. Light in you, Divine in you. When we look at each other, we remember this."

The leaves of the Banyan tree began to rustle as a subtle wind passed through. Allie closed her eyes to listen. It reminded her of her rain stick from home, magical and glistening. Crows cawed from a distance, and monkeys jumped from branch to branch, observing and waiting. She opened her eyes and noticed a petite woman in the distance quietly observing the group. She wore a peach sari and steadied herself on a large cane, appearing almost iridescent as the sunlight glistened around her. *That's the woman who greeted us with prasadam!* Allie recognized her and hoped that she could thank her later.

"Who is number one?" Babaji invited, referring to the pieces of paper from earlier.

Remembering her number, Allie beamed, "I am!" How could she not help but smile back at the radiant Babaji? She glanced again toward the elder woman, but she was gone.

"Perfect! Our organizer is number one!" Babaji exclaimed. "During trip we visit many temples and we hope to have ceremony at each temple to honor one friend each time. Today we each place tilak on our friend, Allieji, and offer her blessing." Tilak was the colored powder that the priest had used to bless them. It was also what was painted on the sadhus' foreheads.

"Tilak is blessing and reminder of third eye, true seeing. Clear vision. We each give special wishes to Allieji, to bless her and her pilgrimage. Use right ring finger to place tilak on forehead. Ring finger, finger of love."

Marianna was the first. "You're special, and I can't wait to get to know you better. Offering you love." She tapped her ring finger into the red powder and rubbed it gently on Allie's forehead.

Doug approached Allie next. "I don't really know you, but I wish you blessings on your trip." He smiled broadly as he touched Allie's forehead with the powder.

"Blessings to you," Gloria said simply as she offered the tilak.

Kurt was next, and Allie saw him place his middle finger in the powder and he gently tapped her forehead.

"Oh no," Allie teased. "I'm not sure what'll happen if you use your middle finger!"

Everyone laughed. Babaji encouraged Kurt with his big smile. "Do again, Kurtji, with ring finger."

Kurt and Allie laughed together as he gently touched the tilak to her forehead and whispered, "You're very blessed. Thank you for all you've done to bring us together."

Pearl approached with tears in her eyes. "Friend, you're so special. I couldn't have wished for a more perfect roommate. I love you." She touched Allie's forehead.

Allie exhaled, "Thank you so much," into Pearl's ear. As they hugged, she was tickled by something. "Pearl, you have a feather in your ear!" Allie pulled out a tiny grey and white feather and handed it to her. "That's crazy weird!"

Unfazed, Pearl took the feather. "Feathers appear for me when something special is about to happen." She twirled the feather in her fingers. "But I've never had one appear in my ear before! Get ready, friend." She winked and moved on.

One by one, Allie received kind words, warm smiles, and hugs. She'd never experienced such a full and complete welcome. Babaji was the last to go, and by now Allie's heart was bursting with emotion. Her tear-filled eyes met Babaji's.

"Dear friend," said Babaji touching her third eye tenderly, "you are beautiful, loved, and so blessed. Thank you."

She was adorned with a red cotton scarf and showered with fresh marigold petals.

Abruptly, a motion caught her eye. Hoping it was the woman in the peach sari, she glanced toward the Banyan tree. Instead, a flash of brown fur rushed into the center of the group and with stealth and ease, the monkeys stole their post-ceremony snack: fresh bananas. With treasures in hand, they returned to the Banyan tree to devour their prize.

"Monkeys have our prasadam! They receive blessings too! Great thieves. Hold on to your sunglasses or they might steal too! Then we have to bribe them back!" Babaji warned.

Allie felt more alive than she had in years. The offering of love that she had just received was overwhelming. A part of her felt that she didn't deserve it, but another part felt desperate for such kindness, and she absorbed it like a parched sponge in a fresh spring. *Thank you. I feel the purification already. Here, I'm safe and so very grateful.*

They took photos of Allie as if she were a rock star, and the contrast of modern and ancient resonated in the air. As the contented group left the temple complex, the peddlers reappeared and quickly followed them in search of their own treasures. Scurrying along, they yelled, "For you! One dollah!" over and over until the van doors closed, and the group merged back into the congested traffic of the streets of Kathmandu.

From the front of the slow-moving van, Babaji made an announcement: "Tomorrow we go to my village! You are finally journeying home with me! We need to arrive early to airport, so we will have simple and fast dinner tonight." He smiled broadly showing all of his teeth. "Oh, and I forget to tell you . . . is small plane and is a weight limit. Only fifteen kilograms each and one purse allowed. We will need leave extra luggage here at hotel. Is free. No worries, we will return here after my village."

Fifteen kilograms! Allie yelped silently as she munched on a power bar. *With all of our preparations how could he NOT have told me that important detail!* Muttering to herself, she did the calculations. That was approximately thirty pounds, and she had almost one hundred in total. *Really Babaji? Now what?* She had planned carefully and wanted to bring every comfort that she had packed.

Back in her room, she had no choice but to organize for the next leg of the journey. *What to leave behind? We'll be there for ten days. It's only just over a week, not the whole trip. Remember, you're an adventurer now. But I'm an adventurer who still wants to look decent and be a little comfortable.* Her thoughts rattled on as she sifted through her disorganized baggage. She'd leave half of her mighty snack bag, half of her medical supplies, and most of her clothing, including the Indiana Jones hat that she would probably never wear.

They planned to purchase clothing for the festival in Babaji's village, so she packed light-weight garments that could be washed easily. *We'll be back soon enough,* she said to herself. It was a challenge, but Allie decided that she was indeed able to leave one full suitcase behind.

─◟◞─

Journal

Aside from having to leave half of my luggage behind, this was an incredible day. I can't describe how special it was to receive blessings from everyone. Even the two couples tried. Maybe I misjudged them? I think Gloria sort of smiled at me once, and Doug was surprisingly quiet for much of the day. John might have had a tear in his eye as he showered me with flowers, and Jane wins the prize for the best hug. We have strong personalities in this group, for sure. To be able to look into their eyes while they offered me a kind word was transforming for me. Uniting. It helped me see beyond the egos (and my judgments) and look for "the light within" as Babaji says. I believe we'll come together as a group; at least, I hope so. Babaji is reminding us that these simple acts of kindness do make a difference.

I've asked for purification and it's begun. Love's pulsing through me, cleansing and offering me encouragement to step into both trust and vulnerability. In this unfamiliar culture, it somehow seems easier. Why not also step into the unfamiliar territory of the heart?

All for now. Early morning.

CHAPTER 12

Travel to Babaji's Village

This was the day they had all been anticipating for months—Babaji's home village.

"Just a few more hours!" Marianna said at breakfast. "Babaji seems really happy to have us all here. He's just beaming."

"It's a rare gift to find a teacher . . . " Kate glowed as she paused to search for the right words, "with such a pure spirit and . . . display of generosity."

"And one you can trust. Truly a gift!" Allie added raising her cup of chai for a toast. "To Babaji."

"To Babaji," the others cheered.

"So, how are you doing with the weight limit for our flight? Thirty pounds is about what my snack bag weighs!" Allie joked, with a hint of truth.

"Oh, I had to leave most of my clothes AND four pairs of shoes," replied Kate "Not to mention my stash of books. What was I thinking?"

"I can't leave my herbs behind. We might need them. So, I'm just going to have to pay extra. " Kurt whispered, unfazed.

"I've just got my backpack. You all travel with too much stuff!" Pearl scolded. "Time to lighten up."

"I'll say," Allie hoped that she'd made the right choice to leave so much stuff behind . . . "but your backpack is about as big as you are! You're gonna make the weight?" They smiled at each other as soul sisters.

"You betcha!" Pearl replied and looked at her watch. "It's time. We'd better check out."

Everyone rose except for the two lingering couples, who didn't appear to be in any rush.

"See you at the van. We're leaving in a few minutes!" Allie said to John, hoping to encourage them to consider the time.

"Yup. We've got time," John retorted.

"We've already checked out," Jane added.

"Don't bother," Kurt whispered to Allie as they left the breakfast area. "He's on his own schedule and will move only when he's ready. Jane will usher him along as best as she can. I've been observing them. They'll make it. Now . . . Doug and Gloria, they're another story. He's oblivious to the needs of others, and Gloria follows along as if he's king." This was the most Kurt had spoken since Allie had met him a couple of days ago. The quiet observer was paying close attention and it was interesting to hear his take on things.

"They'll learn a lot on this trip." Kurt added softly, as if he could see into the future.

I'm counting on it. We need team players here, not divas. Allie kept that thought to herself and instead replied, "You're very observant, oh, quiet one."

"That's what I do." Kurt grinned.

WITH THEIR EXTRA LUGGAGE stored at the Kathmandu hotel, the group boarded the van surprisingly close to schedule and were off to the airport for the next leg of the trip. Sloth-like traffic, however, stretched the short, five-mile trip into an hour. Late to their destination, they were hustled through security only to wait . . . and wait some more.

"We've been here for hours. When do you think we'll board?" Marianna yawned.

"I really don't know. I didn't see this part of the itinerary" Allie replied. "But, I'm feeling a rumbly in my tumbly. It think we should bust into my snack bag!"

The airport didn't have much to offer with just a tiny trinket shop and a bathroom, so Allie pulled out a box of crackers, some raisins, and a precious dark chocolate bar and passed them around. Even the couples partook in the shared snacks. *To the blessings of food. Here's hoping it can soften even the harshest of egos, mine included.*

Yet another hour later, Rajesh's deep bass voice finally boomed, "It's time. Come, hurry, come." The pilgrims went from passive lingering to sudden scrambling as they gathered their carry-on items to board the small puddle jumper to their highly anticipated destination.

Hustling onto the apron toward their chartered plane, they approached a boisterous Babaji who stood confidently next to their unloaded luggage. He spoke in an uncharacteristically firm tone to a woman who yelled back at him in Nepali. A bewildered and stunned luggage carrier waited close by.

Noticing the onlookers, Babaji stopped the debate, smiled widely, and introduced the woman with whom he had appeared to be arguing.

"Ah ha ha ha, meet niece Lumanti! She is here from Chicago and is with us for festival!"

Of course, his niece! Lumanti shared the same round, smiling face of Babaji, but was taller and broader than her uncle. Her eyes were painstakingly lined to enhance their size, and her brightly painted red lips made no apologies for their prominence.

"Hello, hello," she joyfully greeted the group.

"We are in active discussion," Babaji continued. "Pilot is saying that we are overweight. Too much luggage. We must leave behind something to come later." He and Lumanti exchanged a glance and then surveyed the group, hoping for volunteers.

Silence.

"When's the next flight?" Kurt's almost inaudible question floated to Babaji with trepidation.

"Tomorrow, if weather is good."

Silence. Stillness.

Having already left half her luggage at the hotel, Allie wasn't feeling self-sacrificial. It was an unusual situation as they all stood frozen at the belly of the plane, awaiting the fate of their luggage.

Observing the scene, she huffed to Pearl and Marianna, "You'd never see this in Newark."

Marianna chuckled, "Right? Standing outside the airplane, debating whose luggage will make the cut?"

A not-so-subtle movement caught Allie's eyes, and she shifted her focus toward the front of the aircraft. The two couples were slipping onto the airplane as if they hadn't heard the question. *Stealth. Good teamwork. Thanks for sticking with us.* Allie's judgments rose as everyone else continued to stand uncomfortably with the problem still unsolved.

The sun beat down on the group, and the luggage carrier watched patiently. Beads of sweat gathered on everyone's foreheads, and the silence held. Something had to give. Babaji smiled and waited, trusting that it would work itself out.

Finally, Lumanti spoke in Nepali to Babaji.

"Thank you, niece. Is generous and perfect solution!" Apparently, she had boxes and boxes of books that she had brought to be distributed in her home village. She arrived at the decision that they could wait a day or two.

"Is time!" Babaji boomed, "Everyone watch your luggage be put on plane and then we GO!"

Books? That's what we've been arguing over? Allie exhaled

as she watched the carrier load up her luggage. Excitement flooded her. Finally, it was time to begin their true journey.

"Comfy?" Allie quipped with a fake smile, not waiting for an answer as she passed the two couples. *Grace. Give me grace. Compassion too, can't forget that.*

THE PLANE STAYED LOW to the ground for much of the one-hour flight. As they flew away from the densely populated city of Kathmandu, the air and land cleared to reveal the natural splendor of terraced rice fields, pastures, and rolling hills. Allie felt as if she could almost reach down and touch the soft, mossy texture, cool and vibrant with an eco-system vital to all life.

As they rose briefly above the clouds, Allie saw in the far distance the tips of the greyish-white Himalayas. The snow-covered peaks were a stark contrast to the radiant green below.

"Look to left," Babaji announced to everyone on the small plane, "Mount Everest."

Far in the distance, the peak teased her: *You're closer than ever before.* Once again, tears welled up in her eyes. Confused, she silently asked the mountain, *What are you trying to communicate to me? What's this emotion?* The loud hum of the small jet suddenly sounded different. "Mmmmmmm," like the drone of the OM. Allie hummed along as she gazed longingly at the majestic peaks, desperately waiting for an answer.

As they descended below the clouds again, Babaji added, "Notice many peaks not covered with snow. Is new. Never is happened. Climate change affecting us now."

Allie stared in awe at the expansive mountain range that was overwhelmingly more stunning than any picture she'd seen. Rolling far below lay a muddy, mighty river. Even from this great distance, its power roared as it overflowed its banks. The Arun River beckoned them as they began their final descent.

CHAPTER 13

The Village

The Indiana Jones adventure had proven to be smooth so far. Babaji prepared them for a challenging, bumpy ride, but they couldn't have had a better day for travel nor a smoother flight. With a clear, cloudless sky, monsoon season seemed to be a myth, as the pilot maneuvered easily into the dry, tiny valley that housed the single-runway airport. This being the only flight of the day into the remote area, the airport was quiet.

Three words came to mind as Allie stepped off the plane onto the pavement. "Hot, hot, hot." There was no escaping the 100% humidity nor the unrelenting heat of the full sun. Yet here the air was clear and fresh and the land alive with health and vitality—a big change from the city.

The tiny, light-yellow, concrete airport sat at the foot of magnificent and lush layers of ever-flowing rolling hills. A few solar panels perched on the flat roof, and several articles of clothing and sheets hung on the rooftop clothesline, indicating that it served as both the air traffic control center and a small living space. The building didn't look large enough to hold a group their size, so everyone followed a simple path toward the unpaved parking lot. Behind the group, one petite man slowly pulled a tractor-sized baggage trolley by hand. It was nearly overflowing with their luggage. *Poor fellow. As much as we think we've lightened our load, to him, we certainly haven't.*

"Yay! Aha!" A short distance away in the parking lot, a group cheered for them as they approached. Babaji rushed over to greet his relatives who had driven down the mountain to welcome the honored guests. They applauded and yelled, appreciating the effort and commitment involved to finally arrive in this remote valley. Everyone was showered with smiles, hugs, flowers, and bottled water.

Allie, Marianna, Pearl, and Kurt piled into one of the 4x4 SUVs that were hired to take them up the mountain. The fit was tight with luggage shoved all around them. The others loaded into the remaining three vehicles, and the caravan began the trek up, up, up and around the winding, narrow, dirt road, flanked by wandering stray dogs, goats, and chickens. Allie observed yet again, the intentional language of the car horn. With most of the curves sharp, blind, and free from guardrails, the vehicles used several fast beeps to warn of their approach, one long beep to pass, and two long beeps to allow to pass. Or so it seemed. It was another language but one that was effective and necessary for safety.

As they continued their ascent, the airport faded into

distant memory, as the lush jungle embraced them. Time stopped. *Breathtaking.* Allie gazed at the majesty of Earth's bounty, inhaling splendor-filled scents and colors unlike anything she had ever experienced. She could taste the clean, damp air and smell the richness in the soil, so fresh and alive.

Thatched-roofed houses dotted the landscape, with goats, roaming chickens, and intricately stacked piles of wood. Blue butterflies fluttered around the caravan, and crows cawed to announce their ascent and pending arrival.

"Look! A rainbow!" Allie exclaimed as they rounded the last curve leading into the village. *A beautiful omen!* And just as quickly as it appeared, it vanished into a thick mist that rose from the mountains.

"This trip's been so smooth! Can you believe it? We ARE here!" Allie said aloud to whoever was listening.

"The best Indiana Jones adventure we could've had so far," Marianna mused as she playfully flicked the rim of Kurt's hat.

Kurt replied more cautiously, "So far so good."

The little village of thatched houses that Babaji had grown up with were now mostly multi-level concrete homes with many of them doubling as businesses, a storefront below the simple living quarters. China, being a close neighbor, was beginning to pave the major roads, helping to industrialize the simple villages. Allie was shocked and a little disappointed at the modernization.

"I was expecting bare bones and simple, with less concrete and more green," she confessed to her friends.

"Me, too," replied Pearl. "But there's still a beauty and simplicity about it."

The abundant jungle that surrounded the now more progressive village emphasized, yet again, the contrast of ancient with modern.

Children dashed through the streets while locals watched the caravan pass by: some smiled, some looked curious, and others frowned with suspicion. Allie quickly learned that if she made eye contact and smiled, she would often receive a warm smile back. It seemed to shift fear into kindness.

Perhaps she had too vivid an imagination, but, as they drove into town, an ancient healing resonance called out to her from the lush earth, "I am here. Listen. Feel." But there was also an energy that seemed unfamiliar and dark; something new to her, a shadow that lingered in the mist . . .

Abruptly, the vehicle stopped in front of a building, and she was jarred out of her thoughts. Smiling Babaji appeared at the window bursting with excitement, "We are invited to hear children of village practice for my mother's ceremony. Come, come."

Allie's nickname for Babaji was the "Energizer bunny." He never seemed to tire, and he was always ready for the adventure of the present moment. So, rather than the lunch and rest they expected, everyone crawled over their luggage onto the streets of the village. They couldn't help but create a scene with five vehicles, nine towering westerners, Babaji, and his growing group of family members. Everyone clustered on the street, taking in the new scene and waiting for direction. Locals stopped to stare. Some were curious enough to approach closely, as if to touch them to see if they were an apparition. And Allie *was* one, walking in the dreamlike state of fatigue, hunger, and heat.

Children ran up and said a proud, "Hello!" in perfect English. "Hello! Hello!" they giggled. "Hello," they shouted and scampered away only to boomerang right back to them. They began to pull on Allie's shirt. "Hello!" More children noticed the game and ran over. "Hello! Hello! Hello!"

Allie was just as curious as they were, and she was enjoying their energy. But the game was quickly halted as Sunita ushered the group into one of the simple, concrete buildings, up the stairs toward a small room full of the children's choir and town musicians.

There's no way we can all fit into this space! Allie pleaded silently as she peeked into the already packed room. Undaunted, Rajesh waved them in. *Oh, my God. This is too much. It's too crowded.* Allie tried not to kick or fall on the children as she stepped over and around them. All the while, they sang a simple and haunting melody as one-by-one the visitors awkwardly "snuck" in to observe.

The music came to a cadence, and the lead musician respectfully halted the rehearsal to allow all of the honored guests to find a seat. Not a chair was in sight, so they sat on the floor. Allie rested on her heels and felt conspicuously tall in the center of the room. Kurt was stuffed next to her, sitting cross-legged with his knees up to his ears, his hat balanced on his head, and sweat trickling down his cheeks. "Very cozy," he whispered into Allie's ear.

The lead musician gestured to the remaining guests who tentatively hovered at the door. The children packed in even more tightly, seemingly making room. The others sat in spaces they didn't even know existed, touching each other, everywhere, while Babaji and his niece sat leaning against the wall next to the lead musician.

Desperate for fresh air, Allie prayed that someone would think to open the windows, but they were already open. The locals appeared unfazed. Not a molecule moved, even as her skin tickled with sweat. *Indiana Jones wasn't always comfortable, now, was he?* Allie encouraged herself. *I'm looking for purification, so I might as well start by sweating.*

The stifling room afforded no relief to these weary westerners. She sensed her group collectively trying to cope with the challenges of the new environment. But as the music began, the discomfort softened, and they were reminded why they made the long journey—to support Babaji during the festival. The lead musician's fingers effortlessly danced over the keys of the harmonium, setting the stage for a hauntingly simple melody that immediately pulled on Allie's heart strings. Several other men joined in with rhythmic instruments, and the children's pure, clear tones enhanced the captivating hymn.

Allie closed her eyes. The intense heat and fatigue,

combined with the sincere musical sharing, overwhelmed her. She let tears fall unchecked. It was a soft cry, not a bellow, and it was freeing and safe. Although she was aware of the others in the room, she kept her eyes closed so she wouldn't become self-conscious. She wanted to revel in this restful, peaceful state.

As the tears abated, she became lighter and began to feel like she was floating. The music continued, her physical discomforts eased, and the awareness of the heat faded. Colors began to radiate behind her closed eyes, and a pulsing reddish hue slowly morphed into a soft purple dancing light. As she relaxed more, the moving colors began to take on a more organized form, as if a shape were trying to appear. Allie was safe and comfortable—almost embraced—and she became even lighter. The dance of colors moved around her in a rhythmic pulse like a heartbeat. She was somewhere, yet nowhere, a liminal place that pulsed and emanated love from the center of the colors. *This is IT!* Her body disappeared and she became a pulsing . . .

Allie's head jerked and her eyes popped open. She must have fallen asleep. She had been on a long journey, yet all was still unchanged around her. She saw the smiling musicians and heard the children singing the same melody. Babaji's eyes were closed and his cheeks were covered with fresh, flowing tears. *He felt it too!* Kurt was sleeping peacefully and Doug was smiling broadly. Gloria looked miserable with sweat pooling above her frowning lips. Her obvious distress reminded Allie of the oppressive heat in the room and her own soaking wet clothing.

As the song ended, the silence in the room was palpable. Babaji, speechless, brought his palms together at his chest and bowed to everyone.

"Thank you so much," he sobbed. He spoke in both languages in order to include his guests. "Is honor that you sing to support my mother's next journey." He bowed his head toward his touching palms. Everyone held the silence. When he raised his head, his eyes were fresh with tears, "My friends here have travel long distance from all over world to share Gai Jathra Festival with us. You make this very special. We need go to hotel now but we will see you in next few days. Namaste, dear friends. Thank you."

The rehearsal continued, and the pilgrims, as gracefully as they could, peeled themselves off the floor and hobbled stiffly over the children. Their palms touched at their hearts to offer "Namaste."

Even with the hotel just a few blocks away, they loaded themselves over their luggage and back into the vehicles to continue on their way. The hotel was more like a hostel. Not that Allie had ever been to a hostel, but it was what she had always pictured. It was a clean, basic four-story rectangular cement structure. The stairwells and hallways of each floor were open to the outside, and clotheslines covered with linens and clothing hung on every level including the open flat roof. The space was free from screens and window casements and was truly open to the outdoors. A crow landed on the edge of a half wall to offer its greeting.

Eager but drained from jetlag and another full day of travel, Allie and Pearl carried their luggage up to the fourth floor common space where lunch was to be served. Couches, tables, and a mix of chairs marked the area to host both locals and visitors for meals and town gatherings. Near the stairway stood a counter where they could order a soda or water and, if lucky, one could score a cool drink from the small refrigerator. The travelers had been warned not to consume any ice.

Dribbles of sweat inched down Allie's neckline under her already soaked bra, pooled at her belly button, and landed at their final destination, her soaked underwear. For someone who typically didn't sweat, this was becoming all too familiar. An unmoving fan teased her from above. *YES! Flowing air. Please.*

As the hostel worker brought her bottled water, Allie motioned up to the fan with desperate eyes. The worker shook her head, spoke an unrecognizable language, and waved her hands in circles.

"No electricity," Rajesh translated, observing the situation. "Here, in the village, they only have electricity for six to twelve hours a day depending on the charge from the solar panels. It's monsoon season now, so they have to conserve energy."

"Oh." Allie deflated. She pulled out her water purifier to zap the bottled water.

"Well, I suspect no electricity means no internet. I want to disconnect but I'd also really like to let my mom know that we made it," Marianna said.

"We'll figure it out soon," Allie encouraged.

"Friends! Welcome to my home village! Indiana Jones adventure allow us to make it here very easy! Best trip ever!" Babaji introduced all of his relatives. They seemed to multiply. On a good day, Allie wouldn't have been able to remember everyone's names, but today, with fatigue clouding her brain, it was even more of a blur. She simply returned a smile to their welcoming faces.

"Big news! I ask my friend to pass message to Mountain shaman that we are here. I invite him to visit us and offer skull ceremony. He is special teacher and we will see if he can come. Is many days away, deep in mountains." Changing the subject as if a "skull ceremony" didn't pique anyone's interest, he asked, "Did you like music? Is beautiful song blessing my mother. Asking for rest for her soul and safe journey."

A resounding "Yes!" followed.

Suddenly plates of food appeared in front of them. It couldn't have been a more welcome and delicious meal of rice, dal, vegetables, and pickles. Everyone ate plentifully.

"Whoosh!" Unexpectedly, the fan kicked on, indicating that there were a few minutes of electricity. The first moving air in the village was incredibly welcome as Allie's wet, sweaty clothing became cool.

"Aha! Maybe we can connect now!" Marianna jumped up.

There was a moment of frantic remembrance of attachment to small devices that communicate to loved ones on the other side of the world. A bustle to learn the wi-fi password ensued. Just like in the Kathmandu hotel, it wasn't as simple or as reliable as the westerners had hoped. Even with the correct codes, their devices connected only when the sky was clear and free of dense clouds; or perhaps it was when the wind blew the right way. Either way, contact with the outside world was going to be challenging to these spoiled westerners.

CULTURAL LESSON #8
Release attachment to electricity and connectivity and dry underwear.

With text messages sent, bellies full, and many ready for a long nap, Babaji, their personal Energizer bunny announced, "Is time to see tailor for festival clothing. Come, come!"

Wow, the day just keeps going. Typical Babaji. I'd at least appreciate dry underwear. Allie rambled to herself, but since they didn't have their room keys yet, she had to continue with everything very damp.

CHAPTER 14

The Tailor

The group gathered outside the hostel, eager for their first shopping adventure in the small village. The hostel was set near the center of the village, and the town buzzed with activity and excitement in preparation for the upcoming festival.

"Boom, boomboom, boom boomboom, boom."

A constant rhythmic drum beat resonated from all edges of the village, and small parades of locals passed by practicing their formation. Men and boys, casually dressed in shorts, flip flops, and T-shirts played large drums that accompanied costumed men, who danced wildly in circles, spinning their arms in cylindrical patterns like pinwheels. These "Lackeys" hopped from foot to foot and whirled around and around. The practice was a spectacle, and Allie could only imagine what the full festival would offer.

The group walked in their own casual formation down the dirt streets to Babaji's preferred fabric shop, just a few blocks away. The tiny shop overflowed with textiles in all colors and prints, from silk to cotton. Following custom, Allie left her shoes at the entrance and stepped barefoot into the packed space.

What colors! And what fun! She eyed the limitless choices.

Three women shopkeepers sat wide-eyed and frozen on the cushioned floor, as the unexpected guests filled the shop. Squealing in delight, Babaji rushed over and hugged them warmly as old friends and explained their special circumstance. Locals stopped to stare, and some even squeezed in to sit and watch. As the tailor was summoned, Allie began to sift through the fabric, subtly observing the others observing her.

"I feel watched," she whispered to Kate. "Why are they watching us like they've never seen someone shop before?"

"They call you 'white clouds,' or 'ghosts' and are fascinated by you. Have no worries, it's harmless," Rajesh answered, overhearing the question.

Frustrated by her language limitations, Allie tried to make eye contact and smiled. Some smiled back warmly, others diverted their gaze, and a few glowered.

After some time, Babaji exclaimed, "Aha. Here is it!" He held up a soft, light-peach, cotton fabric. "Simple and cool. Is perfect! And white for men. We all will match for festival."

With all of these colors, he chose pale peach? Truly, my least favorite color. Allie was immediately embarrassed by her gut reaction. She longed for something more exciting but couldn't argue with the man mourning the loss of his mother. It was his festival, and this "ghost" was honored to be there and would look even more ghostly in peach.

The tailor arrived and paused at the entrance. A deer in the headlights, looking as if he wanted to flee.

"He's a little overwhelmed," Allie whispered to Kate who held four bolts of fabric. "We must appear to be the giants who took over this tiny castle of fabrics."

"I'll say and rightfully so! I hope he can make me something out of these also!" She beamed, obviously excited to finally be able to shop.

Allie had high hopes as well. She held a bolt of intricately beaded plum silk. He'll have his work cut out for him.

The tailor was flagpole thin, tiny, and young. Without a word, the measurements began. A second tailor was summoned, and, even so, it took hours to measure everyone, both for the festival and for their personal shopping choices.

"Do you think he's ever built clothing for bodies this size?" Allie asked Pearl.

"Only time will tell!" Pearl replied with her arms raised over her head. The traditional style required a tight fit, and the tape measure was wrapped tightly around her bust. "Babaji, can you please ask them to measure more loosely?" she implored.

"Yes, yes . . ."

The shop bustled with purchases while the seated locals silently watched everything. *I should give them popcorn.* The thought quickly passed through Allie's mind.

Eventually, the melted westerners found their way back to dinner at the hostel where they still hadn't been to their rooms.

Allie and Pearl ate quickly so they could settle themselves into their room for the first time. The immediate challenge was unlocking the oversized, old-fashioned padlock with a skeleton key. The clattering echoed through the open hallway.

"This takes me back to my great-grandmother's old basement door, skeleton key and all," Allie said as she watched Pearl fumble with the awkward lock. "And look, I can reach into the room right here, although that doesn't help us with the lock!" She peeked through the decorative metal bars that stretched from the chest-high half-wall all the way up to the ceiling. The bars offered some security but no sound proofing. Semi-sheer, thin white curtains hung behind the bars, giving the false impression of privacy.

"At last!" Pearl exclaimed as she jiggled the lock open.

The room was small and simple. Two twin beds with clean sheets and a thin blanket shared one nightstand and lamp. The ceiling fan remained still as it waited for electricity, and a small unscented bug repellant was plugged into the outlet by the door. Its enormous job was to protect them from the mosquitos that the thin curtain and half wall would not keep out.

Allie was relieved to see that the bathroom had a "western" toilet rather than a "squatty potty." It also had a small sink, bidet, shower head, and floor drain. The showerhead hung almost directly over the toilet, so taking a shower promised to soak the entire space. Allie thought of Gloria and Doug and wondered how they would handle that one. Fortunately, toilet paper was on their list of packed supplies, as there was none to be found.

"Although the sheets look clean, there's a line of tiny ants moving along my bed and up the wall," Pearl said calmly. They watched the small parade move purposefully along the outer edge of the bed.

Allie checked her bed. "I have them too. I guess this wouldn't bother Indiana Jones?" She was a little wigged out. "Just part of the adventure?"

"I suppose so. Let's shake these babies out!"

They carefully removed the sheets and shook them out in the hallway over the edge of the building.

"I've got bug spray. Let's spray the sheets. Maybe it'll keep them from crawling on us in the night?" said Allie hopefully.

"Definitely worth a try."

With the unexpected task complete, Pearl began to hang a rope from one end of the room to the other. "We can use this to hang our clothes up to dry. In this heavy, wet heat we'll be washing them a lot." She looked at the unmoving fan. "We'll see if they dry."

"Fantastic idea!" Allie said. "Ok with you if I hop in the shower?"

"You bet!"

Allie made sure the toilet was flushed before stepping under the shower head. The hint of hot water felt decadent as she washed away the village dust. On the wall a tiny lizard, just hanging out, kept her company. Perhaps the lizard, the ants, and she could coexist for ten days together?

Journal

What a long day! We couldn't have asked for more perfect weather for our flight to the village. So much for the Indiana Jones adventure! Even though I haven't seen any rain yet, the lush green indicates otherwise. Rajesh mentioned that during monsoon season, it typically rains through the night but clears up during the day. I'll take that!

The hotel/hostel is simple and clean, but the dirt

roads make the village really dusty. It's odd that there aren't any full walls in the building to keep out the dust, critters and bugs. I'll sleep with natural bug spray on to repel the mosquitos and my new ant friends.

The village is bustling with festival activity. The steady beat of the drums, ringing of bells, and dancing are adding to the excitement of being here. It's no surprise that the ants are also parading. Everybody, the lizard, ants, and locals seem to be preparing for the festival and watching the white cloud ghosts.

Really tired. More tomorrow.

CHAPTER 15

The Hill

"Adventure begins! It won't be easy but we go up, up up! Everybody ready?" Babaji greeted his friends as they gathered outside the hostel ready to explore.

Since not all members of the group were able to do a strenuous hike, Babaji arranged for them to travel up The Hill, about ten thousand feet above sea level, to experience the beauty of the Nepali mountains without too much exertion. Just in case, he was prepared with an oxygen bag and medicines for altitude sickness. Kurt was also on call with his suitcase of herbs just in case. A caravan of five Land Rovers waited in front of the hostel, ready to transport everyone, including several of Babaji's relatives, to their destination.

The pilgrims bounced along the bumpy, uneven dirt roads in vehicles whose shocks seemed to be long destroyed. Despite the discomfort, the beauty around them was breathtaking. Wet and rich rice paddies dotted the landscape with their meticulously terraced mud dams. Pools of natural spring water glistened and seedlings reached for the sun.

Small, thatched huts scattered across the landscape, and layers of green, brown, and purple mountains flowed endlessly into the distance. On this day, the sky was blue and clear with not a cloud in sight. The well-maintained land radiated life.

After about an hour of a steady and subtle incline, the caravan pulled to the side of the road for their first rest and bathroom break. Some took turns behind a giant boulder to find relief, and others played and posed on top of the boulder that provided a perfect backdrop for a photo session. A cow rested nearby under a makeshift bamboo shelter, casually chewing her cud and observing the excited tourists. She didn't understand the language of these tall creatures but seemed unfazed by her invaded serenity.

Allie looked beyond the cow to see Kate carefully climbing up the muddy incline toward a farmer who was tilling his field with two bulls and a hand-made wooden plow. Kate approached the farmer and gestured with her hands as she tried to communicate. She pulled out her phone and photographed the unfazed farmer, gesturing again. Confused, the farmer offered the plow to her and the two began to till the field together.

She has guts, that girl does. Such childlike wonder that I long to have.

"Okay, everyone!" Babaji boomed. The cow turned its head toward the sound, still chewing quietly. "The Indiana Jones adventure continues! We go up, up, up now! Zum, Zum. Let's GO!!" He noticed Kate in the field. "Haha, we lost Kate to farmer. Come friend, come!" When she didn't come, he let out a loud whistle. The cow responded with a resounding "Moo!"

Kate glanced their way. "KATE!" Allie yelled. "Time to go!" Kate offered a bow to the farmer and slowly returned to the group. Her smile revealed a sweet innocence, as if she had just discovered something very special. And who knows, maybe she did.

Babaji was not exaggerating. The pastures disappeared below, as the winding road indeed went up, up, up, becoming more and more narrow. To the right, tall trees stretched up the steep mountainside, offering Allie an illusionary safety barricade from the long drop down. To the left, protruding boulders rooted into the mountainside, texturing the dense forest that reached toward the open sky. From somewhere high above, varying pathways of water rushed down and around the boulders with the water, at times, running inches deep across the road as it continued its descent to the ravines below.

I can't imagine hiking this. Just sitting here, being driven up the mountain, is a huge undertaking, Allie thought, feeling brave and adventurous.

At that moment, the caravan paused in front of a fast-flowing spontaneous waterfall that crossed the road and cascaded down the mountainside. The drivers were used to the muddy, gaping potholes and rushing streams, but they took their time assessing the present situation. Allie's driver yelled out the window to the car in front. They conversed for a few moments, and then the lead driver proceeded slowly across the flowing water while the others followed. Allie's heart skipped a beat as the vehicle rocked side to side, making its way slowly but safely across the wet road and uneven terrain. A Jersey girl, Allie had been taught to never drive through flooded roads, and yet here, high into the Nepali mountains, this seemed to be a normal and necessary practice.

It was beyond time for another bathroom break, so when the road widened to easily accommodate two lanes of traffic, the caravan pulled over, allowing the pilgrims to happily stretch their legs. They were quite a sight as they jammed up the small, mountainous road. Allie climbed out of the vehicle to the smell of fresh water and realized that she was standing in the clouds. A light mist danced through the air, and an even larger waterfall enhanced the moistness as it tumbled down the bouldered mountainside, across the road and continued down, down, down.

"Friends," Babaji announced as they stood in the clouds, "Is process, not destination. We need to appreciate our journey at all moments. Destination, we don't know. But *this* moment, we do!" Always their teacher, Babaji never missed an opportunity. "Now . . . photo session! Everyone into waterfall!!" he shouted with a broad smile.

It was party time. One of the vehicles blared Nepali music from the radio while the group appreciated the cooler air and icy water, both refreshing and nourishing. The singer's bright soprano sang a simple, repetitive melody that echoed throughout the jungle.

"Om Bhoo Bhoovah Swahah . . ."

That was all Allie could make out. Those words, with each repetition, called to her as if they should be familiar.

"Om Bhoo Bhoovah Swahah . . ."

The lively melody flew over and around Allie while she treaded carefully into the woods in search of a private area to take her bathroom break. In the distance, laughter and loud chatter filled the air.

We're certainly making our presence known. I can't imagine any wildlife would hang around here right now. Hopefully no snakes! She squatted behind a tree and balanced over the ferns.

A movement in the distance caught her eye. Still finishing her business, she realized she was little too far off the beaten path. Allie turned her head in the direction of the movement and held her breath. In the far distance, amidst the dense trees, she saw the figure of woman. Allie froze. She forgot she was peeing. She forgot herself. The figure turned to look toward her and Allie felt familiarity and recognition. *That's the woman from the temple. How?* Allie blinked, and then she saw . . . nothing, just trees.

God, I'm losing my mind. A play of shadows? She blinked again and hurriedly tried to finish, all the while, listening for footsteps; just in case.

Standing quickly, Allie gathered her courage to look back

toward the "play of shadows." One immature, thinly stalked tree with just a few leaves danced in the wind. But there was no wind.

"Om Bhoo Bhoovah Swahah . . ."

The repetitive melody came into her awareness again, drawing Allie back to the group. She turned and ran toward the others.

"Join us, Allieji!" Babaji yelled. He didn't notice her spooked, pale face.

Pearl, Kate, and Marianna huddled playfully in a crevice under the waterfall. They were mostly dry and giggling like children.

John and Jane had removed their shoes and splashed their feet safely in the puddles at the foot of the falls.

Kurt and Gloria took photos while Doug danced on a boulder with his hands confidently pressing into the air with each beat.

"Okay, Babaji, I'm coming!" Allie yelled back. "What's the song playing now?"

'Gayatri Mantra! Mantra of light. Come, Allieji, come." He and Lumanti huddled under the waterfall laughing and tossing water into each other's faces.

In the middle of Nepal, somewhere halfway up a mountain, Allie felt her protective boundaries begin to fall away and her fear of the unknown diminish. She felt daring as she removed her shoes to wade in. With her toes tingling in the fresh, rolling water, a chill shook through her. *That's it. Shaking off the stresses of life.* Although she didn't climb as high as the others, she laughed and played all the same.

> CULTURAL LESSON #10
> Take time to enjoy the moment. Especially if
> it means playing in a waterfall on the
> side of a mountain.

Wet, cooler, and lighter, everyone eventually climbed back into the vehicles to continue up the mountain. Back in her seat, Allie let out a huge sigh. *This is more than a pilgrimage, it's a vacation.* She felt free from all responsibilities and obligations. It was an unfamiliar sensation. *So, this is how being **truly** in the present moment feels.* She liked it.

They drove more deeply into the clouds as they approached their destination; a tiny village of only a handful of homes with one store that could provide basic necessities and a homemade meal. The villagers must have had advance notice of their arrival, because they were welcomed with an extensive, traditional homemade feast. Generous hospitality was a cultural given, and a good meal was a necessary part of the welcome. Typically, there were a minimum of four now-familiar dishes, and this day did not disappoint.

So far, at the high altitude of ten thousand feet, everyone seemed to be okay and ready to hike. However, their hostess, upon hearing that they made the long journey to explore the peak, gave a grave warning to Babaji.

"Oh no!" He translated, "Leeches are too bad right now.

Monsoon make it very wet. Not recommend going on hike. Leeches will fall on head. Get all over. After monsoon is much better."

A collective silence blanketed the group as they processed their disappointment **and** the leeches. The five-hour journey up the mountain for a spectacular view was now just a long journey in Land Rovers to be fed a great meal. One thing Allie was quickly learning: attachment to an activity, event, or specific timing was only a set-up for disappointment. Flexibility and fast adjustment to change were a necessity for her well-being, if she didn't want to be racked with pain and distress. If only she could remember that back home.

CULTURAL LESSON #11
Release attachment to an outcome.

"Hahaha! Is journey, not destination, remember?" Babaji was wise in his advice. However, some would be able to handle it better on this trip than others. In the meantime, five children ran up, shy and excited, and whispered something to Babaji.

"Aha, is good! Instead of leech hike, children want to show you safe area. Let's go. See," Babaji encouraged.

Most of the group was happy to move their legs and easily rallied themselves to follow the young children down the narrow, steep pathway to the local watering hole. Gloria and

Doug were the only two who stayed behind with beers in hand. *Wonder how they scored those?*

CULTURAL LESSON #12
Even the most remote village will have
beer if you know whom to ask.

The natural well that the children so proudly showed them provided water to the entire village. A long pipe had been installed from which people could drink, fill buckets, or even bathe.

Allie was reminded yet again of the ease in which she lived back in the States.

Babaji described, "Is only source of water here. Villagers walk long, steep path many times a day in all weather for drinking, cooking, dishes, and bathing. Your meal, dishes, preparation take great effort." Allie saw Babaji give the villagers and the children extra rupees to express the group's gratitude.

CULTURAL LESSON #13
Plumbing is a luxury. Natural spring
water is earth's gift.

With the impromptu tour complete, the group began the short journey back toward the vehicles. One family generously shared their outhouse with them, a hole in the ground, free from chemicals and toilet paper. The smell was overwhelming, and Allie held her breath longer than she thought she could as she squatted as quickly as possible.

"Before getting in car, check for leeches," Babaji instructed.

"Ah, oh, my God, oh, my God, oh, my God. Get it OFF!!" Gloria yelled. Even though she had stayed behind with a beer, she was the only one lucky enough to score a leech on her pant leg, which was easily removed by the laughing Babaji.

The journey down the mountain seemed endless. That which was magical going up, quickly became monotonous and never-ending as fatigue and car sickness (or was it altitude sickness?) set in for many. Allie was surprised at how well she felt at the high altitude, but as they descended, she began to struggle with a headache and mild nausea. She pulled out a power bar and electrolyte packet from her mighty snack bag, hoping they would help.

"You look pale. Here." Kurt put some scented oil on her wrists.

"Thank you." The soothing scent, a mixture of lavender and frankincense, softened the stale smell of their vehicle. Allie closed her eyes and allowed herself to be bounced into to a shallow sleep.

"Wow, I'M REALLY HAPPY to have my feet on the ground again." Allie couldn't get out of the car fast enough as they pulled up to the hostel and began to adjust to the mere four-thousand foot altitude. She felt light-headed, and her stomach was still topsy-turvy.

"Drink more water and get some rest," Papa bear Kurt suggested.

"Gladly," Allie popped a ginger candy into her mouth.

"Let's do it, friend," Pearl said as she put her arm around Allie. They climbed the three flights of stairs slowly, arm in arm, ready for a few moments of rest before the evening's events.

"Okay with you if I hop in the shower?" Allie asked Pearl.

"Go for it!"

Pearl was snoring softly as Allie and her lizard friend finished a cool shower. *Fantastic idea!* Allie shook the ants off of her sheets and lay down—her head couldn't hit the pillow fast enough.

A DELECTABLE DINNER OF traditional dal bhat, tarkari, spicy relish, and yogurt was served. The pickles added heat to the dish, while the yogurt soothed the burn. Allie was still in a fog from her short, deep nap. She had slept so soundly that Pearl had to shake her awake, and, even then, she had forgotten where she was.

"Looks like something's going on!" Allie observed to Pearl. "I guess I have to pinch myself to wake up."

The meal had ended, and the room began to fill with locals. There were already a few familiar faces. The village musicians were setting up their instruments, and the children from the rehearsal gathered, all dressed in matching outfits. There were dancers, beautifully dressed in long, glossy orange skirts, and fitted red shirts elaborately decorated with gold collars. An elegant golden headdress topped it off. Locals filed in as the hostel workers lined up chairs to face the impromptu stage. It was time for a full cultural welcome, and the space quickly filled up.

The five male musicians played the harmonium, drums, and small rhythmic instruments and sang in unison, "Om Bhur Bhuvaha Svaha . . ." Raw, unrefined, and full of love.

That's the melody from the hike! I've gotta get this! Allie pulled out her recorder.

"Tat Savitur Varenyam Bhargo Devasya Dhimahi Dhiyo Yo Nah Prachodayat."

Most of the words were a blur, but the melody was enchanting. They repeated it over and over, each time a little louder and more joyful. The locals joined in, and the united voices filled the entire space. The melody danced around her, and the tickle of energy combined with the static hot air made her feel electric. Allie felt soothed and relaxed as the last of her barriers softened. Her heart opened just a tiny bit.

Next came the dancers, whose hand positions and eye movements expressed an intricate story. Allie had never seen a dance so detailed and expressive. The children's choir followed, and the sweet folk song told yet another melodic story of the land. With translation unknown, the poignant emotion was still felt by all who listened. Three hours passed, and, by the end of the presentation, the group felt warmly welcomed and culturally informed. It was the best welcome Allie had ever experienced.

Journal

Today was a wild and full day. The cultural welcome was spectacular. It felt like a presentation for a president or a dignitary, but it was for US! I couldn't have asked for a more perfect way to immerse into the culture and learn more about the musical traditions. One melody dominates, and I'm so drawn to it. The Gayatri Mantra. It affects me deeply and is inexplicable. Like I know it already, somehow, deep in my cells. I almost don't want to know the translation, because it might take away from the primal, natural resonance that's so profound. I'll learn the pronunciation though. If I were home, I'd have googled it by now, but I don't want to bother here with access so infrequent and slow. And I'm also content with my phone turned off. So, I'll try the old-fashioned way. By listening.

Now, it got weird on the mountain because I swear I saw someone in the jungle when I was peeing. I watched her turn her head and look at me! I *saw* her eyes. And it totally freaked me out. She not only looked like the stranger from the temple yesterday, but also the angelic woman from the yoga studio many years ago. I totally must be fabricating her in my mind. I'm tired and in between time zones. And I was changing altitudes. That's got to be it. I know I'm not going crazy here already. Anyway, at least if I am being haunted, it's a character who seems loving. Better than the other characters who live in my head.

I'll call her the crone. Night night, old crone. I'm ready for that peace.

CHAPTER 16

Morning in the Village

At six a.m., Allie, Pearl, Kurt, John, and Jane met Babaji and Lumanti for a hike around the village. Birdsongs rang out over the landscape, announcing the new day, while the soft glow of the sun blushed the dark sky. Shutters, doors, and metal storefronts flew open, scattering the goats, dogs, and chickens that wandered the streets.

Allie's heart was light, grateful to be with Babaji in his village at sunrise. He glowed as he tenderly shared stories about his homeland with the intimate group. It was a dream come true.

"Today too muddy and slippery for us to go." He gestured to a path that led from the road up into a jungle of emerald, olive, and jade greenery. "But listen for monkeys. Do you hear? They sometimes chase you or steal sunglasses. Keep watching eye!" The thick trees were inviting, and Indiana Jones called out to them, but, instead, they continued along the village road.

The curious group came upon a large cement structure, similar to that of a tree trunk. It served as a road divider at the small dirt intersection.

"Later today we go Rudraksha hunting to search for special, sacred seeds of Rudraksha tree. But here, see cement? Here very old tree lived. I need tell you story. This tree protected for many generations by families. It grew and grew. The families so connected to land, they understand language of nature, of trees. They know to work with nature, to use herbs for healing, medicine, and food. This tree was Mother Earth connection. They respect it for shade, fruit, protection. To show gratitude, they make offering twice a year with special ceremony. Is said that ceremony for tree so powerful that if stranger not prepared came up on it, stranger get sick and die. The connection very special, magical, and deep. As population grew, others move to area. Others not understand this connection. They say tree 'worshipers' are strange. Call them witches. Some stumble on ceremony by accident, others on purpose. All died right after or become very ill. Fear grow in village and one night, sacred tree cut down. They think will solve problem. Land sad now. Hurt. Mother energy injured. Cement here, honors tree but damage is done."

Allie remembered the movie *Avatar* and how horrible she felt when the mother tree went down. Maybe this is the feeling she sensed in the mist the other day—a sadness or darkness? Is the village haunted by this tragedy? The travelers moved on along the dirt road feeling a little heavier.

"What people don't understand, they try to destroy. Is not good. We need have compassion for each other. Make connection with others, with earth and listen," said Babaji. "Let us stop for moment. Have quick meditation." He closed his eyes and took a long, full breath. "Feel feet on earth. Take deep breath. Smell Mother Earth." It smelled of fresh soil, moss, mushrooms, and grass, crisp and moist. "Now, send love to earth. From our hearts. Thank you, Mother Earth. Please help us understand. Please help us hear and listen. We love you. We thank you." He paused again . . . "Now . . . listen . . ."

The rustle of leaves, the movement of the monkeys, the flapping wings of birds, bells ringing in the distance, villagers chanting, talking, coughing, and laughing, the brush of brooms sweeping dust into dust.

"OhhhhhhhMMMMM," Babaji sang softly. "Listen, can you hear the Om?" He continued so softly so as to lead his friends into it. "OhhhhhhhMMMMM." Long, steady, and barely audible. "The Om is in the wind, the birds' song, our heartbeat. Is here now." The silence within the sounds was palpable.

"Caw, Caw!" A crow called loudly from a distance and landed on a tree branch above Babaji's head.

"Aha! And maybe OM is in song of Crow, too!"

"Caw, Caw!"

They listened.

"Now we return for breakfast." He smiled.

CHAPTER 17

The Flute

That afternoon, the community room bustled with activity due to the dramatic arrival of the monsoon rains that were dropping buckets of water on the once-dusty village. The pilgrims' rudraksha hunting had to be postponed, so they had no formal afternoon plans. Marianna, Pearl, Kate, and Allie were hanging out after the full meal. Kurt sat quietly in a corner reading a book. Babaji gathered with his family, reminiscing and laughing. The two couples were enjoying a boisterous discussion with beers in hand. Locals clumped in small meetings and conversations. Everyone was settling into a new rhythm and comfort with each other.

"Dai!" A sudden excitement filled the room. The endearment of "older brother" rang out in greeting. A strikingly handsome man stood at the foot of the stairs of the community room, and he was joyfully greeted by his friends. Babaji obviously knew him, and, after a long hug, he introduced him to the group.

"Meet Loojha. Is very famous singer in Nepal. So many albums and videos. You will hear. He is home to sing for festival."

The local celebrity stood at a poised 5'5" and radiated a kind confidence. He spoke more English than Allie spoke Nepali, but only slightly. "Hello. Nice to meet you," he said slowly in a thick accent.

"Mero nam Allie ho." Allie tried out her Nepali with a simple "My name is Allie."

"Ah! Hah. Nice to meet you!" And the conversation stopped there. They smiled awkwardly at each other with no more native words to offer.

"Allieji is famous opera singer in America! Her singing so beautiful," Babaji told the town musicians in both languages as he introduced her. "You must hear her chant."

She was embarrassed by the exaggeration, "Oh no, I'm a professional singer, or used to be, Babaji, but definitely not famous! Maybe infamous!" She laughed, but the joke fell flat. The language barrier was too great for nuance.

Okay, she thought, *I guess here in this small village I'll be a "famous opera singer."* This wouldn't be the first time broken English led to an elaborate exaggeration.

The musicians' eyes widened and they encouraged, "Yes, sing, please."

They stood and stared at her with large smiles. They waited.

Now? she thought. "Oh, no, not now, later?"

"Sing, please!"

Babaji stood smiling. Her mind raced. *What should I sing? What style would they like to hear? Opera or chant?* She always took singing for others so seriously, even in a casual situation like this. There was a part of her that wanted to share her voice with them and another part that just wanted to be an anonymous fly on the wall, an observer, a silent pilgrim. But here they were, still staring at her in anticipation.

"Yes, sing, please," Babaji repeated.

She silently raced through her repertoire. She couldn't burst into an opera aria without attracting the attention of the entire village. There were no walls, and an aria required her full voice, which was trained to fill a large auditorium. *What would be the purpose in that anyway? Just to show off?* She chuckled at the thought of her voice resonating through the hills of the village like the haunting sound of a ghost! Instead, she settled on a simple chant that, upon first hearing, made her feel comforted and embraced. She sang it often as a meditation.

Inhaling, she began quietly, "Jai Sita Ram, Jai Sita Ram, Bajarangi Jai Hanuman."

The men smiled widely in appreciation of her choice. The text was obviously familiar to them, and, once they picked up the melodic line, they sang along. The mantra represents the essence of devotion and love, and they all joined with one voice, their sincerity bridging the language barrier and any other perceived differences.

When they came to the final cadence, the lead musician exclaimed, "You know Hanuman Mantra!! How you know?"

"Yoga," Allie said simply.

"Beautiful opera mantra! Sing tomorrow with us!"

Opera mantra? "O-okay," Allie blushed. She felt that old flutter of nervous anticipation rise in her stomach. In a matter of a few minutes, she transitioned from a relaxed anonymous pilgrim back to her stressed professional singer persona. She didn't like it and didn't want to bring those old tensions into the trip. *Relax. You're in Nepal. You don't have to be perfect. You can even make a fool of yourself, and no one will be the wiser. It's okay!* Giving herself a familiar pep talk, she tried to let go and return to the role of pilgrim.

Everyone began to settle into their activities and conversations as Allie sat back with her friends.

"Well-deserved, dear friend. I overheard that you're the famous opera singer from America!" Pearl supported. "I can't wait to hear you sing with them! Your voice always relaxes me."

"Me, too!" Marianna chimed in.

"I wish it would relax me. I haven't sung in so long, and I'm nervous now at the thought of it," Allie grumbled.

"That's ridiculous. You're a pro-*fesh*-ional. That's what you do!"

"I know, I know. And it's my job as a pro-*fesh*-ional to entertain and put others at ease, but singing's become too stressful. Oh, I can put up a good front alright, but the truth is, I've been battling stage fright my entire career, and I'm just exhausted by it all. And since my divorce and the tornado of loss that followed, I don't have the energy to battle anymore."

"You got this. Isn't chanting solely to commune with God? What more could you want?" Pearl encouraged.

"True. This isn't the opera world, now is it?" Allie said.

"No, this is the land of magic!" added Marianna.

The friends settled into a comfortable silence, which allowed Allie to drift into a memory.

The activity in the community room faded, Nepal disappeared, and her mind rocketed back six years to an event in Upstate New York . . .

Allie was attending her first yoga retreat. She was brand new to the culture and had registered at the last minute on a whim. She didn't know anyone, nor did she really know why she was there. She just knew that her life had recently exploded into a stressful climax, and she was desperate to escape and decompress before her head exploded.

After a surprisingly relaxing day of enjoying the grounds, she ran into a man wearing orange. He had a peaceful, joyful energy and spoke with a New York accent, which put Allie immediately at ease.

"Can you play the harmonium?" He asked excitedly when he learned of her profession. He was referring to an instrument that was like a miniature organ-keyboard and accordion all in one. To play it, one pumped the bellows with one hand and played the tiny keyboard with the other.

"A little bit," she said lightly. "I'm just learning." She had only just begun to explore chant more deeply.

He clapped his hands in joy. "Good! You'll lead chant before my lecture tomorrow morning at six a.m."

"But, I'm only just—"

"That's okay. When we chant the holy names," the Swami said intensely, "we're offering to God our love and at the same time, receiving it."

"I understand, but I don't really know what I'm doing yet. I respectfully . . ."

"You've been given a gift," he regarded her seriously, "and you MUST share that gift with others. This is your dharma." His volume increased, "We step out of our personality, our attachments and our ego . . ." he looked directly into her eyes, "and ask to be a servant of God through the music."

She stared back into his bright eyes. He was seeing it so clearly, and yet she was terrified. She didn't take singing in front of others lightly. He must have seen that too. "You cannot run from your dharma. You must serve others by sharing your gift." He grinned. "See you in the morning," and with that, he walked away.

Allie was momentarily mesmerized by his beautiful and heartfelt monologue, but the moment he left, emotions rushed in, and she felt put off by his invitation. *"You cannot run from your dharma." HA! I didn't pay to come on retreat to stress myself out and find my dharma, whatever that is.* All of the characters in her head lashed out at once.

And you nailed it. I'm running. Because if I don't run, I'm going to explode. I'm here to retreat and escape! I just want to forget my "gifts." Enough with my gifts. The mental loop was relentless . . . *He doesn't understand. Maybe I don't have anything left to give. How about that? Maybe I'm sucked dry, and don't WANT to be in front of others anymore. Period.* Her ego was rising to the occasion, and she was experiencing a good old-fashioned temper tantrum. *I just want to be anonymous.*

"Listen to you all!" Allie said aloud to the ranting ensemble in her mind. She didn't remember walking to her room, but there she was. She held her head in her hands. "I need a break from you and your judgments and fears. Shut up!" To her amazement, they got quiet. She wasn't just yelling at herself, she was yelling at her ex-husband, her father, and her failing career.

Deep breaths. Her pulse started to calm down, and she sat on the bed in her tiny room and began to chant. "Om." *Let me connect, God, please. Show me where you are.* She sang quietly. "Jai Sita Ram," her fingers played the melody on her pillow, an impromptu air harmonium. *I can do this,* she realized. *I want to disappear. But maybe I can disappear into the chant . . .*

That retreat was her debut as a leader of chant, whether she wanted it or not.

A sweet voice lulled Allie back to Nepal. The sounds of the community space filled her ears, and Allie followed the melody to Loojha, the handsome man with the confident aura. *I wonder if he ever gets nervous?* He was sitting with the town musicians in a tight circle in the corner of the room. It appeared that Loojha was organizing a rehearsal, and it was obvious to Allie that they had work to do and didn't want to be disturbed. The guitarist strummed softly, and Loojha's sweet voice sang a folk-like melody. Indeed, they were rehearsing. The singing was quiet, and they listened carefully to one another. On occasion Loojha stopped the group to offer suggestions. Then they began again. Allie was all too familiar with the process, and she rushed to pull out her voice recorder. *Perfect research!*

The melody was new to her, but it brought up a longing within, as only a good, tender melody could. And although she had no idea what the song was about, she heard the heartfelt expression and was enjoying being the observer of the rehearsal.

"TOOT, TOOT, TOOT . . . ," the sound of a native wooden flute screamed from the stairwell. Not a fluid, soothing sound but rather, a hollow, screeching similar to what one would hear from a new clarinetist—a beginner's tone. And it entered the room, carried and played by none other than Doug. Proudly he strode to the musicians' circle and stood over them attempting to play along with their music. Loojha glanced at him curiously and went back to rehearsing. Yet Doug hovered, "Toot, toot, tooooot."

Allie cringed and turned off her recorder. The flute that Doug was playing was in a specific mode, and, unlike a keyboard, was limited in its chord structure and melodic notes. The musicians were singing in a completely different key, and the clash was remarkably horrible to a trained ear. If she hadn't been mortified, she would have laughed in exasperation.

The whole room quieted to observe the awkward exchange. "Toot TOOOOOT." The musicians finally stopped. They could fight the clash of key no longer. Doug didn't notice that they had stopped mid-song and were staring at him with wide eyes. He continued, eventually ending on a high, sour note, whereupon he lowered the flute and beamed.

"Please, play," Loojha kindly offered, giving the foreign guest an opportunity to share his music as a solo.

Very generous and diplomatic. Not quite what I would've done! Allie was impressed.

Doug puffed up with confidence. He widened his stance, rocked back and forth until he stood equally on both legs, took a big breath, and began to play a simple folk melody similar to that of "Hot Cross Buns." What Doug lacked in technique and tone, he made up for with emotional expression. His body flowed and moved as he serenaded the captive audience. When he finished, once again on a sour high note, he flicked the flute to the side and bowed as if he had just completed Pachelbel's Canon.

"Oh, yes, yes," They high-fived him. "Thank you." "Nice."

"We practice now, okay?" the guitarist said kindly. Doug looked puzzled. After a slight hesitation, they began.

Doug listened then began to improv along again. "Toot,

toot, tooooot." The musicians hovered together more closely and tried to continue while ignoring Doug. They had work to do. Allie rushed over to Babaji.

"Babaji, they're trying to rehearse, and Doug's disrupting them. And he's in a totally different key."

"I know Allieji. Is really bad! But what do I do?"

"Toot, toot toooooot."

"I don't know." *The obvious,* she thought, trying to be polite. "Somebody at least has to tell him that he's in the wrong key and to let them rehearse!" *Somebody has to reel in his ego!* His insensitive behavior was making her anxious, and her head tingled. *He's so oblivious.* In just a few days' time, she was tired of Doug's insistent need to be the center of attention. The desire seemed so desperate that he was unaware of how his actions affected others. This bothered her deeply.

CULTURAL LESSON #14
Don't be an insensitive ass-in whatever country you're visiting! And if you're not sure your behavior is inappropriate, ask someone.

It was typical of Allie to feel responsible for the well-being of others, particularly as a guest in another country, but was it her place to inform Doug that he was disrupting their hosts' rehearsal? *People can't learn unless they're made aware and taught. But on the other hand, not everyone wants to learn. How do you teach someone who doesn't want to learn?* She and Babaji looked at each other. Stalemate. "Namaste," she mumbled, deciding that it wasn't *her* place to say something in this moment. He was the teacher. Doug already seemed tense around her, and it would be too embarrassing for him. Instead, she huffed to her room to visit the lizard and the ants to blow off steam. Pearl followed.

"I don't understand why Babaji won't say something. He's our leader and teacher! If you can *do* something, you should *do* something. Expert in the flute, ha! He doesn't even know that he's in the wrong key," Allie wanted to scream as she paced around the room, very obviously upset on everyone's behalf.

"Sounds like this is a sensitive subject for you." Pearl said quietly.

"You think? Are you not seeing what I'm seeing?"

"Yes, but what's the big deal? So, Doug sucks at the flute and he's embarrassing himself. Why's it your place to get involved?"

The lizard appeared on the wall, all ears. The ants were in normal formation on the bed, waiting.

"It's rude. It's unnecessary and disruptive," she told all of them. "I'm tired of people being insensitive asses, and what's worse . . . I didn't expect it on this tour."

"Aha. Okay. Got it."

"Nor did I expect there to be such egos on this trip. I needed this trip to be easy, and Doug is just plain rude. I left my egotistical husband, and I don't want to be reminded of him through Doug. Center of attention, always!" Allie threw up her hands. "And this could be easily remedied by *someone* teaching him appropriate sensitivities in a new culture. What's so hard about that?"

Pearl thought for a moment. "Babaji has his reasons and methods. Maybe he has a deeper plan of action? I think you're riled up because of all you're going through. Doug reminds you of things you're trying to leave behind. But here it is in your face. Toot, toot, toooot." Pearl mimicked the sour flute. "So . . . you have choices . . . you can stay suffering, or you can say something to Doug and get it out in the open. Or, maybe you can just let it go? Don't stay stressed over it. He certainly isn't."

"Good points." She took a full breath and looked in Pearl's caring brown eyes. "Being here has its challenges . . . and," she referred to the ants, "you guys are no exception. I guess everything seems elevated," she exhaled. "I guess it's not such a big deal. Thanks for the pep talk."

"Anytime. I'll probably need one down the road. In the meantime," Pearl rose and grabbed her sheet, "how about we shake these ants off?" The lizard ran back into the bathroom.

"Deal. But they'll be back."

"Yup, that's the process. We just keep at it!"

When they returned, Doug was seated with his flute next to Babaji, laughing and talking, and the musicians were rehearsing in peace. How it resolved, Allie and Pearl would never know.

CHAPTER 18

The First Shaman

The second welcome event was to take place that evening at a yoga school, which was nestled amidst the rolling hills just outside the village. The group collectively chose to walk the short distance through the densely forested footpath. Rich green hues greeted Allie's eyes with a newness and freshness that transcended any Crayola superpack. Nothing manmade could match this infinite spectrum, and she couldn't get enough of it. *Now, THIS is the Nepal I envisioned.* Sweet scents of hidden flowers and flowing pollen tickled her senses, while insects and critters scuttled away from her heavy steps.

All too soon, the path led the pilgrims out of the jungle into an open vista of rolling hills, grassy fields, and the modest school grounds. To the left, perched at the top of a crest, stood a portion of the main village, a watch tower over the vast jungle. Although the unseemly cement buildings screamed of progress, they were a stark contrast to the surrounding natural beauty.

Here, tucked in the middle of the mountains, this private yoga school housed and educated boys from the region. Some walked miles each day to attend, while others lived on the small campus.

The founder welcomed the group in perfect English.

"Greetings. I am the master teacher for the school, and we are honored to have you on our campus."

Although only five foot two inches, his presence commanded respect, and Allie could tell immediately that his ego was not lacking in confidence or height.

"Namaste," said Allie.

"Namaskar is the proper greeting." His chest protruded like a proud cock claiming his territory. With such extension, Allie wondered if he slept in a full backbend. "Namaste is informal. Namaskar shows respect to elders," he scolded.

"Sorry," Allie apologized. "Namaskar." She again brought her hands together at the center of her chest, now sunken in embarrassment. She'd greeted a lot of strangers already, and no one else had corrected her, not even Babaji. Allie's scalp tingled. *Bad juju? Another Doug?* She was suspicious of those who lauded themselves as "master" but decided to file away her discomfort in order to enjoy the evening.

The school buildings were scattered around several acres and were freshly painted in uniform blue and yellow patterns. The kitchen and cafeteria opened to a large covered outdoor area that was used for asana, presentations, and dining.

"It is festival season so the school is not in session. Most of the students are home to celebrate with their families but some of our students will return tonight to share their talents with you. We have also invited a shaman to welcome and bless your visit to our village. Come." The master teacher led them to the covered area where they would receive the meal and entertainment.

THE MISTY SKY DARKENED to a purple glow as the honored guests finished a spicy meal lovingly prepared by the senior students. The glowing dusk offered a peaceful backdrop that balanced the forming chaos around them. Word had gotten out that the village shaman was going to bless the "ghosts," and it promised to be a spectacle that the villagers did not want to miss. Locals rushed in from all directions, and the space quickly filled up.

The master teacher stood boastfully. "Welcome, everyone, and welcome, honored guests from all over the world. This is a very special school. Everyone learns English, and students graduate to become scholars, doctors, and engineers. The students become very successful. We are happy that you chose to visit us, and we invite you to enjoy our presentation."

Three elder boys began their accompaniment on the harmonium, kartals, and drum while others set up center stage. The boys' fine acrobatic asana presentation made Allie wonder if their joints would survive puberty. All the while, the master teacher stood strong and firm, barking formation orders. They were confident and focused, as if competing for the gold medal. (And competition winners, they were.) Their sincere display of flexibility and stamina went on for hours.

Babaji could see that his friends were wilting, yet there was more planned.

Standing, he clapped his hands to rally excitement. "Is time for ceremony! This shaman is very special channel of Shiva energy. He is focus on removing obstacles for you on this trip. Come, come. Bring our chairs to front!"

Allie was very happy to stand for a few moments. She was managing her fatigue well, considering the endless days, but her eyelids were heavy, and her body longed for bed. With the invited shaman ready to go, she and the others lined up their chairs side by side at the foot of the makeshift stage and took their seats, packed in by curious and excited villagers. Some even had beers in hand and were laughing and joking loudly, as if they were gathering to watch a sporting event. As the crowd became more boisterous, Allie began to feel self-conscious.

"Look at all the people. Where'd they come from? I feel like they're constantly watching us," the loud whisper was meant only for Pearl and Marianna.

"This shaman must be special to draw such an audience," Marianna whispered back.

"Maybe it's us? I feel on display. It's a bit embarrassing," rattled Allie.

"Overwhelming's more like it; who could've seen this

coming?" Pearl added. "But we're here to support Babaji and learn about the culture. Let's focus on that. And this is a REAL shaman!" She laughed with good humor, ready for the adventure.

Allie sat back and tried to ignore the commotion around her. Instead, she focused on the shaman, who was young, tall, thin, and certainly not what she had expected. She'd pictured a tiny weathered man with wrinkled skin and piercing eyes. The shaman was dressed in white with a red sash around his waist. A feathered headdress enhanced his height and presence, and several strings of natural wood beads swayed and clattered from his neck as he twirled his decorated wand. Nearby hovered his assistant, ready to play the sheepskin drum.

Allie would have preferred to meet with the shaman privately in a quiet location, but instead, while the villagers chattered excitedly, the display quickly began.

"Boom, boom, boom," sounded the drum, steady and strong. The crowd of voices came to a crescendo and then quickly quieted down in anticipation. The shaman's kind eyes scanned the group before yielding to the rhythm of the drum. He chanted softly and bounced around and around from foot to foot in a practiced pattern and formation. Allie became mesmerized by the sound and her heavy eyelids gave way. She lingered between sleep and awareness as she tried to focus on the many personal obstacles she was ready to release.

Purification of . . .

Whack!

Her eyes popped open to see the shaman dancing in front of her. His swirling wand had hit her pointedly on the left side of her head as he bounced by. Although he looked to be in a trance and didn't seem to notice that he had just hit her, she wasn't sure. Maybe he was whacking something out of her or knocking sense into her? Either way, it was shocking and drew her to full attention. It hadn't hurt, and for that she was grateful.

As she tried to take it all in, she wished that Babaji could explain what was happening. *What are we witnessing? What is the shaman chanting? What does the dance represent? The drumbeat?* Her head was full of questions. *Not everything needs to have an explanation. Quiet down. Feel. Experience.* Afraid to close her eyes again, she watched the shaman while the steady rhythm of the drum began to quiet her.

"Boom. Boom. Boom." The beat eventually slowed and came to a stop, cueing the shaman to stop as well. His breath was labored, and he looked as if he had been on a long journey. Everyone held the space in silence, even the rowdy villagers. After he caught his breath, he spoke to Babaji who translated for the group. "Is anyone have any questions for shaman?"

Silence.

"I have a question," John boomed. "Can we dance with him for five minutes?"

Babaji translated the question back to the shaman. There was a collective inhale by the spectators that gave Allie the impression that no one had ever asked that question before. A few locals laughed.

Dance with the shaman? Well, that's ballsy. She pictured all of them up there dancing an awkward western side step or disco dance to the beat of an eastern drum. She easily saw Doug with his protruding chest, confident smile, and flailing arms. *Is John crazy? And in front of all of these people? What's he thinking?* The voices were back. Allie's judges knew no boundaries in the few seconds that they had to react.

The shaman paused, closed his eyes, and settled into a brief meditation as if he were consulting with his inner self or guide or . . . Shiva. The room was silent. After a long moment, he opened his eyes, looked at his drummer, and nodded. Then, immediately, the lights went out. Darkness. They had lost electricity.

"Boom, boom, boom." In the darkness, the drum began to play the steady and familiar beat. The ceremonial ghee candles provided just enough light for the group to see that the shaman had begun to dance. John jumped up immediately and began to hop from one foot to the other, respectfully mimicking the shaman's circles. Jane was next. Then Kurt. *Kurt? Really?* Oddly enough, Allie felt a pull to dance but she was shy to go up alone.

"Come with me?" she begged Pearl as anticipation rose within her. Her body began to pull her out of her seat.

Pearl shook her head.

"Please. I don't want to go alone. Please?" The darkness

filled her with new-found courage, and she suddenly had to experience all that she could.

Pearl held her ground, but Marianna hopped up.

"Let's go." She grabbed Allie's hand.

Suddenly, they were up with the shaman hopping from foot to foot to the steady and mesmerizing beat of the drum. Self-conscious Allie disappeared as she tapped into the frequency of the shaman. She started to spin. It was so easy and freeing. This spin had her feet barely touching the floor, and she knew he was guiding her steps.

This is so cool. I'm not trying, but I'm spinning AND I'm not dizzy. Allie was swirling in joy.

And then, just as quickly as it had begun, it was done. The drumming stopped. The spinning stopped. Buzz . . . The lights came back on. The villagers cheered, and Allie was reminded of the spectacle. She grabbed Marianna's hand, and they rushed back to their seats trying to be invisible.

"That was amazing," Allie said, breathless.

"Yeah. It's as if I were being spun. So easy." Marianna delighted.

"Fun to watch," Pearl chimed. "You ghosts were really getting it! Well done." she continued her playful attitude.

The evening ended with each pilgrim offering the shaman a traditional thank you in Nepali rupees. Then they walked back to the hostel for a good night's rest with their minds lighter, dancing with wonder.

CULTURAL LESSON #15
Always dance with the shaman when the
opportunity comes along.

Allie opened her journal but fell asleep with the pen and paper in hand. At some point in the night, she had a dream, or was it?

Allie was lying on her bed in the hostel. She felt a presence and opened her eyes. Hovering over her was a translucent angelic being with a glowing, vibrant beauty. This young angel in human form swept over her, and Allie felt a soft, cool breeze touch her face.

"Don't you want to be back here?" Allie asked telepathically.

"No." Her voice was like music. "It's too beautiful here."

The angel swept back over Allie, tickling her forehead as she disappeared into the dark night.

But a sweet, familiar melody remained somewhere in the ether that lulled Allie back to sleep.

CHAPTER 19

The Aria

"You sing tonight?" Loojha asked Allie with his mesmerizing smile and warm brown eyes. She had been wandering the village with Kate and Pearl, admiring and purchasing the unique fabrics and clothing of the region when they crossed paths.

"Uh, sure," she stammered as her heart sped up. "Yes, thank you?" *I think. What've I gotten myself into?*

"Good!" He clapped his hands indicating that he was pleased. "Come, please." Marching forward, he invited the three of them to follow.

They walked a short distance through the full streets to a storefront that sold small electronics and music. He led them to a section dedicated to his work and gave them each a CD.

"Dhanyavad!" They yelled in an excited chorus. Allie searched her pocket for some rupees, but he waved away the offer of money.

Laughing, he replied, "Swagatam! Welcome!" And with that, he disappeared into a crowd of friends.

"That was really sweet! So, you'll be singing with a famous performer tonight!" Pearl smiled as they meandered toward the hostel. "There's no better research than that!"

"Please, don't remind me," Allie responded with a sigh. "I'm already nervous. I'm so new to this style. I really shouldn't have said yes."

"You're going to be just fine. Don't you worry," Kate championed.

Allie stopped in her tracks. "That's what my mom always said to me. Those exact words! She made it sound so simple, like it wasn't a big deal to get up in front of hundreds of people. She and my dad were my greatest support." Allie reminisced. "In my early career, my dad would travel to New York City with me for auditions. The competition was fierce, and he always gave me the best pep talks." She paused, and her friends waited patiently. "It was such an innocent time, before everything happened. I really miss them." Pearl put her arm around Allie.

"That's a really sweet memory," Kate said.

"It is. And you know what? It's the first time I've been able to share any good memories of my parents. It's been easier to wallow in the sad and the bad, because remembering the good brings up such feelings of loss, it shuts me down." Covered with a soft layer of dust, she took in the crowded streets, cement structures, and towering trees. "There **really is** magic in this land!" Accepting Pearl's embrace, she whispered, "Thank you." The three friends continued down the street, walking arm in arm, smiling broadly and taking in the enchanted, healing spaciousness of presence.

THAT EVENING, THE MUSICIANS gathered in the community room to offer another round of music to Babaji and his friends. Loojha, true to his word, approached Allie. "Please come. Sing. Come." He ushered her along toward the front.

Here we go! She was actually excited. *This could be fun. Just a small, intimate gathering. Although I AM singing with a famous artist. Yeah, let's forget that minor detail.*

The small gathering, however, quickly turned into another all-village event, as Allie watched the locals pile in and fill up the room. *They're probably here to see Loojha, but they're going to get me. Great.* The old habit of stage fright and doubt kicked in. As her heart pounded, she suddenly didn't feel prepared enough. Well, actually, she wasn't prepared at all! *I thought we were just going to chant together casually! We didn't practice for a town-wide event! We didn't practice at all!* The judge, critic, and worrier were powerful weapons against her, and all the peace she'd found earlier that day was swept away. *Remember, it's all about God. Not me. You don't have to impress or be perfect. You can make mistakes.* The cheerleader was nudging the critic. *You can make a fool of yourself. They'll never see you again after you leave.*

But then the swami from a few years ago appeared somewhere in her imagination and began to chastise her: *You're nervous because your ego's involved. You should know better by now. It's not about YOU. This is about something purer. You're a messenger, a conduit. Get over yourself.*

"Please, come!" The harmonium player's sweet voice burst through the fictional words and kindly invited, "Sit here, sing."

Thump, thump, thump. Her heart beat as loudly as the festival drums of the village. *Ridiculous. You are a freakin' pro-fesh-ional.* The imaginary curtain rose. She looked up at everyone. They stared at her blankly. *Swami said to pray.* She prayed her regular prayer: *"Help!"*

The room fell silent, and she had no choice but to begin to play the melody with tentative fingers. She wanted to disappear. *Let me disappear into the chant.*

"Jai Sita Ram . . . " She sang and they responded. *It's going okay.* As the purity of the chant quickly took over, she started to feel more confident. Her tense shoulders relaxed and the spirit in the room rose. *What were you worried about? Silly Allie.*

"Bajarangi Jai Hanuman" . . . Soon the music began to take on an energy of its own. The musicians merged in timing, and everyone became one voice. A special, ascending musical energy was being created in real time, and the heart of the message revealed itself—love, unity, and harmony. Allie forgot herself and her many critical voices and sang from somewhere deep in her heart. It was easy and smooth, just as one would imagine a chant to the Divine should be, until . . . until a discordant voice began to break the unity. Someone was suddenly singing obnoxiously loud, as if to mock the practice. A quick scan of the room led Allie to none other than Doug, sitting upright, eyes open, literally yelling the melody out of key.

Really? Now? Allie continued the chant without missing a beat. *Is he swept away in bliss, or is he demanding attention?* Although he appeared to be oblivious, Allie suspected that he just wanted to be noticed. The peacock was showing his colorful tail: "Look and listen to me!"

His bellowing was so loud that many locals began to squirm and glance over at him with curious stares. *What do I do?* Allie was genuinely embarrassed.

Can you just shut up! The critic within her yelled. Cheerleader countered, *Give him the benefit of the doubt.*

She met Pearl's eyes and jutted her head briefly toward Doug, trying to communicate telepathically. *Help?* Allie moved her eyes around the whole room as if to say, *Can you ask him to follow what the locals are doing? To be considerate of others?* She brought one hand to her heart, briefly. *To respect this is a form of prayer? Please?*

She continued to lead the chant with Doug wailing over everyone. "JAI SITA RAM" . . . Allie was in multiple arenas of her mind now as she juggled reverence, worry, and judgment.

She smiled and tried to hide her discomfort. *God, please help this awkward situation.*

Before Pearl could act, John, the "master" of chant, not so subtly walked over to Doug and whispered something into his ear. Doug's body language softened and his face flushed.

"Jai Sita Ram" . . . his response was quieter, but he sat taller.

Thank you, God. Actually, thank you, John.

Allie felt the room collectively relax. The chanting started to become a more unified gathering of voices again. She hoped that the ghosts, as guests, could now begin to merge with the locals rather than try to dominate them.

"Bajarangi Jai Hanuman" . . . Allie eventually slowed the music, as is typical in this style, and ended the chant.

The excitement in the room was palpable. Her new friends asked her to stay with the band while the music continued. She was temporarily a *bona fide* band member. *This is awesome! Living the Dharma isn't too bad after all!* Her fears melted away, and she enjoyed herself in ways that she hadn't in a long time. Once again, she sang for the love of music, and it felt wonderful.

"*I've never seen such peace in someone's eyes,*" Allie heard the crone say.

CULTURAL LESSON #16
Sing with the locals whenever you can.
Sing from your heart. Sing, sing, sing.

AS THE MUSICIANS BEGAN to pack up, Allie shared hugs and smiles with the locals, while Babaji fluttered around, saying goodnight.

"Che bella cosa . . ."

Someone was beginning to sing a familiar Italian tune that Luciano Pavarotti had made popular to the western world.

"O sole, 'o sole mio . . ."

The vocal quality was untrained, but it matched pitch, for the most part, and was passionate in emotion. And loud. Really loud. Allie followed the sound and saw the infamous Doug standing in front of his seat with his arms rigidly sticking out to the side and one foot in front of the other. The peacock's feathers were rising to full bloom, and he was now taking the opportunity to display his prowess. Gloria sat next to him glowing.

Although the musicians continued to pack up, a few locals respectfully stopped to listen to Doug's impromptu performance. Allie followed suit. Red-faced and trembling with overdone physical tensions, he sang with full volume and impassioned expression. Gloria mouthed along.

Knowing the climax was coming, Allie stepped back and held her breath. His bright red face turned purple, and every muscle in his neck protruded in preparation for the sustained high note. She didn't know if he was going to survive. He widened his stance, raised his hands, and landed a tight, trembling high B. And as if that weren't enough, he sustained it longer than Pavarotti ever did. So long, that the pitch crept down a half step.

Ouch. Allie cringed. *His poor larynx is as raised as his ego.*

Finally, he cadenced the aria, flicked his hand, and bowed theatrically.

Gloria clapped loudly. Allie stared, speechless. The locals returned to their light chatter and continued on their way. Uncomfortable with the strange power play, Allie tiptoed to her room.

Journal

What can I say? This evening was Divine. Well, most of it. I'm so grateful to Loojha and all of the musicians for inviting me to join them. It doesn't go unnoticed that there are no females in this group. I don't know why that is, but they were all respectful and very welcoming.

I was nervous on many levels, (I know that's ridiculous) but my biggest concern was how we would work together as a group without a rehearsal. Listening is so important, and not everyone knows how to do it, particularly during a live musical presentation. It's such a subtle form of communication, and, thankfully, we all listened to each other well.

When the whole room was singing as one, the sacred essence of the chant embraced the room, and we rose into something incredibly special. Like the whole room was filled with love. It was other-worldly. Maybe that's why the Doug bellow show began. That high frequency can make someone who's not ready for it uncomfortable. Whatever the reason, it was awkward and inappropriate, but I'm trying to take Pearl's advice. I can either say something or let it go. I'm going to let it go. Now his aria, I'm going to let that go too. I don't want to compete and don't want to rise to meet him. I have no idea why he's created this strange duel, but I want no part of it. I was hoping to release judgments on this trip, but man, are they loud so far. So much for quieting the mind. It's screaming right now. I miss my singing bowls. Ironic that we're here to research their roots, and there's not a singing bowl to be found.

The Indiana Jones adventure is presenting some challenges, but the benefits are far out weighing the minor inconveniences. At least, so far.

Okay, all for now. Sweet dreams.

CHAPTER 20

The Arun River

Pearl shook Allie awake early the next morning. "Allieji, let's sneak upstairs and chant together."

Neither the sun nor the rooster had risen, and the hostel was unusually quiet.

"Sure!" Allie chirped, feeling surprisingly refreshed from a restful, dreamless sleep. "We haven't meditated since we arrived, and I really miss it." She rolled out of bed to visit her lizard friend and her toothbrush.

"Tonight is the full moon lunar eclipse, and it'll . . . " Pearl opened their door and gasped. "Oh, sweet! A feather! Again!" she whispered in the echoing hallway. "Remember what I said at the temple? Feathers appear for me when something special is about to happen."

"Ooh, I wonder what today'll bring?" Allie whispered back. "One of my teachers told me that it's a way for the ancestors to communicate with us, to let us know they're around." Allie closed her eyes, hoping to hear something. Nothing. Just her growling stomach asking for a snack.

Pearl tucked the feather into her bag, and they tiptoed up the stairs to the common room.

"What do you want to chant?" Allie asked, sitting on the couch rather than the unswept floor.

"You lead me. You have more practice with this, and you're the *real* singer!"

"Hahaha, I'm not sure about that after last night," Allie referenced Doug but quickly moved on. "So . . . I'd love to chant the Gayatri mantra, but I don't know it well, do you?"

"No. Not yet. If we had cell signal, I'd pull up the words, but we don't."

Allie peeked out over the half wall onto the tranquil village street. All was still. "How about Om Ma . . ."

A flash of color caught her eye. Allie sat rapt and gawking as she watched a petite woman, supported by a long walking stick, slowly round the bend. Her head was covered, but her alluring presence held Allie's focus.

Pearl followed her distracted friend's gaze toward the street. "What is it? What do you see?"

"That woman. I keep seeing her." Allie met Pearl's eyes. "She was at the Temple in Kathmandu, and I swear I saw her on the mountain when I was peeing in the woods. She just appears and disappears. This is so weird. I'd forgotten about her. How can she be here?"

They jumped up to get a closer look. Empty. "Friend, did the shaman's dance get to you? I don't see her. Are you sure you saw a person?"

"I saw her! She was there rounding the bend. Come on . . ." she pulled Pearl toward the stairwell, "Hurry, let's get to the street. Hurry!" Allie rushed down the four flights of stairs two at a time out to the street.

The rising sun had already warmed the abandoned street. The rooster crowed. "This is crazy. I saw a woman. How can she just disappear?"

"The feather? A special sign just for you? I don't know. We **are** in the land of magic. How about we chant to her? Maybe she'll reappear?"

"Sure." They walked back up the four flights to the community room. "Thanks for not thinking I'm crazy . . . yet." Allie was afraid she might indeed be losing her mind.

"Never, friend. We're in this together."

"So, how about *Om Mani Padme Hum*. That's something Babaji has chanted a lot, and I could really use that energy to cope with Doug."

"Perfect! You lead, dear singer. I'll croak along."

"Om mani padme hum, om mani padme hum, om mani padme hum."

The simple chant was said to contain the seed of compassion and all who sincerely chanted it would awaken the energy within them beyond what they thought they were capable of experiencing. And Allie certainly felt compassion deficient.

"Om mani padme hum, om mani padme hum, om mani padme hum."

The friends found their rhythm and pace together as the village woke up around them. In the near and far distance they could hear the sounds of others beginning to rise; doors opened, bells rang, and morning prayers and chants floated through the air to welcome the new day. A crow landed on the half wall, contributing to the chant with a resonant "caw." Pearl and Allie held the space and repeated the mantra quietly until the chatter of people began to fill the room indicating breakfast time.

Allie reached for Pearl's hand, "Thank you, friend." In the peace of the moment, they touched their foreheads to each other.

"That was amazing!" Pearl whispered. "Let's do this again. There really is something magical about this land."

Allie's stomach growled. "There sure is. But, now, let's eat. I'm starving!"

AFTER A BREAKFAST OF dal bhat and hard-boiled eggs, the group piled into their vehicles with the intention of visiting their second temple somewhere hidden in the mountains, but the roads in the region were too muddy to pass. Instead, they detoured to a smaller temple just down the other side of the river bank.

"Here, is very, very special area," Babaji led the group to

the muddy path to the temple and river. Taking a long inhale and an even slower exhale, he whispered in reverence, "Look . . . Listen . . . "

The churning Arun river bubbled and bounced, its current strong and relentless. The right bank boasted mountains of sumptuous, ancient woodlands that overflowed with sounds of its forest inhabitants. In stark contrast, the left bank unfolded into a rockier terrain with two lone boulders standing proud and strong. Allie stood in awe of nature's spectrum, speechless.

"Magic." Babaji wiped tears from his eyes. "And do you hear Gayatri? Gayatri sadhus were here."

The Gayatri? Tingling with excitement, Allie closed her eyes to listen. The group held the silence and Allie waited. *Please let me hear it.* Minutes passed.

"Om Bhur Bhuvaha Svaha," sang a low, guttural groan.

There it is! I hear it!

"Tat Savitur Varenyam." Allie peeked. Babaji chanting reverently. His eyes softly closed and face radiating peace.

"Bhargo Devasya Dhimahi Dhiyo Yo Nah Prachodayat." Babaji sparkled. "Yes, is here. Feel it in land. See it in waters. Very special mantra. You need to learn. We will learn on this trip, maybe."

"Babaji," Marianna spoke up, "I've heard that in some traditions women are not allowed to chant the Gayatri mantra. They say it's too powerful for females. And . . . even for a male student to chant it, it must be a direct transmission from guru to student."

"Oh, no, no, no." Babaji smiled. "Mariannaji, in Nepal, we all chant Gayatri. Is sacred mantra for all. Very powerful." He looked at Marianna and then Allie and held her gaze. "You must learn Gayatri and share with others. You need record too and share."

"Boom, boom, boom" . . . the conversation was interrupted by a familiar beat of the drum that resonated from up the mountain.

Babaji turned toward the sound. "Oh my God, is very auspicious." he almost clicked his heels in excitement. "We came here many times and is never been shaman! And full moon eclipse tonight. Surprise visit from shaman is very special blessing." He bustled away to tell Gloria and Doug, who had wandered ahead of the group.

As the remaining pilgrims followed bubbling Babaji down the slippery path toward the temple, Allie stood, enjoying the fresh smell of the damp, muddy overflowing Arun. Suddenly, overcome with emotion, tears rolled down her cheeks. She had no idea why she was crying, but it felt like something from deep within her soul—a nudging familiarity or recognition.

Welcome back. The words came clearly, even though she didn't "hear" them. She closed her eyes and inhaled. *I've been here before.* She knew it as truth in her very core.

"You okay?" Pearl asked, as she observed her friend.

Allie felt as if she were trying to sense another lifetime. "Yes, just taking it all in. This place seems so familiar."

"Boom, boom, boom." The shaman was getting closer, and Pearl's legs began to kick to the rhythmic beat.

"You're dancing now?" Allie teased. "I couldn't get you to dance with the other shaman!"

"I'm not sure what's happening. I feel the beat so strongly. I . . . can't really control it." Her body began to move more and more with the rhythm of the drum.

"Boom, boom, boom," the shaman and his drummer danced by the group, hopping from foot to foot.

Pearl began to tremble as the strong drumming forced her body to move. It was, perhaps, similar to Allie spinning with the first shaman, but that was her choice. Pearl wasn't in control. It looked like she was being taken over.

"Are you okay? What's going on?"

"I . . . I don't know. I'm fine. I feel okay. I just can't stop my legs from moving and bouncing to the beat. It's coming from inside me but it's not me. I can't explain it," Pearl's voice was clipped.

"Give me your bag and camera. I'll hold them for you. Can you breathe? Can you take deep breaths and try to settle down?"

Pearl handed over her bags. "I'm trying. I'm okay. Really, it's just . . . strange. I've never felt this before. I just need to go with this and let it pass through." She bounced in her body with her feet still on the ground like a child hearing music for the first time, trying to dance.

The shaman went into the temple.

"Boom, boom, boom."

Babaji was close behind, calling the pilgrims to follow.

"Let's follow the group into the temple." Pearl was calm, even though her body was in constant motion.

"Okay." Allie hesitated, concerned for her friend. Was she becoming possessed? *No, we're with Babaji. He said this surprise shaman visit is a blessing. Nothing bad can happen to us.* She wasn't sure she'd convinced herself, though.

They moved on toward the temple. The small, soft-yellow, concrete pagoda was simply built and sparkling clean. In front sat a six-tiered ghee candle lamp in the shape of a spiral, and hanging bells of all sizes decorated the wrap-around porch. Traditionally, each temple has at least one bell to ring upon entry. Here, there was choice aplenty.

The priest stood at the entrance wearing a classic white polo shirt and an orange dhoti wrapped from waist to ankles. A customary orange scarf hung over his right shoulder.

A dhoti and a polo shirt! Allie noted the striking contrast of ancient and modern.

The tiny temple had just enough room to walk down a narrow aisle that offered access to an altar that housed several deities. As they entered the temple one by one, the priest handed them a small pitcher of milk to pour over the deities as an offering of gratitude. This particular puja or ritual wasn't always allowed to foreigners. It was a special welcome from the temple priest to Babaji's friends.

"Offer milk with right hand as gratitude. Say prayer. Ring bell," Babaji instructed with his radiant smile. John and Jane went first, then Kurt, Marianna, and Kate. Allie had done this once before at the yoga retreat. She loved learning and sharing rituals from different cultures. Today, however, she was distracted with concern for her friend, who was usually steady and calm but was now a shamanic pogo stick. The drumbeat continued in the distance as the shaman moved down to the river.

Allie watched Pearl take the milk and gracefully pour it over the deities. *Pretty good for a bouncy ball.* She followed closely behind Pearl and realized that the priest was waving at her.

"No, no, no," he exclaimed loudly, flailing his hands wildly.

Oh Lord! Allie felt the pitcher in her hand. *I used my left hand. Oh, no.*

She was so concerned for Pearl that she hadn't been mindful of what she was doing. Mortified, Allie stood still. She knew that in Nepal the left hand was considered dirty, the bathroom hand, and was never used for meals or offerings. Allie, however, being left-handed, often had trouble remembering to use her non-dominant hand.

The priest ushered her back to the front of the altar as he chanted and waved his hands over the deities. Allie imagined him asking forgiveness for this ignorant, tall, blonde westerner. He then filled the pitcher with milk and offered it to her right hand.

Second chance! She smiled and bowed to the priest. "Namaskar. So sorry!" In response he frowned, waved his hands and ushered her forward. *He's very serious. Thank goodness my God is forgiving. I trust these deities are, too.*

With the task completed, the mortified guest left the temple and sought out her possibly possessed friend.

Pearl was a short distance away, bouncing on her heels in a distinct rhythm, trying to keep her feet on the ground and not make a spectacle.

"What do we do? We need to get Babaji!" Allie whispered.

"Yes, we'd better! It's getting stronger." Pearl was flushed, and her eyes were beginning to glaze over.

Allie saw Marianna. "Marianna, please discreetly bring Babaji here. Something's happening with Pearl."

Marianna's eyes widened at the sight of the flushed, bobbing Pearl. She rushed off to find Babaji.

"Boom, boom, boom," continued the drum. The shaman was preparing to leave. Allie readied both their cameras. *We're going to need to remember this.*

But, the cameras wouldn't turn on. *What the . . . ? I know the batteries are good.* She tried again, and again. They were both dead. There'd be no photos of this shaman.

Babaji and Marianna came rushing over. "What's happening, Pearlji?"

"I can't stop moving. The beat of the drum is so strong. It's making me tremble and bounce. I'm not in control," she said calmly.

Babaji observed Pearl and assessed the situation over several breaths. "Is okay. You connect with shaman energy. This means you have shaman qualities in you! Is actually big, big blessing. But it is new and uncontrolled."

Babaji placed one finger on the center of Pearl's chest, closed his eyes, and became quiet. He went into a deep meditation. Pearl closed her eyes as well, and her body began to settle down. Her skin became less flushed, and the bouncing eventually stopped. After a few minutes, they both opened their eyes and smiled at each other.

"Drink water and walk down to river. Rest there," Babaji suggested.

Allie checked to see if any of the others had noticed. Gloria and Doug had skipped the temple offering and were already down at the river taking photographs. John and Jane were walking hand in hand slowly toward the river. The others were all lingering around the temple. No one else seemed to have noticed.

"Wow, so you have shaman qualities. That's pretty cool. Does it mean anything to you?" Allie returned Pearl's bag and camera to her.

"I'm interested, for sure, in shamanism. But, *hoo-ee*, that was definitely a new experience. When we found the feather this morning, I knew something special was going to happen, but I didn't expect this!" They moved toward the river.

"It's a special message just for you. I'm glad I got to witness it, but I'm more glad that you're okay. Oh, and I tried to take a picture of the shaman for you to remember, but neither one of our cameras would turn on."

"Really? That's strange. It has fresh batteries." Pearl turned the camera on. It worked just fine. Allie's turned on as well.

They met each other's eyes. "We've stepped into a powerful, crazy world here. I guess you weren't supposed to have a picture of the shaman."

"Guess not. I'll remember though, photo or not. That's a guarantee." She took a huge breath. "I'm going to take Babaji's advice and sit under that tree over there and meditate."

"A good idea. I'm going to head to the river."

As she walked down to the banks of the Arun, Allie saw two young local boys watching the group carefully from a distance. No one else seemed to notice, but she suspected they might be up to something.

The boys, however, quickly fell out of her awareness as she approached the boulders. Allie shivered, and her hair stood on edge. *What's this feeling?* She knew. *It's familiarity. But of what?* The boulders were brimming with history, and, somehow Allie was part of that history. *If only these boulders could talk. Did the wise sages who brought the Gayatri to this earth sit on these boulders? Did they bathe here? Did I?* A feeling of coming home overcame her, and she was able to breath more deeply.

The clear, damp air smelled green and succulent, and the shallow water cooled her hot, sandaled feet, as she rock hopped close to shore. For a few precious moments, she was content; a rare and cherished experience.

After a time, however, impatience settled in. "Okay, mighty Arun, here I am," she announced to the water. "I suspect you know how long the journey's been, and I know I'm meant to be here. Right here, now. So what's this feeling of recognition, of coming home? Tell me, please."

Allie waited expectantly for a message. The water rushed past her, and, for a while, she was able to simply be present. Tree stumps and limbs sped past in the powerful current, seemingly weightless. The river showed no mercy to anything in its path.

Allie returned to her plea. "Surely, with such an emotional response, there must be a message for me. Can you please be clearer?" She listened. Nothing . . . just the sound of rushing water and laughter from her group. She closed her eyes. *How about the Gayatri? Can I at least hear that?* Allie, as everyone knew by now, was not an adventurer, and that she'd made it all the way to this very location was a remarkable feat. And she longed to know what had called her to Nepal.

Still, nothing.

Looking down at her feet, she noticed something shimmering in the mud. Mindful of water snakes and other Indiana Jones surprises, she carefully reached down to pick up the small, white quartz. It was the only white stone around her, and, although it wasn't anything spectacular to look at, it felt special.

"All right. I give," she announced. "I obviously can't hear the messages in the ether, but maybe if I meditate with this stone, I'll be able to at least remember this special feeling. Can I take it with me?" she asked the water. She closed her eyes and heard a definitive, *"Yes."* She finally heard something! Was it her mind giving her the answer she wanted, or was it God or the river speaking in the ether? She didn't know, but she now felt comfortable leaving with the small stone.

But, first, she needed to give something back. "Never just take from earth. There needs to always be balance. Always offer something back, even if is just gratitude," Babaji had said during one of their trainings.

She noticed Kurt tossing a coin into the water.

"Kurtji, do you have any extra change that I could borrow? I'll pay you back. I left my purse in the car."

"I just used my last coin but I have a dollar bill."

"That's perfect. Thanks!" Allie took the bill and folded it up. *I'm so grateful. Thank you for the special welcome, for this feeling of ease, and for the deep breaths. As I take this stone with me, I'm open to any messages that will come. Please, please let me hear them.*

She threw the bill out toward the raging water but just at that moment, a gust of wind caught it and stopped it in midflight. *Funny, I hadn't noticed any wind.* The bill floated lightly into a shallow area where the current slowed. Not missing a beat, the two young boys from earlier stealthily rushed into the river after the money. *And I thought I wasn't being watched!*

"No!" she yelled! "That's my offering!" *What happens if my offering is stolen? That's got to be bad karma.*

The boys laughed and continued to wade into the water. She realized that they had been watching the group for this very opportunity. Allie stomped her foot like a frustrated child. "Little thieves!"

"I suspect they need it more than the river does." Kurt's eyes were soft with compassion.

Allie took a breath. "I suppose you're right. But what does it mean if you make an offering and it gets stolen?" She smiled at the irony of it.

Kurt shrugged. "Maybe you're paying it forward twice?" He returned the smile.

Just before the bill was swept away into the strong current, one of the boys belly flopped into a long stretch and grabbed it. *This might be their livelihood, but that's my offering! It's theft!* Her thoughts swirled. *But if they had asked me for money, what would I have done? Would I have looked them in the eyes and given them something?* Allie had so much to learn. With no answers, she shook her finger at them. Their giggles continued as they waded back to shore.

Well, I guess that offering doesn't count. Now what?

She stacked some stones and made a simple cairn. *Will the boys knock it over?* She didn't know. They appeared to be long gone, so, for now, it stood.

"Time for photo everyone! Get together!" Babaji yelled, summoning the group to gather under the Banyan tree.

Well, well, well, Allie thought, as she joined the others. In the mighty Banyon hovered the very same boys, watching and waiting. *How'd they get there so quickly? And unnoticed? They're experts already at their young age.*

"Watch your bags, everyone, we have visitors," Allie announced to her friends as she wagged her finger again at the boys. They were unapologetically grinning and waiting patiently for their next opportunity.

The group and the perched urchins smiled broadly. "Perfect!"

As she slipped her way back up the muddy path to the waiting Land Rover, tears fell unchecked from her eyes. She wanted to stay until she had answers, but, instead, lovingly pocketed the little stone. *See you again, great Arun. Somehow, someday. Thank you!*

CULTURAL LESSON #17
Make an offering from your heart. But
remember, you can't control where it ends up.

The Temper

After returning from a full day at the Arun River, the ladies gathered in the common area to search through the pile of identical peach-colored garments until they located their name written in blue fabric chalk. It was the night before the festival, and the tailors had worked as fast as they could, given the hasty deadline. Marianna, Pearl, and Allie shared a room as they tried them on.

"I can't get this over my head," Allie grunted.

"Mine is huge." Marianna modeled the draping fabric with the pants hanging to the floor. Pearl's was too tight in the bust.

"They must have confused names and measurements. Here, try mine on." Pearl handed her outfit to Allie. It was a perfect fit.

The three women went back up to the common area and discovered mass confusion.

Gloria was yelling, "How can this be! This is unacceptable. I purchased the outfit and I want to know where it is!"

Marianna calmly gave Gloria the set that she had just tried on. "Try this, I think there's been a mix-up." Red-faced, Gloria grabbed it out of her hands and stomped away to try on the wrinkled garment.

Everyone swapped clothing until they all found something that came close to fitting. It required a lot of patience and flexibility, but it was, after all, Nepal! To add to the confusion, dinner was served before everyone was ready, and tension floated in the ether. Cold food, exhaustion, and general third-world adjustments were taking their toll on the best of entitled western temperaments.

By the end of dinner, however, tensions settled down, and excitement began to fill the crowded space in anticipation of festival day. Drums beat in the background, "Boom, Boomboomboom, Boom," while locals reminisced and laughed with old friends.

In contrast, Allie noticed Babaji sitting across the room looking exhausted. He'd been holding the space for all of them while also helping his niece prepare for tomorrow's festival.

"Babaji, are you okay?" she crouched in front of him. Allie glanced at Lumanti, who sat next to him holding his hand. She smiled back, wordlessly trying to reassure Allie that all was well.

"Is ok, Allieji. I don't feel well but rest will help," he responded. This was very unusual. The Energizer bunny had never shown fatigue.

"Please, can you let friends know plan for tomorrow?

Rajeshji and Sunitaji not here to tell others. We meet outside at 7:00 a.m. dressed for festival. Bring water and anything they need for day. Okay? I think I need rest now."

"Yes, Babaji. You rest. Can I bring you water?"

"Yes, thank you."

Allie got him a bottle of water and zapped it with her purifier. She was getting good at having the lightsaber with her at all times. "You're doing so much for us. Please, go, rest. Tomorrow's a very special day. We'll be okay."

She scanned the bustling hall for her group. Most were seated toward the front, so she began with the closest table and moved from table to table, relaying Babaji's message. Everyone wished him rest and agreed with the morning plans.

"Thank you so much for all that you're doing, Allieji!" said Pearl.

"Yes, thank you," the others agreed.

"I'm not doing much, but you're very welcome," Allie replied, still flying high from her tender experience at the river.

Happy that, so far, all were in agreement with Babaji's plans, she approached the last and furthest table to see Gloria and Doug glaring at her.

Gloria must still be upset about the clothing fiasco, Allie thought.

"What's going on?" Doug was curt.

"Friends, Babaji's not feeling well, and he asked me to pass on the schedule for tomorrow."

Without hesitation, Doug slammed his fist on the table and jumped to standing, "HE MUST BE HERE! I DON'T CARE IF HE'S SICK!" He yelled at full volume.

Gloria stood and added equally as loud, "HE NEEDS TO BE HERE WITH US NOW!" Her face distorted into an angry gargoyle.

At the sound of the verbal earthquake, the entire room fell into surprised silence. The locals flashed glances at Allie as she stood in front of the barreling Doug and Gloria. Allie was jolted. She had never been the recipient of such aggression and ferociousness. Her face flushed. *Why such rage? And over such a little detail? Babaji,* **our teacher,** *needs rest. What's the big deal? Aren't we here to support him?*

"He needs rest. It's his mother's festival tomor . . ." She was cut off.

"HE WILL BE HERE. THIS IS UNACCEPTABLE!" Doug bellowed.

Allie raised her volume to meet his, "BABAJI IS EXHAUSTED."

"HE CAN BE EXHAUSTED AND SIT RIGHT HERE WITH US."

Shock trembled through Allie. She was mildly aware of all eyes observing the uncomfortable scene, as she found herself in yet another awkward situation with Doug and Gloria—this time, as a public recipient of their bullying. *How could they show such a lack of compassion for the man who shared everything to bring us here?*

Denise Mihalik

Allie kept her volume level high to meet his: "LET HIM REST." She was not going to take his bullying.

Doug pushed away from the table, and his chair crashed to the floor. He slammed his fist again. "HE WILL BE HERE!"

Allie froze.

"HOW DARE YOU SPEAK TO HER LIKE THAT," boomed a strong male voice from behind her as a protective arm embraced her shoulders: Kurt, the gentle giant, to the rescue.

"I CAN SPEAK TO HER AS I LIKE!" Doug bellowed.

"YOU ARE OUT OF BOUNDS." Their eyes locked. Tears welled up in Allie's and the trembling increased.

"I DON'T CARE!" Doug puffed up his chest and shoved his face into Allie's. She smelled his beer breath but didn't dare wipe the spit from his words. Silent, she met the bully's glare.

Kurt whispered through clenched teeth, "Back off and apologize." He reached for Doug's shoulder and started to push him away.

Just then, Babaji appeared.

"Please, friends, sit down." How much he heard, they didn't know.

The trio held their ground, frozen in space as if the tiniest blink would shatter the situation. Babaji walked over and lightly touched Doug and Kurt's shoulders. He repeated quietly, "Please, friends, sit down."

After a suspended second, everyone sat down, and the room heaved a collective exhale. Flushed and shaking, Allie swallowed tears. She did not want to give Doug the benefit of seeing her cry. Kurt gently grasped her hand.

What's going on? Today was such a sacred day. I felt so safe and at peace. How could they act like this? Treat Babaji like this? Me? They're ruining everything. This display didn't bode well for the reputation of westerners, and as Allie tried to calm herself, mortification rushed in, both for her and the group. *One bad egg can certainly spoil the entire dish.* Allie often mixed up her metaphors, but this confused cliché never seemed truer.

Babaji spoke quietly and slowly: "I don't know what is the problem, but I realize that I have contribute in some way and for that, I am sorry." His eyes were heavy with exhaustion. "Is something for me to learn here, so I can be better. You," referring to Doug and Gloria, "yell and show great anger and that is not acceptable. Is not. But, I am sorry for my part. How can I help you?"

Again, the room seemed to exhale and local conversation resumed.

Allie was impressed by Babaji's grace, compassion, and humility, which was something she lacked. His calm demeanor and gentle words were slowly steering them back toward the spiritual essence of their journey.

The group was quiet.

After a beat, Allie knew what she had to do. She stared first into Babaji's eyes for strength and then glanced toward

Doug and Gloria who were seated closely holding hands. "I don't know what I did, but I apologize," she told them.

Kurt exhaled in a tight whisper, "I, too, apologize."

Doug and Gloria nodded proudly, absorbing the apologies. Allie waited in anticipation for theirs.

They whispered to each other and then Doug took a deep breath. "We realize that we are not welcome here and we need to leave. We'd like to leave tomorrow morning, the first flight out."

Allie didn't follow their train of thought but certainly wouldn't stop them from leaving. *That'd be GREAT,* her thoughts swirled. *Things'll be much easier without their negativity. I didn't journey halfway across the world to pacify egos and coddle a spoiled couple, nor do I want Babaji to have to do the same.* She wasn't proud of her thoughts, but they were honest. *A pilgrimage is supposed to be a time to simplify, quiet down, and listen to the still small voice within. Not the booming voice of a raging ass.*

"Whatever you need, I will do to make you happy," Babaji replied, pulling Allie back to the awkward moment. "But, why are you feeling unwelcome? You are friends, and here in my village, you are family. We will like you to stay, but if you want to leave, we will help you."

Please don't talk them into staying. Allie now felt desperate for them to leave.

"We don't fit into the group. You don't want us here. We'll leave," Doug snapped.

"What have we done to make you feel that you don't fit in?" Pearl spoke with firm consternation.

"We eat alone. We're always the last to know things. We never know the schedule."

"Ridiculous," Allie muttered. Kurt squeezed her hand.

"When you eat alone," Marianna explained, knowing that they often ate with John and Jane, "it's because you choose to, not because you're unwelcome. You've made choices this entire trip to isolate yourselves. You cannot put that on us."

Well said! Now, feeling she had to speak up to defend her recent actions Allie quipped, "I approached you last simply because you sat at the table furthest away. It wasn't a conscious choice. Information is constantly changing here, and either Sunita, Rajesh, or I have made sure that **everyone** knows the updated schedule. You've been told by me or others about the changes. I know that as a fact. It's been a group effort to be sure everyone is informed."

"We need to have it in writing," Gloria said slowly. Allie met her cold eyes with disbelief.

"That's impossible." Flames shot from her eyes. "We're in a third-world country and you want changes in writing?" Allie was exasperated. *Entitlement!*

"Yes."

Kurt squeezed Allie's hand three times quickly as if to say, *Don't bother arguing.* Taking his cue, she merely stared. Her fire was rising. She squeezed Kurt's hand back. *Lord, I'm not passing the test of grace here.*

Babaji jumped in. "We honor your request, Doug and Gloria, and will do my best to honor."

Allie glared at Babaji as she vise-gripped Kurt's hand. *Are you kidding me? This is beyond ridiculous.* Any bit of compassion she'd been trying to muster quickly fell by the wayside, down, down, down, like the water cascading down the mountains yesterday.

"We need to go and talk this out. But we'll prepare to leave tomorrow." Doug and Gloria rose to go to their room.

Please, please DO let the door hit you on the way out.

"Babaji, I'm sorry," Allie said once they were gone.

"Allieji, is difficult situation. Thank you to apologize. That was a right thing to do. We don't know why they are angry, but they are yelling at me much of trip, so far! Even though you feel you didn't do nothing wrong, apology is good start." Babaji advised as he stood and retired to his room for his much-needed rest.

The remaining group stared silently at each other. Allie scanned the room to gauge the an encouraging smile. Loojha winked at her. She tentatively shyly smiled back, but she was so embarrassed for everyone.

"This is such a shame," Allie said. "The festival's tomorrow, and here we are yelling and carrying on. I'm mortified."

"They've been a simmering cauldron since the start of the trip. It'll be better for them to go. Better for all of us," Kurt exclaimed in a surprisingly strong voice.

"Thank you for helping me." Allie squeezed Kurt's hand

CHAPTER 21: THE TEMPER

and let it go. "I've never been hit with such rage and I'm so grateful to you."

"Anytime, and hopefully, never again," said Kurt.

Remembering that the full moon lunar eclipse was that night, Allie asked, "Is anyone interested in going up to the roof to offer Babaji and his mother special blessings with a chant? And to clear the negativity."

"A great idea!" "Yes!" "Perfect!"

"Let's meet in fifteen minutes?" Allie suggested, having no desire to share this pop-up plan with her agitators. Desperate to be alone, she discreetly climbed the cast-iron staircase that led to the roof.

At the top of the stairs, the mighty mountains surrounded her on all sides, illuminated by a bright glow of the risen moon. The beauty stole her breath. *Majesty.* She held Mother Nature's gaze until her trembling body could sustain the trauma no longer. It knew no mercy as it rushed out of her like the flowing current of the mighty Arun. She had no control as her body released disappointment, trauma, embarrassment, anger, and shock.

She bellowed for the first time in her life, falling to her knees and crying out to the moon. Its bottom edge was already hidden by the earth's shadow. "I came here to find peace. To find something that doesn't hurt! Why? Why are you doing this to me?" Weighted by the rising pain, she dropped into fetal position, hugging her knees into her chest. "I am here to HEAL," she sobbed, "and this is what you give me?

This is WHAT YOU GIVE ME? What am I supposed to do with THIS?"

She was in a foreign country surrounded by unfamiliar customs, food, people, clothing—you name it—and one of her own group had attacked her in her most vulnerable moment. This wasn't how it was supposed to be.

Suddenly, years of suppressed memories rose to the surface. She clenched her eyes tightly only to see a policeman handing her her dad's wallet and drivers license. The old photo showed the father she longed for, with his sweet, kind face staring back at her. How could he have taken his own life? Allie held her head, trying to block the images, but they were now unleashed. She heard her ex-husband, confessing his love for someone else and saw her mom taking her last breath, not ready to die. Fighting against the approaching darkness of the eclipse, the depth of her own bottomless void was turning her inside out. Shards burned her chest, and her head throbbed, "Aaaaahuuu!"

"Are you okay?" Kurt, her knight in shining armor, rushed up to her.

"I, I don't know." She could hardly say the words. "I'm SO . . . disappointed, It was supposed to be different here." She gasped, "It's too much. I try to be kind. I love, I help, and it just doesn't matter. It's, it's all just . . ." She could barely whisper. "I can't escape it and it's so, so painful." Kurt didn't say a word but just held her as she soaked his shoulder. He gently rocked with her and let her cry until there was nothing left.

"I'm a mess." Allie held her head, trying to hide, embarrassed by her bellowing. "Do you have a tissue?"

"I'll go get one. Hang tight." Kurt rushed off downstairs.

Depleted, Allie lay on her back and gazed at the open sky.

"This life is chaos." A soft female voice cooed. Shimmering in the light of the moon, the mysterious woman appeared over her. An iridescent light-blue aura glowed around her shoulders and head. Allie blinked. *Am I hallucinating?* Her crone was dressed simply in a flowing peach cloth that covered her from head to toe, concealing the radiant beauty that masked her age. The long staff steadied her ancient form. "But there is a magical beauty in this life, if you can see it. And infinite love. You feel shards in your heart, you feel loss, but in Truth, you are whole. Nothing, nothing can take that wholeness away." She somehow knelt over Allie and touched two fingers to the center of her chest and sang sweetly. 'Om Bhur Bhuvaswaha, Tat Savitur Varenyam, Bhargo Devasya Di Mahi Deeyo Yo Naha Prachodayat."

Allie felt completely safe during the stranger's lullaby. She closed her eyes and floated, light and free, like she was flying—away from the pain, away from the memories that haunted her, away from the confusion and disappointment. The shards in her heart softened, and the pain disappeared.

"Here you go." Kurt was back with a handful of toilet paper and his gentle kindness.

Allie popped up. "Um, thank you." She gratefully took the toilet paper and blew her nose. "Did you, uh, by chance, see anyone when you came up the steps?"

"No, just you, lying on your back. You looked so peaceful. Actually, you look much better. Did you catch a quick nap?"

"Maybe?" Allie did feel much better. She decided to keep the vision or dream to herself. Whoever this angelic lady was, Allie didn't want to spoil the magic by telling anyone about her. Yet. "Thank you, again for helping me."

"Ready to chant?" Kurt asked.

"Oh, yes!" Allie sighed. They sat down near the center of the roof as the others came up to join them.

Allie led the simple "Om Mani Padme Hum." It was the perfect night to step into the essence of compassion. *Thank you, Babaji's mother, for sharing your son with us, Thank you for the honor of sharing your home village with us. Thank you, mysterious crone. Thank you.*

As the moon disappeared behind the earth's shadow, their soft, sincere chanting radiated from the rooftop, over the village, and out into the ether.

ALLIE FELL INTO BED, too exhausted to journal or even shake away the ants. They all slept peacefully that night.

CHAPTER 22

Festival Day

Hours before sunrise on the day of the festival, Babaji and his family gathered at his brother's home to begin meal preparations for hundreds of friends who would be passing through, offering their respects for a smooth next journey. He didn't tell his western friends about the early-morning preparation, because he wanted them to sleep in and feel rested for the full day ahead.

A cool evening rain had blanketed the village, but the rising sun was already warming the streets. It was promising to be a hot and dusty day ahead. Back at the hostel, Allie and Pearl were awakened even before their alarms by the sounds of the festival drummers practicing their rhythmic beat.

"There's no mistaking that it's festival day," Allie said softly as she rolled over in the bed, trying not to disturb the ants on the far edge, which she knew would already be awake. They were their own village now, and, despite the mad, mysterious sheet-shaking storm that came each night—last night being the exception—by morning, the ants always returned to their regular route, never trespassing into Allie's space.

"I hope Babaji was able to get some rest," Pearl responded and then, barely audible, added, "Do you think they'll leave today?" referring to Gloria and Doug.

"I sure hope so, but I have no idea. It'd certainly be easier if they did. I feel for Babaji. He doesn't deserve to be disrespected when he's been so generous in bringing us here. And, to top it off, they never apologized to me or any of us."

"It didn't go unnoticed. You okay?"

"I think so. Particularly if they really leave. I'm tired of his weird competition with me. He's gobbled up my compassion like a Pac-Man. I came here to grow it, not have it stolen from me, and that makes me feel like a failure. It'll be easier when he's gone. At least, I hope."

"You're being hard on yourself. You're not a failure. I think you've handled him quite well. You could have punched him smack in the nose last night, and you didn't. I'm not sure I would've held back."

"Now that's an image," Allie laughed. "Thanks for that. Anyway, like you said, I've got to let him go or he'll ruin my trip even in his absence."

"You got it, friend. Here's hoping they're on their way down the mountain to the airport. Now, something tells me you're hungry. How about we go to breakfast?"

"You know it. I'm starving."

Allie and Pearl dressed in their matching festival outfits

and headed up to the common room. No sign of Doug or Gloria. *Thank the Lord!*

"Here's to a special day." Pearl held up her chai for a toast.

"May it be so!" They winked at each other in relief.

Promptly at eight a.m. they all met in front of the hostel to wait for Babaji, excited to begin the big day. Kurt and John were dressed all in white, and the ladies wore their identical peach outfits. The group would definitely not get lost in the crowd.

You're kidding me. Shit. Allie melted in disappointment as she watched Doug and Gloria pridefully walking down the stairs toward the group wearing their matching outfits. *Dammit. Why are they still here? Maybe they have an afternoon flight? Lord, I pray so.*

Allie grabbed Pearl and Kurt's hands. She was NOT going to be a victim of their rage again. *I hope they'll at least be kind for today and let Babaji honor his mother in peace.*

Everyone looked confused, but nobody said a word. The day was now going to be different than they had imagined and even hoped.

"Friends! Is festival day!" Babaji appeared looking radiant in his white top and pants. He greeted everyone warmly, including Doug and Gloria, and acted as if nothing inappropriate had happened the previous evening.

"We are preparing big meal at brother's house for entire village. Come, come, you will help . . ." He began walking only to stop suddenly. "Oh, and I give you all money. Is good luck for you to give to Lakhe for dance." He passed out American dollar bills and Allie put them into the pocket that was conveniently built into her outfit. "And there is umbrella at house for shade from sun. Don't forget!"

The house was just down the road near the center of town. Not surprisingly, locals paused on the street to watch the parade of ghosts in matching outfits walk behind their teacher.

The simple backyard patio of the multi-level cement home overlooked the jungle and school. Here the stage was set for the meal preparation. A large tank of cooking gas fed into several portable burners that heated two large pots full of dal and rice and two giant frying pans for deep frying. The hot and bubbling oil sizzled perfectly, as Babaji's brother made Sel Roti by squeezing rice flour batter into simple circular designs, similar to that of a tiny, thin funnel cake.

Friends and family sat in groups on the ground, chopping bowls full of ginger and garlic, hundreds of potatoes, tomatoes, cucumbers, and other seasonal vegetables. There were pounds and pounds of flour and buckets of dipping batter and yogurt. A feast was sure to be had!

A floral scent filled the air as Lumanti placed petals of jasmine, rose, and marigolds into intricate brass bowls as offerings to the Divine. Others folded piles of American dollar bills to be offered later to visiting family members, friends, and Lakhe dancers as a symbol of prosperity and good luck.

There was so much commotion that Allie didn't know what to do. She asked Lumanti if she could help with the meal.

"Yes, yes!" Lumanti waved a cousin over, who happily gave Allie a giant bowl of fresh ginger root, a plastic cutting board, and a knife. Sitting on the cement ground, Allie observed how the others were cutting the ginger. She'd only used powdered at home, so this was yet another learning experience. Trying her best, she peeled and chopped awkwardly as if she were tearing apart a tough piece of meat with a dull blade.

"Ah, ha ha, no, no, . . ." The cousin smiled widely, took Allie's knife and turned the ginger so she was cutting with the grain. The demonstration looked as easy as cutting soft butter. They smiled at each other and Allie tried again. Just as she was getting the hang of it, and with only about eighty more pieces to go, John approached her. He hovered over her a little too closely. "I'm a chef, you know."

"No telling, really?" Allie said, wondering where this was leading. "I'm not and I'm new to ginger."

"I don't know if I'd do it that way."

"How would you do it?"

"How about I just take over?"

Allie paused. "Sure." With no desire to hold onto her new-found terrain against yet another "expert," she stood and willingly handed over the reins and the dull knife.

John began to charm the ladies with his smiles and chopping techniques. Giggles faded into the distance as Allie dared to return to the busy village street.

In front of the house, Babaji's friends were decorating a four-wheeled farm cart that would transport the musicians during the procession. Orange silk fabric perfectly framed the base, and freshly made garlands of marigolds, jasmine, and mixed berries adorned the entire vehicle. To honor the departed, framed photos of Babaji's smiling parents were attached to the front and back of the cart.

"What's this, Babaji?" Allie asked, referring to a large bamboo scarecrow-like structure that supported an oversized photo of his mother.

"Ah, is symbol of cow figure. Cow is believed to guide soul. Long ago is said that our people waded through mythical Baitarani River holding onto tail of cow to reach heaven. Some use real cow, but when you have no real cow, we make bamboo figure."

Allie noted that it did not resemble a cow at all but seemed more like a spiritual totem intended to lead his mother's soul to heaven.

"Hey, Allie! Up here!" A familiar voice resonated over the crowds from above. Pearl and Marianna waved from the second-floor balcony. "Come on up." The anticipation was growing, and Allie rushed up to meet her friends.

"Wow, what a view and what a crowd." Allie was breathless. Like the ants on the edge of Allie's sheets, the crowd just suddenly appeared, each with great purpose. "We're going to step out into that rush?"

"Yup! It's festival day, and our Indiana Jones adventure is going to kick up a notch," Marianna rejoiced, already glistening from the sticky heat.

A stunning rush of colors filled the narrow streets as far as the eye could see. People, decorations, clothing, costumes, Lakhes, drummers . . . all packed, standing shoulder to shoulder, with not an empty space to be had. Allie searched the crowd for her crone. Nothing. Not yet.

The town musicians, all dressed in white, loaded their instruments into their traveling concert hall for the day, while the singers and drummers gathered behind, ready for the procession. Two men stood in front of the cart, waiting to pull it around the winding, hilly village road, from one end to the other.

"Come, come! Join procession!" Babaji called to his friends.

As the group slowly gathered around the musicians, Babaji gave each pilgrim a large circular picture pin of his mother's smiling face. "Please, wear pin today to honor my mother and wish her an easy journey on other side. It shows too that you are my friends."

Like they didn't know that by now! Allie laughed as she eyed the matching peach and white uniforms.

"Here also is gift." He handed each of them a folded dollar bill. "Wishing you abundance, joy, good luck, and love."

"Thank you so much, Babaji," Allie offered and tucked that special bill into her other pocket to take home with her.

With a softer, more contemplative smile, Babaji radiated a soulful peacefulness that transported Allie to a place of reverence—reverence for this life but also for those whom she so dearly missed. She slipped into quiet reflection and allowed herself to feel the love and loss of her many loved ones who had passed.

It was an exceptionally hot day and the mash of people stood and stood, waiting for what seemed like hours in the torturous heat for the procession to begin. Allie was profoundly grateful to remember the umbrella that she mindlessly held in her left hand. Once raised and opened, the blonde giraffe didn't go unnoticed by the petite locals, and, suddenly, her closest neighbors squeezed in to her to share the welcome shade.

How can so many people fit under one tiny umbrella? Her giraffe self was overwhelmed by the odors and heat of the unexpected bodies pressing close into hers, greedy for shade. The body connection only enhanced the temperature, and Allie dripped with perspiration. She wanted to levitate above the crowd to find relief.

So much for the festival. I've anticipated this moment for so long, and here I am, miserably hot, soaked with sweat, stinky, and already exhausted. The moment is finally here, and I can't wait for it to be over!

Just then, the crowds parted in respect for ten women who had formed a U-shape in front of Babaji and his family. These Sherpa wives had walked a full day from their village to offer their condolences. They were simply but beautifully dressed in basic full-length skirts, solid tops, and intricately woven strapped aprons. A circular hat perched on top of their heads, and they appeared to be unfazed by the oppressive heat.

A quick glance at their offering revealed a gold plate with a chaliced ghee candle, flowers, food, and perhaps something else. Allie saw their mouths moving and heard a faint melody, but the street sounds masked their voices.

Next, the Lakhes presented their ritual dance to bless the departed. With a lion's mane of long, dusty white yak hair, the red 3-D clay mask was at least six times the size of a human head. An enormous joker-like smile with laser-sharp teeth swirled up into protruding rosy cheeks like a spinning mustache. The cleft chin and huge, flaring nostrils competed with bulging, white, pupilless eyes and overdone eyebrows that fanned out like angels' wings. As if that weren't theatrical enough, supplemental stripes of green, orange, blue, white, and black textured the red face, reminding Allie of war paint. Add to that the unkempt yak hair, and it was frightening, almost otherworldly.

The Lakhes hopped and swirled with the giant head both leading and following like a feather duster sweeping and cleaning all around it. And, indeed, that was their purpose, to clear the path. The colorful skirts fanned out during the dance, creating a whirling spiral effect. In their hands, they held long strips of red and orange cloth that flowed over and behind their heads emulating fire. The persistent beat of the drums was meant to scare off negative energy while also helping to clear the path for the soul as it passed to the next journey.

It was a primitive and wild display, and, as they passed

by Allie, they bumped her purposefully, it seemed. Allie was already feeling hot and dehydrated, and they might have knocked her over if it hadn't been for the jam-packed crowd holding her up. They bumped again with the scary, huge mask just inches from her face, and Allie remembered the money in her pocket from Babaji. She threw a single into the dancing hand, and they all moved on. *Message received.*

At last, the children began to sing and the cart began to move. The melting ghost pilgrims filed behind as the procession finally began.

Ah, the glorious music, Allie thought. *It almost feels cooler. Thank goodness we're finally moving. Things are going forward.* She took a long drink from her purified water bottle.

As they moved, the crowds opened up, and Allie gave her umbrella to her shade-seeking friends. She would rather brave the beating rays of the sun than be a sardine sticking to the sopping skin of those so tightly packed around her. As it was, her peach garment and underwear were soaked through, and she was sure the sour smell that followed her was the betrayal of her own body odor.

"How ya doing?" Pearl yelled over the music as she successfully located her friend in the crush. She was equally wet and dripping.

"Melted. How 'bout you?"

"The same. I guess the bright side is that it's not torrential rain? It could be worse."

"Oh, I'd take rain right about now." Allie took another

swig of water. "I feel guilty saying this but . . . I'm miserable. And I know I should be grateful or impressed or reverent, but . . . all I really want right now is a cool shower, a coke, and a nap, and I don't even drink coke."

"It's been a full journey so far and not without drama. I have to admit, this is anti-climactic. We've been waiting for this for a year, and here we are . . . not able to really be present." Pearl was equally honest.

Their conversation was interrupted by a steady beat as more Lakhes danced by. They bumped the women and danced into them until they once again produced the magic dollar.

"They're persistent. I'm glad Babaji told us about the dollar bills," mumbled Pearl.

"Ooh!" sighed Allie as the children began to sing a familiar melody. "This is from the rehearsal. I loved this melody! Let's get closer." The women inched forward and followed quietly.

The pictures of Babaji's parents stared down on them from the cart, and Allie was reminded of her reason for being in this very location in Nepal—*What's wrong with me? This discomfort is no comparison to losing one's mother.* "I'm sorry," she said aloud. "I'm here. I'm back."

"I'm here too." Pearl held Allie's hand for a few moments.

The procession inched slowly up and over the hilly village roads. Bottles of water emptied, and sunburns settled in, until, finally, two hours later, they landed back at the house.

Here, Babaji greet his honored guests, "Friends, please go

to hotel for early dinner. I will meet you soon. Rest, enjoy. Thank you, friends, for being here."

Allie and Pearl didn't have to be asked twice. They worked their way through the active streets back to the hostel and up to the fourth floor.

"The joint is jumping. I guess we aren't the only ones ready for a coke and a break from the heat." The area was definitely a meeting hub, and it was filled with the hustle and bustle of the local meet and greet.

"I'll take a cold coke," Allie said to the worker.

"Me, too!" added Pearl with a wink.

Journal

Festival day! I have to say, we're finally here, and I was too exhausted to really enjoy it. The full schedule, the dynamics and tensions between our group, the constant eyes of the villagers, the intense heat and restless nights have been overwhelming.

How to describe the festival–I've been to the state fair. I've been to parades, and the circus, and a funeral procession. It was all of these in one, on both a small and large scale. There was the simplicity of the procession with the tender music and reverence for Babaji's mother. Also, the sincere belief that this ritual guides her next journey. There's the magical energy that adds mystery, mystique, and a Harry Potter feel. Then there's the mash of crowds that goes beyond any New York City rush-hour subway experience. Not to mention the persistent drumming and dancing of the Lakhes that frequently bumped past. Add fertilizer and water, and you have the perfect storm of feeling one hundred percent overwhelmed.

I had the best-tasting coke ever, and the meal did not disappoint, even though it was Dal Bhat. Again. Pearl and I chilled out with Kurt, Marianna, and Kate. I hadn't talked to Kate in days. She seemed blissful and childlike, with wide eyes and a huge smile. Part of me longs for her innocent perspective. Babaji and his ever-growing crowd of family and friends showed up and laughed and talked long after we had left for our rooms. Funny thing, Babaji had Rajesh tell everyone the new schedule for tomorrow so that I wouldn't have to deal with Doug and Gloria, who, unfortunately, seem to be staying. I SO wish they would go. I haven't had a healing around that yet. Anyway, we all now know that tomorrow is our day to go back to the yoga school and hear a presentation from the "master" teacher. Not sure what that's about. Request for donations? We'll find out. For being so tired, I'm writing a lot. One other big thing! The Mountain shaman will be arriving tomorrow as well to offer us a greeting. I look forward to more mystical magic! Until tomorrow . . .

CHAPTER 23

The Transmission

"It's way too early," Pearl yawned as she rose for yet another full day. The rooster crowed, and a pink glow warmed the hovering mist.

"I'm thinking of skipping this one. I feel almost hung over, and my body needs a break." Allie covered her head with the sheet. Temple bells rang, welcoming a fresh, new day.

"Sorry, friend. We're in this together, and if I'm going, you're going. If you don't get up, I'm going to shake my ants on you!" Pearl joked and ran over to her sheets.

"Okay, okay! I'm up! Let me go say hi to the lizard, and I'll be right back." Allie brushed her teeth, and the lizard appeared in its usual place. "What do you think? Should I shower, or is it not worth it this morning?" The lizard stood frozen. "Gotcha. No shower until later." She didn't feel like fighting the shock of cool water, nor did she care what she looked or smelled like this morning. This marked a big change from the start of the trip. Was it a good one? Probably not.

She fluffed her hair, swiped deodorant, and threw on cotton pants and a new kurta.

Surprisingly, everyone in the group, Doug and Gloria included, met out front to walk to the school for their VIP breakfast. Upon arrival, the headmaster and his two assistants greeted them.

"Welcome back! Does it feel too early today for our western guests? Yesterday was a full day." The master scrutinized everyone, one by one. He caught Allie's gaze and furrowed his brow. Or was she imagining it? *I'm seeing things. I desperately need more sleep.* She tried not to show her instant disdain for his blantant ego.

He added, "We have prepared a breakfast that I hope will be to your liking. Please, come. Sit." He gestured to two long tables that were covered with exquisitely detailed tablecloths.

At the buffet, they were served hard-boiled eggs, fresh bread, sweet cookies, and pressed coffee and chai.

"We trust that you are ready for a good cup of coffee!" He'd intuited the truth.

"The coffee's delicious." Allie reveled in the familiar smell, warmth, and taste.

The two couples sat with the master teacher and appeared to be schmoozing quite nicely. Doug's chest was thrust forward as he told everyone about their easy first-class flight to Nepal. "I'm also a master flute player."

Allie chuckled as she refilled her coffee. *He's earning his VIP status, for sure.* She suspected that there was going to be a request for donations before they left the campus, and Doug's boasting would leave him no choice but to lighten his pockets.

After the simple but nourishing breakfast, the group was led to a small square building perched on top of a hill that overlooked yet another glorious view. The structure reminded Allie of a simple chapel that often accompanied a large church sanctuary. And yet inside it was bare, with the exception of several wooden pews, the predicted donation box, and a framed 8x10 photo that stood front-and-center on a podium. Allie couldn't see what the photo showed, but from the distance it appeared to be a building. *Curious.*

"Welcome to our unique space for invited guests only. My assistants and I will share with you a transmission that will elevate you and help you focus."

Interesting. What's it called? Allie, the compassionless rebelling pilgrim, was suspicious.

"This is a special honor for you and is not to be taken lightly. I am offering you this gift as special guests of Babaji."

Ah, no guilt there. Or pride. Allie caught herself. *Allie, you are failing. Stop the judgment!*

"Today we invite connection to each other and to a higher power through respect, fear, and obedience."

Fear? Allie was on alert.

"Fear is important. Through fear, we learn to respect and be obedient. Now, please, close your eyes."

Obedient to what? Allie glanced around the room, eyes

wide. *Did anyone else hear what he just said?* Babaji stared straight ahead, no longer smiling and slightly pale.

Will Babaji save us from this unnamed technique? No movement. Babaji closed his eyes.

While Allie greatly respected Babaji, she was becoming frustrated by his passivity. *He's my teacher, and I need to trust him. Right?* Allie grabbed Pearl's hand, hoping for support. Trust or no trust, she didn't like where this was going. Pearl squeezed back. Her eyes were closed, her head was bowed, and she was smiling.

Okay, Pearl's listening as well. Comfort in numbers. We'll be okay. He must have brought us here for a reason.

Allie felt the burning glare of the master seconds before her eyes met his. He smiled, but his dark beads pierced her like a laser. *Wow, intense.* She glanced down. *He's on to me. Caught being disobedient.* Her forehead burned. Allie squeezed Pearl's hand again. She was suddenly her young self stuck in church, desperately wanting to flee a bad sermon. Giggles rose within her. Perhaps it was good old-fashioned exhaustion, or the challenges of being in the third world, but, just like Mary Tyler Moore at Chuckles the clown's funeral, she just wanted to laugh. A huge, loud bellowing laugh. *This is not good. Behave.*

Pearl heard her struggle and gripped her hand tightly. *Hang in there, friend.*

Bowing her head deeply, she tried to mask her discomfort

and rising laughter. Her shoulders shook, and Allie grasped for control.

"With your eyes closed," instructed the master, "take a full, deep breath and follow your exhale. We will offer you the technique after a few moments of silence."

Silence.

Good god, this is hell. When will this be over? She wiggled her toes trying to distract herself, but instead choked on her suppressed laughter, snorted, and then, coughed to cover it up. *Get it together. You are a meditator!*

Pearl pulled her hand onto her lap and started to breathe deeply. Allie followed her rhythm. *Settle. You got this.* And somehow, perhaps through the grace of God, she did.

"Now, focus on your third eye and draw your breath there. Feel trust and open your third eye to receive this transmission." Allie slammed her third eye shut and squeezed Pearl's hand again. She squeezed back.

"Now, we move to the heart. Open your heart and receive this in your heart, yes, that's it."

Allie's chest became warm and her third eye burned.

"Feel the sensations resonating in your heart. Now, embody this in your feet and feel the earth. Yes, yes. Now, take a deep breath and open your eyes."

Allie glanced around. The master and his assistants appeared peaceful. Doug was grinning, Gloria was asleep, and the others looked serious. Including Babaji.

"Here," said the master, referring to the framed photo, "we have a photo of the home building. The energy is rooted there."

Well, it's simple, that's for sure. No deities, no "stuff."

"Now, we invite you to make an offering from your heart."

There's the request . . .

As the master stood firmly and waited, Babaji hustled to each of his friends and whispered, "You make small offering. Is okay. One dollar, is okay." One by one, the pilgrims awkwardly walked to the front.

Allie wanted to ask, *Is this for the school or this building? Or you? I'd happily support the students but this is confusing.* Instead, she remained silent, as she placed her dollar in the donation box.

"And now, to complete our program, we will offer each of you a few minutes of an individual transmission. Please, come forward."

Allie thought of church again and pictured them placing their palms on her forehead saying, "You are healed!" She'd tumble backwards into the arms of the others, and all would rejoice. She'd go home full of compassion, fully purified, and ready to embrace the world. But this was not a healing service. Everyone paraded up as if in a funeral procession. Allie followed along. What choice did she have? She couldn't be the only one to leave. That would be rude. *Maybe not as rude as snorting during the transmission.* And as much as she disliked his strong egotism, she felt strangely curious. *I'm here. Why not? I'll keep my third eye closed and see what I feel.*

Allie purposefully got behind Marianna, who stood waiting for one of the assistants, not for the master.

"Come, I will offer to you," said the master, beckoning Allie to the corner.

Allie looked around.

He searched her eyes and smiled. "I feel your resistance. But come, please." Allie thought she saw kindness somewhere beyond the pomp. They stood face to face, and Allie closed her eyes. *Okay, Darth Vader, I'm ready for you.* She tried to appear relaxed but put up her imaginary shield. "Take a deep breath." She couldn't. "Now, focus on the center of your forehead." Allie felt pressure there, like a soft pushing, as if an eye were glued shut, trying to open. Allie wanted to receive a sincere message. She wanted to trust, she wanted to relax but just couldn't. She wasn't willing to let the master in. The uncomfortable pressure continued in her forehead, like something trying to burrow in. And then it stopped.

"Now, open your eyes and take a deep breath." He didn't smile but didn't frown. "I felt resistance from your energy field, but with practice, you can learn."

Allie faked a smile, afraid to say the wrong thing. "Namaskar."

"How'd it go for you?" Allie asked Pearl after they were outside.

"Just fine. I didn't feel much. I was just going through the motions. Didn't want to insult anyone. I saw the big ego come for you. Couldn't get out of that one, now could you?" Pearl smiled. "How'd it feel?"

"It's fine. It was no big deal. He's harmless." Allie was convincing herself. "I felt something trying to pry my third eye open, but I didn't allow it. I don't trust his energy, but I was curious. Call me deliriously tired and stupidly curious."

"Okay, deliriously tired and stupidly curious friend. We have some free time. Let's head back to the village and finish our shopping,"

"A good plan."

"Friends!" Babaji interrupted with a booming announcement, "Exciting news. We just learn that mountain shaman is close. Because of monsoon he had delay and took wrong path, but he is now arrive tonight, and we will have ceremony. Get rest. Is very special night! What time, we don't know yet. We must be flexible because he comes on foot. The journey continues! Destination unknown."

The five friends, Allie, Pearl, Kate, Marianna, and Kurt, gathered together and trekked back up to the village to finish their shopping.

"We finally get to meet the mountain shaman!" Pearl exclaimed.

"Are we ready for this adventure?" Kurt replied.

"I think so," Marianna added. "We have no idea what to expect."

"I can't wait! But right now, I need a long monsoon nap! Somebody didn't let me play hooky today." Allie leaned into Pearl.

"Nap sounds great!" Kate joined in.

Boom boom boom. Lingering Lakhes from yesterday's festival passed by and bounced into Allie, then Pearl. *Lord, I'm not prepared for this.* Allie tried to dig into her bag for a dollar. They bounced into her again and again, so aggressive that she couldn't get into her bag fast enough.

"Okay, enough," Kurt yelled as he stepped in between them. "Just hang on." Whether they understood English or not, they must have felt the towering presence of the gentle giant and backed off.

Boom, boom, boom.

The drums continued, and they bounced in place from foot to foot with their large masks offering a barrier between human and mystique. It was easy to forget that there was a small person under there, maybe even a boy or teenager. Kurt pulled two dollars out of his pocket and gave it to them. "Take it easy next time," he yelled after them as they danced off.

"I don't mean for this to sound ungrateful, but I've about had it." Allie felt her throat start to choke up—not with tears— but with an uncomfortable tightening sensation, like there was something suddenly in the way of her swallowing. She pushed it aside and continued, "That Lakhe dance didn't feel 'sacred' to me at all. It wasn't a dance to send off the dead.

That was just about getting a dollar and intimidating me. I'm tired, and I want to be somewhere where I feel steady and safe. So far, today has not been that day."

"I'm with you on that. I don't think that we're unsafe, but it's all unfamiliar," Marianna replied. "Some seem to welcome us, but others seem threatened by us. I don't know if it's just that we can't communicate with each other or if there's really something in the air."

"We only have a day or two left. I've lost track. But we'll be moving on soon enough. This is harder than we all anticipated, but we'll get through this," Pearl added, ever the encouraging one.

"I realize now that I romanticized this village all these years. I pictured an unpopulated land with huts scattered amidst the jungle. Fewer people and less chaos," Allie said.

"What I didn't anticipate is the power of this land. The magic and beauty but also the shadows here," Marianna whispered.

Kurt agreed, "It's powerful for sure. I felt someone brush into me yesterday, an older woman with a walking stick. She touched my hand and I shivered." Allie perked up as he continued. 'Keep an eye on your friends,' the old woman told me. 'You are their safe keeper here. Your teacher is distracted. He is not seeing everything.' Then a crowd of people pushed through us, and she vanished."

"Can we pop in here?" Kate said, not paying attention to the conversation.

As they mindlessly followed Kate into the small jewelry shop, Allie had to ask, "Kurt, what did this woman look like?"

"I don't remember. It all happened so fast. I just remember the large walking stick. And her kind eyes. Oh, and her perfect English."

Allie shivered and knew to keep her previous visions of the woman to herself. She'd tuck the information away for another time.

As they browsed, the tiny shop filled with villagers, who sat on the cushioned benches—meant—for customers to simply watch them. They were very curious.

"See what I mean?" Allie felt on display again. "It's harmless, but enough is enough," she whispered to Pearl, as they paid for their goods. After almost a week of this, Allie'd had enough. She didn't feel threatened, but she was ready for some personal space.

"My throat suddenly feels horrible. It's not sore but it's tight. Like something is gripping my larynx. Do you feel anything?" Allie asked Pearl.

"No, I feel fine. Maybe you're dehydrated?"

"Maybe so. A nap should help." Allie knew her body, and this was a new and unpleasant sensation, and she was willing it away. *Whatever this is, you're not welcome, and I'm going to sleep you off.* She thought she felt it lessen, or was it her imagination? Things were getting strange.

CULTURAL LESSON #18

"Curiosity choked the cat." Avoid suspicious transmissions from people you don't trust.

CHAPTER 24

The Mountain Shaman

That afternoon, the monsoon rains began to pour down with a fierce intensity. The thick, dense clouds prevented any whisper of cell phone connectivity, and the fetid smell of diesel fuel hovered in the thick humid air as the generator worked to power the hostel.

Babaji had spread the word (and slipped a note under Gloria's door) that the group was to meet the shaman at 8:00 p.m. in an undisclosed location. The event was to remain private. If word spread in the village that the "Mountain shaman" was in *their* village, there would be a frenzy to have audience with him, and another spectacle would ensue.

The pilgrims walked the short distance to a private home in the torrential downpour. Even with their umbrellas, upon arrival, they were still soaked from the bottom up. Earlier that day, Allie had taken electrolytes, a power bar, and a good nap and was feeling more enlivened and energized. Her throat, however, was still gripping, and a shallow cough added to her discomfort.

The second-story room was already filled with about thirty invited villagers when the pilgrims entered. *Secret event, huh?* Allie recognized several of Babaji's family members, a few town musicians, and the master teacher.

The pilgrims left their shoes at the entrance and were invited to take the remaining chairs that hugged the walls of the small space. Allie sat between Kurt and Pearl as they tucked tightly into the damp, stuffy room. Feeling the now familiar sensation of sweat trickling down her chest and pooling at her belly button, Allie gazed longingly at a small fan, trying once again to will it to turn on. But, there was no electricity. Candlelight was their only light, and that added to the magic, mystery, and sweat.

In the center of the space lay a large tattered rug that set the scene for the ritual. Carefully placed ghee candles and copper vessels filled with flowers lined the edges of the rug. In the middle sat a huge, empty tortoise shell.

Excited chatter combined with an orchestra of coughs, electrifying the air. Like the childhood game of "telephone," the cough passed around the room. With each pass, the cough changed, some deep, some dry, some long and tortured; others just a tickle. It was a building symphony and one that Allie was unfortunately beginning to join.

"What's with the cough?" Allie whispered, sipping from her water bottle.

"I just noticed it, too." Pearl huddled into Allie and Kurt. "I'm not sure. Do you think it's the diesel in the air from the generators?"

"Could be. My throat feels so tight. It's a new sensation. Not sore. More like a choke." Allie tried to clear her throat.

"I'm feeling something in the air, and I don't think it's diesel." Kurt looked around, easily towering over most of the crowd from his seat. "Let's put on our protective cloaks and see where this is going to lead. Did you bring your wands?" Kurt winked. He was sort of joking with his Harry Potter reference but mostly not.

"Okay," said Allie. "This is weird, but the master teacher is here. 'Coincidentally,'" she gestured air quotes, "I started to feel a choke shortly after I got a transmission from him. Do you think he's like the Voldemort of the village or something?" She peeked over at him to see if his piercing eyes were peering her way. So far, so good.

"Your imagination is getting the best of you, friend. There's no Voldemort here, except in our minds. But maybe the cough is clearing energy? You know, sometimes with energy healing, physical symptoms come in?" Pearl tried to see the broad picture and remain positive.

"It could be a collective clearing," Kurt added. "The master preaches fear and obedience. That can be choking, particularly if you fight it. Maybe it's a symptom of their fear of him?"

At that moment, the shaman appeared as if out of nowhere. He knelt reverently over the tortoise shell, carefully filling

204 || Denise Mihalik

it with rice, spices, and a touch of water. His subtle chanting quieted the room, and all became mesmerized by the simple and sacred act of preparing the "skull."

This shaman was everything Allie had envisioned. At barely five feet tall, his skin was well-tanned and weathered from exposure to the elements. He was slender and appeared to be strong and healthy and rightfully so; he *had* just walked four days across the mountains in treacherous conditions. Dry, cracked, and callused feet told the story of the challenging mountain trails. He dressed simply in an off-white kurta, matching pants, a solid maroon vest, rudraksha seed mala, and a Nepali topi—the traditional hat. Moving quietly and quickly, he prepared the space for the ceremony. Babaji approached to help and was greeted warmly with laughter and loving recognition. The shaman's translator facilitated smooth communication.

The coughing, which had ceased momentarily, began again as Babaji addressed the onlookers.

"Friends," he spoke seriously to the group, "is honor to have Mountain shaman with us. He walks four days from deep mountains to meet us. Is very special honor. Our visiting friends is invited to spin on skull of his teacher, highest incarnation, the tortoise shell. You set intention for skull. But not everyone spins. Only if you connect to spirit of shaman's guru, you will spin and receive special message. Ceremony is begin now."

Allie wasn't able to pay much attention to the

opening ceremony. Although she heard the chanting and the drumming, saw the movements of the shaman, and smelled the incense, her mind was elsewhere. *Spin on the skull?* One part of her felt ready—*I came all this way . . . I **have** to do this—* but another part of her was suddenly terrified. *What if nothing happens? What if I don't spin? And why do all these people have to watch?* Fear and negativity rose again to dominate her internal dialogue. Allie gulped a full, smoke-filled, stale breath and coughed through her tight throat. *I'm an adventurer now. I'm not going to stay in this chair because of fear. This is different from earlier. This is special.*

After the opening ceremony, Babaji was invited to step onto the skull first. It all passed quickly. He balanced on the shell, and, when the music started, he began to spin slowly. There was an assistant next to the shell to keep him from falling over as he spun. He was the "weeble who wobbled but didn't fall down." Babaji looked vibrant and renewed as he stepped out of the skull. The shaman spoke with him quietly, and Babaji received his translated message.

His broad smile had returned, and he looked at Allie. "Allieji, you are next!"

She saw her teacher's mouth move with the invitation, but her pounding heart drowned out his words. Allie rose tentatively, as if the curtain were rising on a performance she had forgotten to prepare for. *This is Indiana Jones stepping into the unknown cavern, the black abyss, the pit of awakening . . .* Her mind raced as fear tried to drown her.

Soaked both from rain and sweat, as all eyes followed her, she hoped it didn't look like she'd wet her pants.

Babaji took her hand and instructed, "Step careful. Slow. Feet together, bend knees." Whispering and coughing rattled in the background.

The grains of rice felt both comforting and painful on the soles of her feet, which barely fit into the large shell. It felt brittle, and she was concerned that her weight would crack it.

She tucked into a deep, awkward squat but couldn't find her balance. *This is impossible!*

"Breathe, Allieji, is okay." Babaji and Lumanti knelt next to her, offering support. Their fingers tapped her shoulders gently at various times to help her remain upright. She was an apple floating in a wild river current, destination unknown.

The shaman's penetrating gaze hooked her, and, although she had no idea what was about to happen, she knew that an intention was needed.

Purification. She forced a smile.

Silence. Not even a mosquito dared to buzz by.

As if the shaman sensed her intention and readiness, he began to intone a deep, guttural chant in an unfamiliar language. The primordial, soothing groans put Allie at ease. A conch sounded loudly, then a rattle and a drum. Suddenly, pressure pushed into her forehead, like a tug from some radiant force above. Not uncomfortable or frightening, just new, strange. She began to spin—slowly at first, as if this new energy were testing the waters.

"Oh my God, I'm spin . . . ," words died as she simultaneously felt tension in her forehead and steadiness through her feet.

The spinning quickened and thinking-Allie disappeared. There was no other place to be. No body, arms frozen around her knees. She could feel Babaji tapping her occasionally to keep her upright. The room, a blurry, spinning vortex of energy, she went 'round and 'round, and time ceased. No control, nor did she know who or what was making her spin.

"Oh, my God! Oh, my God!" whispered Babaji.

At the sound of his voice, a thought moved through her in slow motion: *What - is - happening?* She hadn't been scared, but his reactions were not comforting.

The faster she spun, the faster and louder he repeated, "Oh my God!"

Faster and faster and faster. Out of control but not dizzy— an observer, feeling and hearing the room gasping. Suddenly the chanting stopped—as did her movement—and she flew off the shell onto the floor.

Silence.

Breathless, she lay on the carpet looking up at everyone. They silently stared back. *Whoa, that was wild.* She was winded. *And fast! What does it mean?* Her thoughts were returning. *And I'm not dizzy! How can I not be dizzy?* Surprised that she didn't throw up, she knew that there was something magical about the experience.

Sitting up, trying to catch her breath, she caught the

shaman's eyes. He gazed deeply into her being and held her with his eyes. It was just she and the shaman. She forgot everyone else and simply sank into his warm eyes. He spoke directly to her in a language she didn't understand. After a moment, she looked at Babaji. A translator translated the shaman's words into Nepali and Babaji translated it to English. "Were you spinning yourself? He say no one is ever spin that fast."

"No, I don't know what was spinning me. It was some other energy. In my forehead."

Babaji relayed the message to the translator, who translated it to the shaman. He looked less intense, closed his eyes, and paused. He nodded his head as if he were hearing something in the ether. Having had some kind of confirmation, he opened his eyes and began to speak.

After two translations, the message came through as . . . "Stay true to your spiritual roots. You are searching, but you have all you need already. Stay true to your roots . . ." He paused. "And . . ."

Ooh there's more . . .

". . . be careful with natural gas."

Natural gas? That's random. Not quite the deep spiritual message she expected. The first message, however, did speak to her. She missed her light, happy self, and her recent challenges had her questioning everything. Why else would she find herself spinning on a tortoise shell in the middle of Nepal?

"Kateji, you are next!" Babaji smiled and clapped his

hands. The village coughs resonated again throughout the small space.

"Okay, now," she said slowly, "here we go!" Kate flushed as she stood. Her broad smile and wide eyes reflected the innocent excitement that Allie so admired.

Babaji helped Kate step into the skull, and a similar process began. Kate hugged her knees while Babaji and Lumanti tapped her at times to keep her upright. The conch sounded, and the chanting and drumming began. A slow force began to move her. It was subtle. She moved to the right and then back to the left as if the energy were deciding to go clockwise or counter-clockwise. Then Kate began to spin clockwise; the same direction as Allie and Babaji but much more slowly. Not even a minute had passed, when Kate slowed to a halt before the chanting finished. With the help of Babaji, she gracefully stepped out of the shell and sat near the shaman, looking at him with a trusting smile. The translations began and eventually, the English message was communicated: "You have goddess energy from many lifetimes that you bring into this body. You are very wise and will bless others with the ancient knowledge within you."

Now that's a message. Allie thought, a*nd look how graceful she was! She just stepped right out of the shell. I was spat out like a watermelon pit.* Allie felt like she had succeeded in some way though, having spun so fast. *There must be a message in speed, right?* She took a sip of water. The still air wasn't any cooler, nor was her underwear any dryer. Unexpectedly, a passing cough overtook her, and she choked out a dry, whooping sound. Her wet bottom stuck to the wooden chair, and Kurt patted her soaked back. *Ugh, not pleasant.* She was now used to being smelly and wet from sweat. That she could manage. But the cough was unnerving and had to go. Now. There was a little something sitting at the base of her trachea, and it was squeezing it shut from the inside like a slow-moving vise. Taking another drink, she willed it away. *Go somewhere else, please.*

Marianna was next to step into the shell. She spun at a velocity slightly faster than Kate and lasted the duration of the chanting. Allie didn't know if that meant anything special. Her message was: "You have a deep connection with your mother. She has challenges now that will resolve. Do not neglect your meditation practices."

"Pearlji! Please come!"

Pearl balanced easily on the shell and waited the duration of the chant to spin but never did. Her message spoke of the shaman within her and encouraged her to return to Nepal to study.

Kurt respectfully refused the invitation to spin as did Doug and Gloria. John and Jane had remained at the hostel to rest.

As the long evening drew to a close, Babaji spoke quietly with the shaman while the group waited and watched. They laughed and hugged like the old friends they were. Babaji then spoke in English to include the pilgrims. "Is great honor that you meet with us, and we are very blessed."

Babaji turned to meet the eyes of his group. "Friends, monsoon rains is getting bad, so we leave tomorrow. Change of plans. Early flight. We meet at 8:00 a.m. with luggage ready, okay?" Doug's face reddened with the last-minute change, but he remained silent. Allie saw Gloria grip his hand. She, too, didn't say a word. They all peeled themselves out of their seats and headed back to the hostel. Although Allie had a lot to organize and pack, she was very ready to leave the village and return to the familiarity of the Kathmandu Hotel.

It was close to midnight when they began the short walk back to the hostel. Allie's feet splashed through muddy puddles, her pant legs heavy on her ankles. Rain battered her umbrella, and exhaustion blanketed her like the full moon eclipse. With each sopping step, her throat gripped more and more. She was desperate to lie down.

"Oh, no!" Babaji exclaimed.

As they approached the hostel, they saw the metal gates closed and tightly chained with an oversized padlock. They were locked out.

"They didn't know we were out?" Allie said.

"Is secret meeting," Babaji responded and then began yelling toward the hostel. No answer.

"We break lock. Is okay! I get hammer from my brother." Babaji hustled off down the road.

A hammer. That'll wake the whole village! The padlock and chains would more likely need a grinder.

Rajesh pounded on the gates. No answer. *How can they not hear us? How many more obstacles can we have?*

The group waited in the rain until Babaji returned and began to hammer the lock. Allie had to laugh. *Pure chaos. And LOUD. Just us "ghosts" sneaking back after secretly spinning on a tortoise shell.* She wanted an adventure, and she was getting it.

Then, just as quickly as the mini-crisis began, it ended. One of the staff workers peeked sleepily out of the third-floor window down at the crowd below. Yelling and more yelling ensued, until eventually he rushed down to unlock the newly dented gate. *Thank goodness.*

It was now close to 1:00 in the morning. Allie ignored her hunger, washed her face and rang our her drenched clothing. No lizard in sight. It was beyond time for rest, and she needed to sleep off the "village cough." She fell into bed without shaking away the ants.

THE DREAM STARTED ALMOST before her head hit the pillow.

Allie was spinning on the tortoise shell, and she was alone. Guttural chanting resonated in the background, and the spinning shell, with her on it, began to drill into the earth. She spun faster and faster as she went down, down, down until she hit a plateau. Suddenly, the spinning stopped, and she was thrown off the shell into the void. Her body began to buzz as she floated in nothingness. Only the shell, in the far distance, was illuminated by a soft light from overhead.

In the limitless open space, Allie struggled to get back to the shell and the light. She tried to swim in the void, but that only pulled her further away. She yelled, but the void absorbed it, and she felt her throat tighten. She couldn't breathe. She yelled again, but there was no sound. She tried to grip something, but there was nothing to hold onto, and she continued to be pulled further from the light. From a distance, she heard a soft, familiar voice begin to call into the void. It was so far away and getting farther . . .

"Allieji, it's okay. You are okay. Wake up." Allie was thrashing and gasping in her bed. The ants didn't know what to do, and Pearl was trying to wake her.

"Wake up, Allieji, wake up." Pearl shook her awake.

Allie inhaled as if she had just come up from being underwater for minutes. "Whoa, where am I?" she gasped to the dark room.

"It's Pearl. You're okay." Pearl searched for the flashlight. "You were dreaming." She shined light into the room.

"Oh my god. That was terrifying."

"What happened?"

"I," Allie was soaked and breathless, "was . . . in some void. I couldn't get back to the light. I think I was on the skull. I . . ."

"It's okay, shh." Pearl rubbed Allie's forehead. "You're okay now. We're in Nepal. It's been a HUGE day and you're overtired." Pearl tried to calm her. "It's okay. The light's here. You're safe." She kept the flashlight on.

"Yes, thank . . . y—" Allie fell back into a deep, dreamless sleep.

CHAPTER 25

The Descent

The next morning the collectively fatigued group rallied to be ready by 8:00 a.m. They piled into their hired vehicles and began their drive down, down, down the mountain to the airport in the now unrelenting flowing monsoon. There was no excited chatter in Allie's vehicle. Instead, the sound of crashing rain assailed their ears while the wipers scraped and screeched, fighting to keep up. Mud splashed around them, and they bounced from side to side as they optimistically moved forward toward the next part of their adventure—a flight to Kathmandu, lunch, and then travel to an elephant refuge.

Allie gazed out the window and thought back to her earlier conversation with Pearl:

"I slept like a log last night. It was my deepest rest so far," Allie said as they'd packed their suitcases.

"Fantastic! You really needed the rest." Surprised that

Allie hadn't mentioned any nightmares, Pearl asked, "Have any cool dreams after your skull adventure last night?'

"Hmm, not that I recall. It was one of those nights that went by in a flash. One minute I was asleep, and the next, it was morning. I feel pretty good except for this uncomfortable grip. It feels like someone's sticking a spear right through my throat from front to back. Any suggestions?"

Pearl decided not to mention Allie's nightmare episode and instead focused on the question at hand. "Okay, so we can try and boost your immune system." She pulled out a vitamin C packet that contained electrolytes. "This should help. There also might be some emotional stuff moving through you, so, once we're on the plane, we can talk about any energetic blocks that might be choking you."

"Sounds like a good plan. Thanks."

They'd finished packing and said goodbye to their room. "This is it. I don't plan to ever return, so take good care and thanks for the company," Allie said to the ants and lizard. She padlocked the door.

CONDITIONS HAD TO BE close to perfect to fly out of the valley safely, and the monsoon was not letting up. Even so, the caravan continued its descent and rounded the last curve into the valley. Allie was jarred back to the present moment, and, surprisingly, her throat felt less tight. She swallowed more easily and could breathe more freely. *Am I imagining*

this? It was a welcome relief, and she decided not to question it. Here, about sixty minutes away from the village, she felt lighter and very ready to leave this part of the journey behind, choke and all.

"Friends." Babaji peeked his head into their vehicle, hopeful. "Is no airplane from Kathmandu yet. We wait one hour and see."

Allie rested her head in her hands, *Lord, please, help us get out of here.* She remembered being hit in the face by the first shaman's wand, the master's piercing eyes, the spinning shell, and her imaginary crone. *I'll take a canoe, a raft, a helicopter, anything.* Allie laughed out loud in spite of herself.

The hour passed and there was still no action. There would be no airplane that day, nor a canoe, raft, or helicopter.

"We go back to village and try again tomorrow," Babaji announced to each vehicle. He didn't seem bothered to be the soaked messenger.

Damn, Allie was more than disappointed. "I guess I shouldn't have left my hat in Kathmandu," she said to Kurt, Pearl, and Marianna. "It feels like I need it now." The Indiana Jones adventure was requiring more of her with each passing day.

"How about you borrow mine?" Kurt reached to his head.

"No, thanks," Allie giggled. "It's become part of you. Wear it with courage for all of us!" She tried to lighten her mood, but, as they drove back up the mountain into the village and to the hostel, Allie felt her throat tighten again. Bone-tired exhaustion settled in. The van may have been going up, but she was going down fast.

"I'm really not feeling well," she moaned.

"We'll be able to rest soon. Can you make it up the mountain or do we need to pull over?" Kurt whispered.

"No need. It's not nausea." Allie closed her eyes and tried to take a deep breath. "I'll make it." She willed the bouncing vehicle to lull her into a light sleep.

BACK AT THE HOSTEL, Allie jiggled the familiar padlock and opened the door to her room. "Did you miss me?" she whispered weakly to the ants, as she plopped her suitcase on the extra bed and lay down. Pearl and Babaji decided that it would be best for her to have her own room for this one night, just in case she had something contagious. Allie didn't care, she just wanted to sleep. The strength and freedom she felt at the foot of the mountain one short hour prior was now being replaced with a full-flaming apocalypse. Weakness pulsed through her veins, and her head throbbed. Some invisible force was wrapping around her neck, and she struggled for breath..

I'm stronger than this, I can will this away. Roots, the shaman said. Trust your roots. Allie tried to envision the white light that she knew so well as a child and young adult. She had been steadfast and strong in her faith, and that light of love informed her path through life, until the one day in her twenties when it went dark.

"Thump, thump, thump," a slow hammer pounded in her head. *Please, let me remember the light.* Allie closed her eyes and saw only a dark void. She tried again to envision the rising sun, the shining moon, anything. Nothing. *The crone! Please, sing to me?* Silence; just the choke and the skull-shattering pain that was stealing her breath.

Through shallow gasps, the darkness behind her closed eyes began to morph into shifting colors. They were pulsing and turning like a living kaleidoscope, and she was being enticed into another dimension. A reddish-orange shape swelled toward her like a giant embrace trying to engulf her. But then it retreated, and all became dark. "Thump. Thump, thump," pounded her head. The swelling color began again, and, like a seashell at the mercy of a rolling wave, she was pulled into a riptide of color and darkness, swelling and releasing. With each swell, she was drawn further into an unknown void, far from the safety of land. Fear kicked in as she began to lose her bearings. The choking around her throat subtly tightened, and she was overcome by a black, muddy image that was threatening and physically uncomfortable. Allie wasn't hallucinating, and she wasn't dreaming.

She called out silently again to the Light. *The light always illuminates the dark.* Her entire being tried to fight this darkness, but instead she was overwhelmed by a deep cough that made her head want to shatter. The grip tightened. Some kind of invisible battle was beginning inside of her. Every time she attempted to call in the Light, a cough would rise from the depths of her lungs, and the choke would hold its grip. *The light's strong enough, The light has to be strong enough!* In spite of her determination, her body was too weak to move, and her mouth was dry and pasty. The cough burned her throat, and the fire of pain in her head had her feeling like she was feverish, even though she was not.

"Help," she whimpered. *The light is being choked out of me.* It was an epic battle that felt like life or death.

"Help," she called again, barely a whisper. Allie tried to get up but was weighted into the bed.

"Oh, my God, what's happening?" Pearl burst through the unlocked door.

"It's too much. The dark's too much. It's taking over," Allie whispered. "It's choking me."

Pearl remained calm, "You're going to be okay. We'll get Babaji. You'll be fine," she encouraged and yelled out through the open wall, "We need help here, someone, hurry!"

"The light isn't strong enough. I'm scared." Allie heard people gathering around her; shuffles and whispers.

"Will reiki help?" Kate whispered into her ear.

Allie didn't have words to answer as the question echoed around her. She felt warm hands on her head, and Kate offered her support.

The black, muddy image transformed into a swirling skull. Again, she called in the Light only to be answered by a guttural cough that racked her entire body. This repeated . . . over and over.

"Stay strong, Allieji," she heard Kurt's familiar warmth touch her consciousness. "Whatever's happening, you'll get through this," He rubbed scented oil on her wrists and forehead.

"Yowadi yadawehy om uuuhyowahehyokuh," Allie felt herself chanting; it was a deep, guttural throat chant in a language that she didn't recognize. Perhaps it was a non-sense language, or some ancient dialect, she didn't know. It simply had to come out as she exhaled. The chanting actually felt good, and, for the length of the chant, she wasn't choking. Allie wasn't afraid of the sound or the feeling of it. Maybe this was her inner shaman. "Yowadi yadawehy om uuuhyowahehyokuh,"

"Allieji, I am here," she heard the soothing sound of Babaji's voice as it floated in from a distance. She was beginning to lose consciousness.

"You are safe and you are strong. I die for you if I need. You are safe. You are pure light, Allieji. You are strong," Babaji soothed, over and over again.

Allie felt the familiar weight of a singing bowl on her chest, and the subtle sound and vibrations momentarily soothed her.

"Yowadi yadawehy om uuuhyowahehyokuh," Allie exhaled the deep, uncontrollable syllables.

"No more chant. Stay quiet. Take deep breath," Babaji whispered. "You are safe. Light is strong in you. Listen to bowl."

At his beckoning, Allie stopped the chanting, but the

coughing started again, so much so, that Babaji had to catch the bowl as it flew off her body.

"Allieji. Hear me, my voice. You are safe. I am here. Light is so strong in you. Breathe, friend. You are safe."

Allie heard a bell and smelled incense. Babaji was chanting quietly.

Suddenly, as if something were being pulled from her, Allie felt the cough turn into a retch. Someone grabbed a garbage can and she threw up so strongly that she was almost turned inside out. She collapsed back on the bed.

Babaji continued to chant softly and ring the bell. A singing bowl played in the distance.

She retched again. Allie had never experienced such a violent expulsion of bile. Although some food came up, she was not throwing up food. It was deeper than that. Whatever she hadn't been able to swallow earlier was coming up. She retched a third time so deep that her viscera felt bruised. The choking dissipated, and Allie took a shallow breath. It was gone. She knew it, but had no energy left to rejoice. The only evidence was muscular strain from the retching, a pounding third eye, and a throat that finally felt open and free.

"You are sick from food?" Babaji asked with hope.

"No. Stomach's fine," Allie croaked weakly. "I was being choked . . . by something. It was so dark. It was suffocating me." She rested a moment. "It's gone. The choke's gone. Thank you." She closed her eyes, and, as she fell asleep, she heard Babaji's soft voice . . .

"You are safe, Allieji. Rest now."

ALLIE WAS STARTLED AWAKE by the loud and sudden rumble of the generator starting up. Diesel fumes floated into her stale mouth and hovered in the stagnant air, reminding her that she was in Nepal.

She opened her eyes to the dark room. *Time, what time is it?* "Oh God," she moaned, grabbing her head as she tried to steady her throbbing skull.

All was strangely quiet. There was no chatter or clatter, just the constant tat, tat, tat of the generator.

What happened to me? An exorcism? She didn't know; she'd never been the recipient of an exorcism.

Click, click, click. The fan came to life but provided minimal relief from the stifling heat.

Allie was dehydrated but had to pee and didn't have the strength to do anything about either. Instead, she fell back into a light sleep until her cotton mouth and nagging bladder forced her awake again.

Trying not to move her heavy head, Allie stretched her arm toward the bedside table and fumbled in the dark for her flashlight.

Clank. It crashed to the floor. *Damn!*

Her wandering hand continued the search until she heard the subtle crunch of a plastic water bottle falling onto its side. *Yes!* She sipped it from her supine position, dribbling some of the precious liquid down her chin and onto her chest. The coolness chilled her.

She needed to pee badly but was blanketed by a heavy unrelenting weight. The effort just to move a limb took all of her energy. With the excruciating slowness of a sloth, she rolled onto her side, dropped to the floor, and crawled on her hands and knees to the toilet. She pulled herself up onto the cool porcelain throne. *Thank goodness.* It was too dark to see if her lizard friend was there, and she felt totally alone.

Mission accomplished, she fumbled for toilet tissue that wasn't there and had to use her hand to brush away the remaining liquid. The sink thankfully supported her weight as she hauled herself up to wash her hands and splash her face with cool water. Allie had never felt so primitive. Having no strength to walk, she dropped back onto her knees and inched to her bed, breathing heavily and sweating from the exertion.

Too much. This is too much. She easily succumbed to the exhaustion and felt as if she were floating away from her body. She moved her fingers but could hardly feel them. *It's okay.* Sensing she was leaving her body, Allie pictured her ashes being scattered at the Pashupatinath Temple. *I'm ready. I can go now.* A bright light shimmered behind her closed eyes, or were they closed? *I can go to the Light.* The light got closer and closer until her entire being felt luminescent. *There you are!* Finally, Allie was overcome with a feeling of peace, and with a soft smile, she fell into a deep, safe sleep.

CHAPTER 26

The Evacuation

Allie awoke to the sounds of nearby shuffling and movement. Her eyes popped open to Pearl packing her bags for her. The natural light indicated early morning, and Allie slowly became aware that she was still alive and in the tiny hostel room. She could feel her fingers and toes and the light sheet covering her body. The headache had lifted, and she had some strength. Shocked that she was still in her body, she sputtered, "I'm still here?"

"Of course, you are! What do you mean?" Pearl asked.

"I thought I died. It was so peaceful. I was ready. My head. It was too much." Allie grasped for words.

"Glad you didn't!" Pearl replied flippantly, thinking that Allie was kidding. "You slept all of yesterday. It's been wild here. But before I fill you in, drink this." She handed Allie a glass of murky brownish-red liquid. "Drink all of it. It's from Rajeshji. It's his mother's special recipe, and he's literally been searching for two days all over the village to locate the ingredients.

Allie was so thirsty she would drink anything.

If I could have an exorcism, I might as well drink a magic potion, too. She chugged half of the drink.

"Well, now," she gasped, "that's disgusting." She'd never tasted anything like it. Although it smelled of fresh ginger, it looked and tasted like rancid, year-old black bean juice.

"Drink it all. Whatever you're experiencing, it's supposed to be a miracle cure."

Allie held her nose and chugged it. "Phew," she said with puckered lips, "as terrible as that was, it's actually a thirst quencher." A comforting warmth filled her chest and stomach as her body absorbed the tonic.

"Good!" Pearl replied quickly. "Now, we need to hustle. We're leaving in half an hour. The monsoon rains are getting worse, and there won't be any flights in or out of this region for days, if not weeks. Babaji's hired vehicles to drive us to the next closest airport. The plan is to catch a flight to Kathmandu from there. How do you feel? Can you get dressed?"

Allie rolled upright, draped her feet over the side of the bed, and felt them hit the cool floor. She stood slowly, testing her strength. "I feel stronger." Surprised, she added, "I think I'm going to live!"

Pearl stepped back, "But woo wee, *I* might not. You stink. You'd better go shower, friend. I'll finish packing for you. Go visit the lizard!"

"Haha, gotcha. I probably look as dirty as I smell."

While the cool water washed away the grime of the last few days, the tonic continued to soothe Allie's dehydration and increase her strength. The lizard scuttled up the wall. "This is it, for real," she said to her companion as she finished her shower. "You take good care now. I do NOT plan to be back. Ever. Thank you," she added, "for being here." The lizard scuttled away.

"Here's some food. See if you can eat some of this." Pearl handed Allie a plate of Dal bhat as she came out of the bathroom.

She sat on the bed and started gobbling.

"So, here's what's happening . . . ," Pearl explained while continuing to pack. "Unprecedented flooding is devastating much of Nepal. Babaji just wants to get us back to Kathmandu.

"Why don't we just stay here?"

"He says we'll be safe from the waters there. He canceled our trip to Chitwan because of mud slides and impossible travel conditions. We've been told that hundreds of tourists had to be rescued by elephants to escape the rising flood waters there."

"This is crazy! I think I really did die, and I'm now in hell." Allie pinched herself to be sure. *Can it get any worse?* She knew better than to ask. "How does he plan to get us to Kathmandu?"

"He considered helicopters, but that's impossible. Instead, he hired four military-grade vehicles to take us five hours to the next town. Wait until you see. They're ready for anything; they even have snorkels. And the drivers are highly trained and know the terrain. The airport there is not in a valley, so we should be able to fly out later today," she said matter-of-factly.

"Sounds like I missed a lot over these past couple of days."

"Oh, yes. Now, we really need to hustle. How's your strength? Do you need my help with anything?"

"No, I'm slow but doing okay, thanks." Allie ate the last few bites, finished dressing, and tentatively headed out of the room.

Outside, the normal activity of the village buzzed around them as the visiting "ghosts" prepared to leave for a second time—this time, traversing the challenging mud roads of the jungles. Some locals stopped to stare, and other new friends, including the musicians, came to say their goodbyes. Allie had grown quite fond of them, and they each smiled warmly. Loojha walked up to Allie with a wide smile and opened his arms. Allie took the cue and shared a hug.

He said, "Sing, sing!"

She replied, "Yes, sing, sing! Dhanyavad."

He laughed. "Swagatam. Welcome!"

Allie was ushered into the second vehicle along with Marianna, Kurt, Babaji, and Pearl. Someone shoved a pillow into her arms just before closing the door, and she didn't argue. She was ready for a nap. Some of Babaji's relatives were joining them, including Lumanti, and they easily filled all four vehicles.

Soon the caravan began to make its way out of the village.

Thank goodness. They were now moving forward to safety and rest just a half day away. *I'm so ready to be somewhere else.* Allie immediately felt the familiar guilt. *You're so ungrateful. It's Babaji's village! You should LOVE it!* She recalled the many welcome events, generosity, and the smiling musicians. But in this moment she felt beat up, and that was overshadowing the good. *This village kicked my ass.*

"This isn't so bad!" Marianna said to Allie from the seat next to her. Pearl sat in the front with the serious frowning driver. Kurt and Babaji sat sideways in the small covered back facing each other. Kurt, with his knees up to his ears and his Indiana Jones hat, was hunched over trying not to hit his head on the low roof.

Suddenly, as if on cue, the driver veered right off the surfaced road onto a tiny, one-lane dirt road.

"Now adventure begins!" Babaji yelped from the back.

"What's happening, Babaji?" Allie asked with wide eyes.

"Is road to next village!" He smiled.

"Oh!" She and Marianna locked eyes. *Not so bad? Spoke too soon.* Allie's initial relief shifted to dread.

"UGH!" The passengers had no choice but to groan as they bounced along the new terrain. To the western eye, the roads appeared impassable, but the experienced drivers continued inching forward across the slippery, pitted surfaces. Setting the pace, the lead vehicle rocked at deep angles through the thick sludge, leaving cavernous, muddy ruts for the following vehicles.

"Ouch! Argh!" They randomly grunted as they were tossed into the air and thrown from side to side.

"Watch . . . out!" Pearl warned over and over again from the front, trying to prepare her friends for the shock, but it didn't matter. The group flew up and hit their heads on the ceiling only to land hard on the worn, firm seats. Upon landing, the vehicle would rock at a deep side angle, knocking Allie's head into the window over and over. Neither the seatbelts nor their anticipatory preparation spared them from the rollercoaster ride.

"My . . . chiropractor . . . is going . . . to . . . love . . . this!" she grunted to Marianna, trying to cushion the blows with her pillow.

"Watch . . . out!" Pearl yelled as it started all over again.

The discomfort had them all laughing . . . at times.

"No need . . . for warning!" Babaji said in between bumps. "Uh! Road . . . is . . . very . . . good today!" he laughed.

The bouncing, slipping, and sliding along the three-foot-deep muddy mountain road was a challenge for everyone, especially those battling car sickness and fear of heights. As the winding roads became narrower and curvier, the dense treeline opened up to reveal a sharp drop on the right with a mighty river far below. Even at their distance, one could see it overflowing its banks; the raging water appearing to race the caravan toward an unknown destination.

Rounding another bend, the lead vehicle sank into the mud at an angle so great that it looked like it was about to tumble down the mountain, but the skilled driver knew how to manage the terrain. He righted the vehicle, and, unscathed, they continued on their way as if it were a normal Sunday drive.

Inside Allie's vehicle, however, hearts pounded almost audibly. A mix of moans, groans, and nervous laughter passed about another hour of swaying, hopping, and jerking. The group couldn't help but settle into a collective fatigue.

"How . . . long . . . did . . . you say . . . the trip . . . is?" Allie asked Babaji tentatively.

"Five . . . hours . . ." Babaji croaked.

Weighted silence.

"It's journey . . . not . . . destina . . . ouch . . . destination!" he instructed, laughing. "Find stillness in . . . uh . . . ouch . . . present moment . . .peace . . . in . . . chaos."

Allie wondered what her mother would say if she were a fly on the wall of the swaying vehicle. Old judgments easily flowed in . . . *Is this what you've been looking for? How can this be helping you?* This familiar voice was trying to rise again, and she realized, in between the bumps, that it wasn't her mother's voice, but her own. *Are you at peace now?*

To distract herself, Allie searched for the beauty outside the vehicle. There was a sparkle of majesty in the mystical fog that floated up the sides of the mountain, touching the land with a subtle moisture that seemed to cushion the unrelenting downpour washing the mountainside.

The caravan slowed. Just ahead, a spontaneous waterfall flowed down the steep incline from the left, across the narrow road and down, down, down the other side. There was no option but to continue through the moving water and to try to stay on the road.

The lead vehicle inched forward revealing a depth of about six inches of water, and passed through without incident. The others easily followed, and the road continued its bumpy path for another hour, until, eventually, a small village appeared before them. It rose out of the fog and seemed to be waiting for them, like Brigadoon.

"We rest here for a breakfast!" Babaji said with relief showing through his smile.

Everyone was grateful to stiffly pull themselves out of the airless vehicles and onto the puddled street. The small town showed signs of progress similar to Babaji's village. Thatched huts had been replaced with two- and three-story cement structures that now served as the hub of the town. The group ambled into a small room in the center building and was served a hearty breakfast of boiled eggs, dal, rice, and chai. The villagers shared all that they had with the unexpected visitors, and Allie was stunned by the bountiful Nepali generosity.

> ### CULTURAL LESSON #19
> Be open to unexpected visitors and give what
> you can to make them feel welcome.
> Practice seva–give with love.

> ### CULTURAL LESSON #20
> Don't travel to Nepal during Monsoon season.

Allie felt queasy but knew that she needed to eat. "Well, I guess we're finally manifesting our Indiana Jones adventure, and I must say, I'm officially stretched beyond my comfort level," she admitted to Marianna and Pearl as they peeled eggs. They all had to laugh. What was the alternative?

"Me, too. I thought we were going to have a closer view of the river as we tumbled down the mountain," replied Marianna.

"At least we get to see more of the land!" Pearl burst out, always the positive one. "It's gorgeous!"

"You're ever the adventurer, friend, but aren't you the least bit scared or even uncomfortable?" Allie asked, hoping to uncover a hidden truth.

"Not really. These drivers know what they're doing. What's the point of being afraid? Fearlessness is more fun," Pearl replied indifferently.

"Fearlessness is scary," Allie exclaimed.

And with that, everyone burst out laughing.

Allie took a long, deep breath. "Speaking of fear, I'm noticing the further we get away from the village, the better I feel."

"I feel lighter too," Pearl added. "I think that's why I'm enjoying the ride so much. There was a strange energy in Babaji's village. It definitely seemed to hit you particularly hard," she said to Allie.

"We never really talked about it, but what happened to you, Allieji?" Marianna asked.

"I've no idea, but it was unnerving, and I haven't had a chance to talk to Babaji about it." She leaned in across the table and spoke firmly, "I can tell you this, though. I won't choose purification again as an intention. It's been way too intense. And please hear me, Universe," Allie gestured to the heavens, "I've had enough. That first ceremony we had in Kathmandu was so special, and it felt so safe to set that intention, but now . . ." Allie paused and realized, "Hey, no one else had a ceremony, did they? Why not?"

"Wow, that's a good point. I guess there's been too many other distractions? Darn, I was looking forward to that!" Pearl said.

"I'll just be happy to get back to Kathmandu, at this point. I'm ready for some rest," Marianna chimed in.

"Speaking of rest." Kurt overheard their conversation as he walked toward the door. "I'm going to lie down in the jeep for a few minutes." With dramatic flair, he took off his hat and bowed in exaggerated deference to his friends. Turning toward the door, he clicked his heels and walked off.

"We're all getting punch happy," Allie laughed. "It's nice to see a silly side of Kurt! I like his idea. I'm going to try and rest as well. We have a lot more bouncing to do."

"I might as well join you." Marianne followed.

"All in," Pearl added.

Kurt was already huddled up in a fetal position with the hatch open as the others quietly entered the vehicle so as not to disturb him. Just then, however, a young villager cradling a tiny baby crawled into the back and squished in across from Kurt. The sudden motion jarred everyone to attention. The stranger began to nurse the baby and looked at the "ghosts" silently with wide eyes.

"No, no, no," Allie said instinctively, knowing that they were already short of space.

The mother turned her head slowly toward Allie. Her wide eyes were blank, void of emotion as she continued to nurse the quiet baby.

Kurt, coming to awareness, said, "Let's hang on here and see what she needs." The mother slowly turned her gaze toward Kurt.

This is not New Jersey, Allie reminded herself, *it's not a car-jacking. I don't think we're being threatened.* She settled down.

A young man, most likely the father, then squeezed in

next to his family. Kurt folded his legs to make room. *Was it normal to hop into a stranger's vehicle uninvited?*

Everyone stared at each other. The baby continued to nurse.

"Ah, you have visitors?" Babaji walked up and observed the situation. Able to speak the language, he engaged them in conversation and soon learned that they needed a ride to the hospital; the baby was ill.

"Is okay we bring to hospital? We can do . . . is just a few more hours and is on our way."

They collectively agreed to help the little life.

Babaji said something else to the incredibly young couple, then fluttered away to gather the rest of the group. Allie closed her eyes to rest while she could.

"They're gone!" Marianna gasped. Just as quickly as the young family had appeared, they left, with no words or explanation.

"Babaji, they're gone! What happened?" Allie asked when he returned.

"I don't know. I say you were sick in my village. Now they rush off." He paused. "We pray for baby." He sang "Om Namo Bhagavate Vasudevaya," three times.

Allie hoped that this chant for protection would indeed make a difference for the ill baby. She was ashamed to admit that she felt relief when they left, which was followed by guilt for feeling relieved. *I definitely have more purification to do, but let's wait until I'm home, soaking in a steaming bath, drinking a cup of hot tea. How about that, Universe? Deal?*

The caravan eventually began to move forward, and Allie rallied herself for the rest of the challenging journey. Somehow time passed. All vehicles managed to stay on the "road," and a few passengers even slept lightly. Finally, after the full five hours, they pulled into the next village, their destination. With the most challenging part of the journey complete, they were safe.

CHAPTER 27

The Obstacle

While the weary travelers ate a nourishing lunch, the locals updated Babaji about the airport and road conditions. His grave expression revealed that more changes were to come.

"Friends," he announced, "Rain makes more delay. We learn that airport is under water."

NO! Allie's mind screamed in the shocked silence of the room.

"Is no other way. We need drive to Kathmandu. Two days."

Silence.

Allie held her head in her hands. *Please, make it stop.*

"We have also more delay . . . only road ahead has mudslide. But no worry, villagers can clear fast."

Silence.

Allie rocked her head side to side. *It's not stopping.*

"Now, we wait here for few hours for mudslide to be cleared. Rest and be comfortable, friends."

"WE WILL NOT WAIT. WE WANT OUR OWN CAR. NOW."

All eyes shifted to Doug and Gloria, flushed, sweating, and angry. In a piercing whisper, Doug hissed, "We will be driven directly to Kathmandu. This is not what we signed up for and we DEMAND our OWN driver NOW to take care of us personally and get us to safety."

"Is not recommended. Is very dangerous. You must stay with us, please," Babaji said quietly, absorbing the outburst and trying to dispel it. They had been so calm and reserved since the last explosion.

Here we go again.

"FIND US A DRIVER," the red-faced Doug demanded. His protruding, panting chest, combined with Gloria's frowning jack-o'-lantern expression, made them look like caricatures from a video game. Allie was beginning to think she really did die and was in hell.

"We will try. But you put your safety into your hands." Babaji met Doug's glaring eyes and walked off.

"I can't believe those two. We're all scared. We're all tattered and sore. Why do they think they're so special? It's ridiculous," Marianna whispered to Allie.

"Let 'em go." If Allie was already in hell, she might as well be honest. "I hope they get home quickly, and I hope I never see them again." She had wanted to grow and rise above these harsh judgments and feelings, but her filters were gone and compassion long lost—probably thrown up in the "exorcism."

"They have no gratitude for all Babaji has done and is still doing. Who knew the floods would come in?"

"Well, he did warn us, didn't he?" Kurt, the observant one, chimed in.

"Yeah, we joked about it, but did we REALLY expect this? He'd never knowingly put us in danger." Allie wouldn't have agreed to this Indiana Jones adventure if she'd known how really threatening a monsoon could really be.

Feeling too fatigued to dwell on the drama, she returned to her task at hand, choking down the Nepali food that her taste buds were now rejecting. Her body was craving something familiar: pasta, pizza, or anything but rice and lentils.

"So, plan B didn't work out and we move to plan C," Pearl suggested. "Let's hope the mudslide will be cleared soon. Then it's just two more days in monsoon rains through the mountains on treacherous roads and um, it'll be just fine." She looked at Kurt, "Better keep the hat on."

"Oh, Pearl, that sounds so appealing! How about instead, we stay here, eat pizza in a hotub, and then sleep for days?" Allie said, mustering a smile.

"I second that," Marianna agreed.

"I'd take my Jones hat off for that one, too!" Kurt added as the friends settled in for a long monsoon's nap.

AFTER A COUPLE OF hours of waiting in the dining room, everyone, including Doug and Gloria, ran through the pouring rain and climbed into their vehicles to begin the next leg of the journey.

"Babaji, what about Doug and Gloria?" Allie inquired as the convoy crawled forward.

"Is no driver or car for them. No one is drive to Kathmandu in floods. This much better. Is too dangerous for them to go on own."

"You're doing so much. I'm sorry they're acting as they are," Allie said.

"Oh, is no worry, Allieji. They are hurting. We need to offer them compassion of Om Mani Padme Hum. They will learn."

"I'll try." Allie sighed.

"You must. Is no choice. Or you suffer, too."

Babaji began to sing the village melody, "Om Mani Padme Hum, Om Mani Padme Hum, Om Mani Padme Hum, Om Mani Padme Hum," and they all joined in. Babaji always had a way to make difficult situations lighter. He was a true healer.

THE TWO-LANE PAVED ROAD out of town was a welcome change from the muddy terrain of the last five hours. Although it was built into the steep mountainside, it was smooth and easy until they came upon the chaos of the mudslide. Just ahead, on the mountain with its peaks rising high to the left and falling sharply to their right, was a traffic jam like none they had seen before. Rain poured down on buses, taxis, tuk-tuks, vans, people, goats, dogs, and cows. All were moving in confusion trying to figure out how to cope with the developing situation.

"Here is location of mudslide. I'll go and see. Please, stay in vehicle. Is not good to wander right now," Babaji instructed as he rushed out of the vehicle. Their driver jumped out as well, leaving them parked in the middle of the frenzied disaster area.

The small expanse of road had indeed burst into chaos. Men scuttered around and directed traffic. A bus was attempting a ten- or twenty-point turn, while cars tried to back out of its way. Locals calmly wove through the mayhem, one balancing a huge, full burlap sack on his head, another carrying a crate of chickens. Tuk-tuks and scooters squeezed through tiny spaces, easily leaving the pandemonium to go back to the town. A colorfully dressed young mother snuggled a baby close to her chest, while the rain beat steadily down on her. The father held the hand of their toddler, and they walked at a slow but steady pace.

And I think I'm suffering . . . Dry and safe hugging a pillow. Where are they going on foot? Allie wondered. The town was long behind them.

The yelling men took notice of Allie's vehicle, smack in the middle of the unfolding madness and began to bang on their hood. They waved their hands and yelled at them.

"What do they want?" Marianna cried out.

"I don't know." Allie stared out the window at the men.

"Maybe they want us to move?" Pearl questioned.

"Where would we go?" Kurt boomed. "We shouldn't move. Babaji needs to find us,"

"This is craziness," Allie affirmed.

In apparent frustration, the yelling men threw their hands up and ran away toward another vehicle.

"Tap, tap, tap," A different man with wrinkled, tanned skin and no teeth knocked on her window. He stared into Allie's concerned eyes and spoke as if she should understand his request.

"What's he saying? What do I do?"

The yelling men returned and banged on the hood again. One of the strangers jumped into the driver's seat, started the vehicle, and, without a word, began to move the group forward, closer to the mudslide.

Frozen, the pilgrims sat in shocked silence.

He yelled out the window at pedestrians as he raced ahead through the battering rain for what felt like eternity but in reality, was only about thirty seconds. They stopped short behind several vehicles that were tucked into the mountainside. Their kidnapper turned off the four wheeler and hopped out. Not a word. Not a backward glance.

"He was just moving us out of the way!" Pearl observed.

Allie was now rattled. "But now we've lost the others!"

"They'll find us. We didn't go far," Kurt encouraged. "I guess it's normal for strangers to hop into other people's vehicles unannounced."

"It's a norm I'm ready to leave behind," Marianna sighed.

They sat in silence for another eternity, each immersed in their own thoughts. Allie watched a steady stream of pedestrians pass her window. Some carried sacks on their heads and backs, others bags of fruit, and another a stack of wood. *Where are they all coming from?*

"How are you get here?" Babaji appeared out of nowhere, seemingly unfazed by their new location. "I have news." He was grave. "Is more than mudslide. Much more."

It's definitely not stopping.

"Mudslide take road down, down, down. Is no more road. We need to walk to other side."

There will be no driving across . . . not today, not for weeks, months, or maybe even a year.

WALK to the other side? HOW? Allie looked up the mountain on one side and down the sheer slope of the other. *Are you kidding me?* This would probably not be a problem for seasoned trekkers, but she was NOT a trekker. And she was afraid of heights.

Allie burst, "You want us to abandon our safe military vehicles, walk across what's left of the road, and hope to find transportation to the next village?"

"Yes."

"And our luggage?"

"Sherpas will help. "We don't know where is our drivers. We will wait for them return and then will we go."

Allie had never seen him more focused, and his eyes were filled with trust and confidence. And trust, she must.

And wait they did . . . for hours in the unending rain. They relieved themselves in shifts on the side of the bustling road, taking turns holding up scarves and fabric to create the illusion of privacy. They were the only tourists on this road with a one-way ticket toward the unknown.

Why are we not turning back? Allie wanted nothing more than to be in Kathmandu, the familiar hotel, and one step closer to returning home, but she was innocently trusting Babaji, who was pushing forward and hustling from vehicle to vehicle checking on everyone. Focused and steady, he returned to his smiling, bubbly self.

Allie closed her eyes. Horns honked around her, men continued to yell, and the rain beat relentlessly on the vehicle, tat, tat, tat. The chaotic orchestra of sounds lulled her easily into a deep sleep.

She dreamed she was in a parking lot and was late for her event. She jumped out of her car, flushed, and rushed to load the singing bowls onto the elevator. No one was helping her, and she was angry and frustrated. With barely enough room for her to squeeze into the tiny, clear, glass elevator, the doors squeaked closed around her. Unexpectedly, she saw her dad appear out of the shadows and run toward the closed doors. "NO!" Allie pressed the "door open" button frantically, but the elevator began to ascend. She hit her fists on the glass doors and gazed down helplessly.

Unfazed, her dad reached into his pocket. In his hand, he held
a large skeleton key. He raised his hand high as if he wanted to
give it to her. He mouthed, "Here's the key!"

"Thump." A random sound startled Allie awake. *Where am*
I? She didn't care. She closed her eyes and willed herself back
to her dream to be with her dad. She was so happy to see his
smiling face, at ease and alive. *And he had a key! What was it*
for? The smell of the stale, humid air pulled her reluctantly
back to the chaos of the moment. The vehicle rocked from
side to side as their driver settled into his seat. Allie vaguely
remembered that he had been missing for several hours. It
was all coming back to her—the mudslide, the floods, the
collapsed road.

Babaji again appeared out of nowhere and calmly spoke
with the driver. He translated to the anxious passengers,
"Our drivers walk to the other side and hitched ride to next
village. They work miracle for us! They say that most vehicles
are under water, but somehow they find drivers to take us to
Kathmandu! We have ride coming to meet us on other side,"
Babaji was almost clicking his heels. "Wait here. I will tell
the others." He hustled off.

Silence blanketed Allie's vehicle. There was no need for
words or much space for thoughts. For once in her life, Allie's
mind was quiet. None of the characters in her head were
trying to think of an alternative plan or anticipate what was

yet to come, or even judge the situation. Maybe this was the precious "Sunyata," an emptiness that emerged from a dull, exhausted presence.

"Allieji, get your purse and let's go, quickly. Everyone else, wait here. We'll do this one at a time," Rajesh said in a shaky but resounding bass voice.

"What about my luggage?" Allie asked.

"The Sherpas will carry the luggage across. Now, we focus on getting each of you across safely."

Allie grabbed her purse with her passport, money, phone, camera, and water purifier and left the safety of the vehicle. She didn't think to thank the driver, grab her snack bag, or say, "See you soon!" to her friends. In stunned shock, she followed Rajesh through the mash of vehicles, mud puddles, and people rushing in all directions.

They tentatively approached the disaster area. An entire portion of the road had cascaded down the mountain, and all that remained was a four-foot-wide dirt path about ten feet long. A line of people were taking turns crossing in both directions. The narrow pass was bordered on the left by the steep rising mountain and on the right by nothing, just open space that once was a paved road. The missing pavement was gone, gone, completely gone, absorbed somewhere below the tiny tree tips that seemed miles down the mountain.

"Are you afraid of heights?" Rajesh asked.

"Yes!" Allie wheezed. She was stopped in her tracks, unable to move forward.

He grabbed her hand, yelled, "Don't look down!" and pulled her forward.

Walking side by side, with Rajesh on the outside edge, they carefully stepped onto the remaining road. Allie was very aware of the mud below her feet, the amount of pedestrian traffic that this parcel of road had already sustained, and the possibility that this might collapse as well. *Others have already made it, and we will too*, she hoped. Time seemed to stand still, and all sounds around her silenced, even as their steps inched them forward.

After what seemed like a lifetime—and Allie just might have shed a life or two—they were safely across, and she realized that she hadn't been breathing and certainly hadn't looked down.

"Thank you!" Allie exhaled. They met eyes, but there was no time to linger, "It's a good thing that you're not afraid of heights."

"Oh, I am!' he yelped as he ran back across the muddy pass to get the others.

With both feet planted firmly on the safe solid ground and some distance between her and the path, Allie looked back toward the collapse. It was as if a giant monster had taken a bite out of the mountain. A few locals stood right on the edge of the remaining *U*-shaped road, staring down. They were so high up that there was no bottom or flowing river visible, only a descending jungle that had received Mother Nature's wrath for as far as the eye could see.

CULTURAL LESSON #21
Adrenaline and the will to survive
will override fears.
Don't look down!

After a time, everyone was safely across. The group huddled under shared umbrellas trying to protect what little dryness they had left, while Rajesh and the Sherpas worked hard to carry their luggage across. *Why did I pack so much?* Allie remembered the other half of her "stuff" that she left in Kathmandu and was embarrassed by her need for so many things.

CULTURAL LESSON #22
Lighten your load. Simplify.

John and Jane sat on their bags, solemnly holding hands and quietly conversing. Doug and Gloria stood arm in arm under their own umbrella, hair soaked and clothing not much dryer. Gloria's forlorn eyes and frown could have stopped the Dalai Lama in his tracks. Doug stared blankly as if he had checked out to another place. No private car could have saved them from this. Soaking wet, like everyone else, they stood in the reign of their own misery. The two couples were no longer battling for alpha but were struggling for survival just like the others.

Time crawled past while the pilgrims waited and waited.

"Do you think they're coming?" Allie asked Pearl and Kurt under the shared umbrella.

"What if we don't really have a ride?" Marianna whispered to Allie from another umbrella.

There were no answers. Babaji stood with Rajesh and Sunita looking confident and trusting. What was the alternative?

They heard them before they saw them; the subtle sounds of the engines and the kick of mud splashing through the tires. Two white vans and a jeep raced up and stopped short in front of the group.

Vans? Where are the all-terrain vehicles? Allie wanted to feel grateful but instead was skeptical.

With no time for questions, they were ushered into the vehicles while the drivers' assistants loaded their wet luggage on top of the vans without any protective covering. With one less vehicle, Doug and Gloria silently joined Allie's group, and the newly formed caravan began the next leg of the journey to the next town.

CHAPTER 28

The Bus Depot

The day, the road, the rain, and the mountains seemed endless, and Allie was riding a hamster wheel of uncertainty. *What time is it?* If Allie could see the sun, she could guess, but it was well hidden behind the dense cloud cover. *But what does it matter? We have farther to go, so why count the time?* Her mounting weariness drew her more and more into the discomfort of the moment. Her stomach gurgled with a mixture of hunger and motion sickness, and she longed to lie down. Instead, she gazed blankly out the window and watched the blur of fog, rain, and trees fly by.

At some point, they descended into a valley, and the jungle opened to reveal a city before them. As they drove into the outskirts of the town, Allie sensed a shift in energy that hit her like a brick in her gut. She didn't know why, but she felt danger. Perhaps it was the monsoon dusk that made the dirty buildings look darker and the thick smog feel heavier. It was a remarkable and unexpected change. The locals momentarily stopped to watch the new arrivals creep into their town. All was frozen but for the slow-moving caravan as they meticulously wove through the markets, stray animals, and pedestrians. Allie was in a modern-day western, the desperate stranger stumbling into a bad situation.

Babaji spoke cautiously to the exhausted group. "We need stay in town for night. Road ahead is dangerous. Thirty people die trying to cross today. Many others lost. We wait until morning to try."

All remained quiet, including Doug and Gloria, as they parked in front of a small, grimy building that appeared to be a hotel. Instantly Allie's gut burned, and she was flooded with dread.

Babaji must have felt it as well. "Oh, is not good here. Does not feel right."

"I agree," Allie screeched.

"Me, too." Pearl added.

"We can't stay here. I'll go tell others." Babaji popped out of the vehicle.

Moments later he hopped back in and said, "Zum, zum, go, go. We leave now." And then they heard and felt . . .

Boom, Bang, Boom, Boom.

A large group of gauntly thin men wearing stained tank tops and skinny jeans surrounded their vehicle, yelling, pounding, and rocking the van. The driver yelled back, and a new type of chaos ensued. Babaji caught on quickly.

"Oh, God, is local gangsters. We leave NOW! "ZUM, ZUM!"

Gangsters. In Nepal?

The driver flailed his arms and yelled out the cracked window. Babaji yelled at the driver, and the passengers sat in quiet shock as the van started to shake more.

They're going to flip us!

"Go now! Zum!" Babaji yelled.

The driver accelerated quickly and the men jumped out of the way. Allie didn't know how they got past the crowd, but they sped away toward a new unknown location. The other two vehicles thankfully followed.

"Oh my God, We didn't know is gangster town. We will find another hotel," Babaji was thinking out loud.

Plan D was set into motion, although no "plan" was formulated yet.

They sped through the dark, wet roads and landed at a bus depot on the other side of town. A mix of open-faced storefronts, tents, and shacks formed the active square, offering travelers necessary items such as cigarettes, packaged snacks, drinks, plastic toys, and clothing—it was a city unto itself. Allie's unsettled gut still hinted of danger while the rising fog added to the unsafe atmosphere, like an alleyway she should not pass through alone. The drivers left the caravan parked in the middle of the square to purchase the necessary toll pass to leave the town.

Buses and vans crowded the area, and the now-familiar chaotic scene continued to test their western sensibilities. Babaji tried to call his niece, but there was no signal.

"Do not leave vehicle!" He ordered as they all sat in silence trying to process the latest events.

No worries on that one.

Someone tapped on Allie's window. A tiny, young woman with long pulled-back black hair and an aged face met Allie's eyes and drew her fingers to her mouth.

"She's asking for food! Babaji, what should I do?"

"Please, ignore her. If we feed one, our van again will be surrounded. We need to stay safe. Instead, we pray for her." He closed his eyes and chanted softly.

Allie shook her head at the woman who continued to bring her fingers to her mouth, imploring silently with fatigue and sadness. Allie knew that some beggars were professional con artists, and others were sincerely in need. She stared helplessly ahead, hoping the woman would move on. It was awkward, and Allie felt at odds with the entire situation. The woman moved to the other side of the vehicle, and the situation repeated itself until she silently moved on.

Allie searched the area for her crone, craving the peace this apparition brought her, as well as a message that all would be well. Nothing. The group waited and waited as they observed the three drivers sitting in a tiny covered cement shelter that served as the toll office. It was a simple square building with no obvious door, just an open storefront. One uniformed man sat rigidly at a tiny table that served as the desk, while several men lingered in the shadows. Their driver gestured strongly. Although she couldn't hear the dialogue, she could tell that the conversation was becoming heated.

"What's taking so long, Babaji?" Marianna asked.

"I don't know. Is way too long." Babaji tried his cell phone again. "No signal. I need to see Lumanti."

Yes, please do something, anything. If Allie'd had an ounce of energy, she'd be clawing the walls of the van, impatient and frustrated, but instead she stared mindlessly out the window allowing others to be in control. Until she noticed the water starting to puddle around their vehicle.

"Babaji, I think the water's starting to rise around us. Are we in a flood zone?"

He jumped up. "Oh, my God. We need to go now! Everything is flood zone. There is hotel outside of here. On more higher ground. We will rest there for the night and be safe, I promise. Please, lock door. Stay here." He rushed into the torrent of rain toward the arguing men.

Allie's famous snack bag had ended up on top of the vehicle, and she was weak with hunger. She also didn't want to drink anything, since they couldn't use the facilities anywhere or get out to find a tree.

"The waters are still rising," Allie said.

"Yes, they are. I feel like a sitting duck that can't float or fly," Marianna added.

The waters weren't just rising. They were beginning to move in a current. And yet, the activity around them continued, as if all were normal. Or maybe not. Maybe everyone was preparing to leave. The sitting ducks didn't know.

Babaji returned with packages of butter cookies.

"Here is dinner," he encouraged, tossing them to everyone. "Sorry. I will do more later. Right now, drivers are fighting to pay toll. They want more money. Is CRAZY!" Babaji shrank into his seat and closed his eyes.

All was quiet but for the crinkle and crunch of dinner. The scent of buttery vanilla shortbread filled the vehicle, and for a moment, time was suspended and all was well. Allie chewed slowly, reveling in the sugar rush.

"ZUM ZUM!" Babaji popped out of his meditation and yelled out the window. "WE NEED TO GO NOW!"

"PLEASE!" the others yelled.

Babaji settled back into his meditation and the pilgrims finished their "dinner."

Finally, with the water now covering about four inches of the low-lying vans' tires, the drivers returned to the vehicles with the prized toll pass. As Allie's driver silently slipped back into his seat, two strangers hopped into the front next him.

AGAIN? Who are THEY?

"They are not part of our group," Babaji said firmly in good English and Nepali. "Hello, who are you? What do you want?"

No answer. The van began to move forward out of the bus depot.

Babaji repeated himself. Still no answer.

"Why are you ignoring me?" He addressed the strangers,

two slight, very skinny men. They wouldn't turn around so no one could see their faces.

"Who are they?" he yelled to the driver. "Why are they with us?"

Nothing. They pretended not to understand any language.

With a renewed fire under them, and Allie's vehicle in the lead, the caravan sped out of town.

"These guys are assholes, they're not answering me!" Babaji yelled to the back of the van, speaking freer than ever and assuming that they didn't understand English. Allie had never heard Babaji raise his voice, let alone curse, so to hear him call someone an asshole was serious business.

Babaji continued to hound the driver until he finally responded. "Oh . . . ," Babaji didn't translate the answer. He continued in Nepali but raised his tone. A heated discussion continued and then . . . silence.

We're speeding out of town with two strangers. Who knows if they're armed. Indiana Jones has nothing on us. Allie's gut burned.

The fast pace slowed to a halt. Traffic jam.

Should we jump out? Allie pleaded to silently Babaji.

"Is okay. We are close to hotel," Babaji encouraged.

Did he hear me?

The westbound half of the bridge ahead had partially collapsed, and only two lanes remained open with a weight limit. No buses were allowed to cross, only cars and vans. As they inched over the remaining sections of the bridge, Allie's skin tickled with the now familiar sensation of dread. *When will this side of the bridge collapse?*

Safely over the bridge, they passed lines of buses and trucks that were pulled over to the side of the road. Westbound traffic was backed up for miles.

For the eastbound pilgrims, however, the traffic cleared, and the pace again quickened. They flew past the hotel, their perceived destination for the night, and continued along the dark, unlit country road, flying into the darkness.

"Is hotel." Louder, "You miss our hotel," Babaji repeated in Nepali. "They drive past hotel!" he translated.

Silence.

"Turn around NOW," in Nepali.

Nothing.

They sped ahead. Babaji yelled in Nepali. "This asshole NOT listen to me. We head to flood waters! Many die today ahead, asshole. Turn around!" He tried to call his niece in the other vehicle but there was still no signal.

The two other vehicles followed close behind. Apparently, all of the drivers were in on whatever was happening. Allie wasn't sure why they wouldn't stop or listen to their pleas, but she suspected that it had to do with the new strangers who joined the caravan. Why would they be driving dangerously fast into the flooded waters?

Babaji tried his cell phone again. Rain poured down as they rushed forward. Time let go of its grip, and Allie stepped into the empty void, conserving what little energy she had left for what lay ahead.

Unexpectedly, the jeep carrying Lumanti sped past them and stopped in the middle of the road, blocking their path. The vans were forced to come to a sudden halt, jostling everyone and everything in the van. The pilgrims were thrust forward, and their bags crashed to the floor.

Somewhere along the fast-flying dark road, Lumanti had transformed into a raging dragon and had gained control of her driver. Through fierce eyes and an unyielding tone, she screamed out the window at the drivers in Nepali.

"You turn around NOW! I am on the phone with chief of police. Roads ahead are under water; barracks are under water, and police are in the trees. If you put our friends' lives at risk, I will have you arrested and your license taken away, and that is only the start of it." Her seething voice fed the fire in her eyes. She repeated, "You already put our friends' lives at risk, and the chief of police knows this. Turn around NOW!"

The van slowly began to turn around. *"Thank God!"*

The two strangers remained still and silent while the driver appeared deflated. Whatever was fueling his desperation to flee town took a huge hit, and he was temporarily honoring the instructions from Lumanti, who saved their lives that night. The caravan drove back past the pulled-over buses and trucks and inched their way through the backup until they found the hotel again. Fortunately, they didn't have to drive over the damaged bridge, which was still partially standing.

The shocked passengers piled out into the hotel lobby. It was the largest hotel so far, similar to a western conference center with marble floors and an expansive ballroom. With the tingles of danger now past, Allie, Pearl, and Marianna walked slowly toward their single room accommodations.

"Rest well, friends," Allie mumbled/murmered over her shoulder.

"You too."

"Enjoy the hot shower they promised!" Pearl encouraged.

Allie locked the door behind her, relieved to have a clean room, large bed, and fresh linens. The gangster town at least offered nice accommodations. As she waited for her luggage to arrive, she turned on the heating device in the shower only to find that it was broken. Desperately attached to a hot shower, she dialed the front desk.

"Yes ma'am, someone will come shortly," they responded.

A good half-hour later, her soaking wet luggage arrived along with the hotel manager.

While the hotel manager fussed with the shower, Allie laid her clothing out over the cooling unit and all around with hopes of having something dry in the morning. Pearl had the clothesline.

CULTURAL LESSON #23
Travel with a hard-shell suitcase during
monsoon season, dummy.

"Sorry, ma'am. Broken. We will fix tomorrow." He offered Namaste and left smiling.

Tomorrow is too late, Allie thought desperately as she shivered in the cold shower.

Goosebumped, clean, and dry, she set her alarm for the early-morning departure and sat in bed with her journal.

Journal

Longest day ever.

Survived skull shaman exorcism to face deep mud journey, flooded airport, mudslide, gangsters, and "asshole" drivers, who, for whatever reason, won't listen to Babaji.

Questions:

Why didn't we just turn around and wait out the rains and mudslide in town?

Who are the hitchhikers, why are they with us, and will they be gone in the morning?

What's the panicked rush? Why did the drivers try to drive us into the flood waters in the dark?

Why didn't we fight the drivers for control or jump out? Too Indiana Jones dangerous?

Wishing for new drivers in the morning and all-terrain vehicles.

Oh, and my dad!!! The key. What's he trying to tell me? Please, Dad, come back.

Allie could stay awake no longer. As she fell asleep in the comfortable bed, free from ants, in a dry room with a creaking air conditioner that blew warm, stale air, she felt grateful to be alive.

CHAPTER 29

The Floods

The next morning, Allie and Marianna stood in the open external hallway, watching the early-morning deluge.

"Look at this rain. Do you think we'll be able to travel?" Marianna asked.

"I really don't know." Allie had slept through the night but still couldn't think clearly. If she could have, the chaos of plans B, C, and D would have driven her mad, but as it stood, she was mindlessly doing as she was instructed.

Breakfast was served, and, as their leaders decided on plan E, the group chattered freely, not listening for answers, because there were none.

"Why can't we just stay here until things settle?" "We could die here in the floods." "Do you really think we could die? It seems safe enough here." "Where are we? Has anyone looked at a map? What body of water's rising?" "They say Kathmandu is the safest place to be. But can we get there? SHOULD we get there?" "We have to trust our guides and

Babaji. They know this land." "We'd better be getting new drivers." "They were terrible." "Who were the silent strangers in the front?" "And what about the gangsters?"

"Friends," Babaji interrupted. He looked solemn as he clapped his hands in Namaste position. "All is okay, we need to continue on. Locals think rains stop later and the flooded road is reported clear now by travelers who just arrive here. In twenty minutes, we will meet at van. Bring then luggage to load."

Everyone jumped up to prepare for the fast departure.

"Allieji." Babaji met her eyes with warmth and care. "How are you?"

"I'm okay, Babaji, but feel really shaky." Allie held up her trembling hands. "I'm still recovering from what happened in your village. We haven't been able to talk about it. Was I possessed by something? What really happened to me?" Babaji closed his eyes. Allie thought she saw the subtlest nod of his head.

He was quiet for a full minute, then opened his eyes. "We will talk later, okay?"

"Of course." Allie smiled. "You're doing so much for us. Are you okay?"

"Yes, Allieji, I am well. Indiana Jones adventure much more than we expect. Present moment offers us all new opportunity. We need grow and rise up over obstacles, or we will fall down, down, down. We need rise. We need trust. Now is time to continue. Come, Allieji, come!"

Allie dragged her wet luggage to the waiting vans and was disappointed to see the same drivers and engineer pairs at the vehicles with the two hitchhikers hovering in the background. Her heart sank. *Why are they still here?*

In the heightening monsoon, the engineers loaded their already soaking-wet luggage onto the tops of the vans and jeep, while the hopeful leaders remained confident in their decision to continue toward Kathmandu.

"Are we that desperate to travel with the same drivers and hitchhikers?" Allie whispered to her friends as she considered whether or not to get into the van.

You are their protectors here. Kurt remembered the advice from the wise crone: *Your teacher does not see everything.* He had thought that wisdom was intended for the challenges in Babaji's village, but the choices made so far for their evacuation seemed questionable. He remained on his guard.

"It's all or nothing, it seems. We don't want to pull a Doug and Gloria, do we?" Pearl advised.

Allie saw Babaji. "I'll be right back."

"Babaji, you said we need to trust, but how can we trust these drivers? They won't listen to you, and they almost got us killed."

"Is no other drivers, Allieji. No one. Earlier I speak with them. They will keep us safe."

Allie wanted to be reassured. "And the hitchhikers? Who are they?"

"They need to come. I will tell you later."

Everything is later. Allie wanted to know everything now, but she had no choice but to climb into her seat in front of Marianna. Although she was fresh from a decent night's sleep, a dull fog of shock and exhaustion blanketed her. Blanketed everyone. They were all moving forward, numbed by their new itinerary, blindly trusting the journey, and desperate to reach their destination.

Their driver, engineer, and the two strangers once again remained silent as they began the next leg of the trip. Travel was slow, but the roads were surprisingly passable.

"Here is area where others died and gone missing yesterday. We are okay here! Better that we didn't do it last night." Babaji repeated this in Nepali loudly so the driver could hear.

Even with the flooding of yesterday and the continued downpour, the water in the flatlands had miraculously receded enough for the caravan to easily drive through. They continued forward, feeling relief and hope.

Allie searched for evidence of the floods in the fields that extended as far as the eye could see. Several trees dotted the landscape, standing strong and full. She didn't see the police barracks that Lumanti had mentioned but tried to imagine the police finding shelter in the trees during the flood. If houses, people, and animals had been there, they were all gone now.

Continuing on, they approached a two-lane metal-framed bridge that typically rose high above the river, but on this day, the raging river rose into it, splashing its wild waves onto the roadway.

If this rises any higher, it's going to overtake the bridge. With the fast-flowing mud water crashing against the strong metal, Allie sensed that they were making it over the bridge just in time. She tried to steady her breath. *We made it through the worst part. We're okay. We're outrunning this.*

Rushing forward, they sped through a small village with its one convenience store and cluster of thatched homes. This normally would have been a welcome rest stop, but with the river still rising, they couldn't stop. Or so they thought.

As they rounded the next bend, they had no choice—an ocean of brown rapids had risen high enough to submerge the road ahead with no land showing in the far distance. Villagers stood in front of their homes, barefoot and helpless as they watched the river rise. Whatever had been ahead was now submerged, and there was a good chance their houses were next to go. The expanse of unending water reminded Allie of Lake Michigan with an added angry and destructive current.

"Wait here." Babaji hopped out of the vehicle to speak with the locals. There was a town ahead, but everything leading to it was submerged by the flood waters. They didn't know the depth of the water, the strength of the current, nor did they know how much of the town on the other side remained. There was a road under the water, and if they were to go through, it would have to be now. But it was not recommended, because there was no one coming from the other side.

Allie kept a close eye on Babaji from the van. In the time that he spoke to the locals, the water rose from Babaji's ankles up to his shins. He rushed to the jeep to talk with Lumanti, and then to the other van. It was decided. They would turn around and find higher ground to wait out this part of the storm. Knowing they shouldn't return to the flooding bridge, they'd have to find somewhere else. Plan F.

Babaji returned to his seat, directed the driver, and then turned to his friends, "Is way too dangerous. Locals not recommend. We need turn around now and find a safe place to wait. Tide needs to go out again, and then we will try. You lead others," he told the driver. "Zum, zum."

They turned around and backtracked for a half mile. Then, unannounced, their driver stopped at the convenience store. One of the silent strangers hopped out, and the driver followed.

"What's going on? Is no time to stop!" Babaji yelled out the window in exasperation. The two continued walking. "Assholes don't listen!"

Allie had a fleeting image of Indiana Babaji jumping out of the van to wrestle the key from the driver, and then driving them to safety. And, as if she were manifesting that action, Babaji opened the door and jumped out but stopped in his tracks.

"Oh my God, the others are not with us! Where are they?" Babaji exclaimed.

At this realization, the scoundrels returned without comment, as if nothing was impending.

"We lost others! How do you lose others! We need to go back. Turn around. Now!"

And to everyone's surprise, they began to head back to the flooded area.

Allie's heart pounded. The silent van returned to the scene of the flood. There, they saw the jeep—but not the van standing in a foot of water.

Where'd the van go?

Babaji rushed out and waded through the water toward the jeep. All Allie could do was watch.

She saw Babaji talking to Lumanti, who remained in the jeep. He threw his arms up into the air and put them on his head. His head shook side to side, and he flailed his arms, turning in a half circle. His face showed it all. Grief. Loss. Despair. It was an expression of anguish that Allie would never forget.

"Oh, my God, oh, my God," Allie moaned. "Look at Babaji. Are they gone? What happened?" Observing his body language, she began to cry.

"No!" Marianna yelled. The van became dead silent as they watched Babaji walk toward them, head hanging, eyes lost. They were terrified to hear the news as he got back into the van.

"They are gone," he cried. "They drove into waters. Lumanti saw them go. Driver is determined to get to other side."

"Babaji!" "NO!" "Did they make it?" "Do you know?" Everyone spoke at once.

"How can we know? Oh God." The grief.

Suddenly, the van lurched forward. They were now moving toward the flood waters.

"Turn around!" Babaji commanded. Silence. Forward motion. No control.

The driver continued to move forward directly into the flood waters.

ALLIE HAD NEVER TRIED to imagine what it would be like to drive into Lake Michigan, but there she was, somewhere in the middle of Nepal, about to find out. Yet again, they were hijacked by their driver. Had she been Indiana Jones, Allie might have tried to wrestle the wheel away from him, but it didn't occur to her now, nor, apparently, to anyone else. *Why are we all just sitting here allowing this?* she thought in slow motion. *Have I truly survived an exorcism only to die in flood waters?*

No one, including the driver, had any idea where the road was, how deep the water was going to get, or if they would make it to the other side that wasn't even in view. Marianna, who was sitting behind Allie, reached around the seat and hugged her. Allie welcomed the hug and placed her hands on Marianna's.

Time stopped. Thoughts stopped. Allie became aware

only of the present moment . . . the sight of the raging, muddy brown water surrounding them as far as the eye could see; the sound of the river rushing around the van—splashing, rolling, and roaring; the feel of the water pushing into the van from right to left; the warming fear and tingle in her fingers as the driver slowed to a stop, unable to feel the road; the water pushing the van more firmly from right to left; the collective screams, "Zum, Zum, Zum," as they felt the van start to give way to the pressure; the slow crawl forward as the driver tried to fight the current; the feel of her heartbeat, fast and steady.

I am good swimmer, Babaji thought. *I will get out everyone before I drown.*

I'll die back here, Kurt thought. *But I'll do what I can to get everyone out.*

I'll save my love or we'll die together. Doug grabbed Gloria's hand.

I'm too young to die. Gloria held Doug's hand tightly.

My mom. Marianna silently cried. *She won't survive my loss.*

We'll get out of this. I know it. Pearl held onto hope.

Allie thought nothing. Blank and fully in the moment. Her breath was minimal as she watched the relentless current rise higher and higher, sloshing into the van. The windows were splattered with droplets. All she could hear was the splash and rush of the water.

Time stood still. No thoughts of death. No fear. This moment was all. No prayers, no visions of loved ones. Empty.

No past, no future; no pain or emotion; no memories and no worries. It was just she and the water that sounded a steady pulse, as if she were returning to the womb.

The van inched forward.

"Look, look!" someone yelled.

Allie snapped out of it, whatever IT was.

Up ahead lay part of a submerged, capsized bus. Land appeared before them, and in the distance, villagers stood at the water's edge, watching the "ghosts" rise out of the expanse of water. They stared as if they were seeing an apparition. Unbeknownst to anyone but perhaps the driver, the jeep was following behind. They had both made it!

Relief as they had never known it overcame everyone.

"Oh my God. We made it!" Babaji yelled. They cheered! "If we made it, maybe others did too? We will find the others!" he yelled to the driver.

Barefoot villagers stood in shin-deep water and watched the anxious ghosts drive slowly past in search of their missing friends. Allie didn't know what had been submerged by the flood waters that they had just stupidly braved, but here, storefronts were beginning to see inches of water. Some families in the distance were now on an island of slightly higher ground as the waters rose around them on all sides. *What'll they do?*

Cows munched casually on garbage piles while dogs, chickens, and goats ran in random directions, sensing the impending danger.

"Look! LOOK! There they are!"

Up ahead about a half a mile, they saw, with great relief, the missing van pulled over on the side of the road, everyone standing solemnly under shared umbrellas, watching the road, hoping.

"There they are!" Babaji yelled! "Oh my God, oh my God."

Blissful tears, laughter, and hugs marked their reunion, until the drivers erupted, yelling at each other. Babaji rushed over and began yelling at the drivers. What they were saying, the group would never know. But with the addition of Rajesh and Sunita, the highly heated discussion turned into a dog fight.

Jane and Kate, now reunited with Allie's group, filled them in: "The drivers are only after money and more money. The sooner they get to Kathmandu, the sooner they get more work." "They don't care about putting us in danger. They're reckless and don't understand the power of the flood water. We were almost pushed over to the side. It was terrifying. And we could do nothing."

"We were, too! We didn't ask to come after you, but our driver heard that you went across and must've decided that he could make it, too. We shouldn't have survived," Allie said.

"None of us should have. It was by the grace of God," Jane added.

"Did you see the bus? Did the people survive?" Allie asked, but the question remained unanswered.

The heated debate subsided temporarily, and the drivers returned to their vehicles.

"Okay, we need to hurry now. Flood waters is rising quickly. Is still danger and more floods ahead," Babaji spurted. "But here, we are very low land and so we must continue on. These assholes don't care. They demand more money now to continue. We have no other choice. We need keep going. Zum, Zum!"

"Babaji, what about bathroom? It's been hours." There was no privacy in this location.

"We will find soon. Can everyone hold? Let's find somewhere up ahead!"

After settling into the vehicles, Babaji sighed, "Oh, Allieji, is bigger Indiana Jones adventure than ever." He started singing. "Om Namo Bhagavate Vasudevaya," over and over. Allie, Pearl, and Marianna joined and invited the rest of the van. A few mumbles rumbled from behind. Babaji held steady with the chant, until eventually Pearl and Marianna fell asleep. Then Babaji. Allie continued the chanting quietly until exhaustion finally took over, and she also dozed off.

The illusion of safety didn't last for long. They were jolted awake as the traffic came to a sudden halt. A police officer spoke with the drivers.

Babaji translated. "Is okay, but bridge is damaged. We need to get out of van and walk across bridge. Van will drive over after."

Allie mindlessly got out of the vehicle and followed the procession. The "what ifs" were too overwhelming to consider.

They tiptoed onto the structure—as if that would lighten

their collective body weight! Babaji burst into the melody, "Om Namo Bhagavate Vasudevaya!" Fearful of a collapse, the pilgrims all joined the chant, "Om Namo Bhagavate Vasudevaya, Om Namo Bhagavate Vasudevaya" over and over until they were back on solid, flooded, but manageable road. The vans and jeep crept over one by one, testing the structural integrity of the bridge as well as the courage of the cavalier drivers.

The land was devastated. As they drove through village after village, only those on higher ground were safe in the active, rising water. Houses and shelters were already submerged; cows drowned, crops destroyed.

Shouldn't we stop and help? Allie was too overwhelmed to vocalize the question.

As the caravan continued forward, the top priority for Babaji was the safety of his friends. The top priority for the drivers was fast and full payment, and the top priority for Allie was a good, long pee.

They drove through two more badly flooded areas but nothing, fortunately, as extreme as Lake Michigan behind them.

"Stop here," Babaji instructed the driver and, surprisingly, he stopped.

After five hours of outrunning treacherous conditions, they were finally on higher ground for the much-needed potty break. Bursts of fog rose over miles of open fields, but one lone boulder called out as Nature's restroom. While cars breezed past, the pilgrims, one by one, walked into the veil of foggy privacy to find relief.

"Wowee, that was the best pee I've ever had. I didn't know I could hold it that long or, for that matter, if I'd even live to pee again, so this definitely ranks as the best ever!" Allie delighted to no one and everyone.

She was grateful to be alive, and with a looming eight hours still in front of them, Allie knew by now that anything could happen. The engineer retrieved her snack bag, and she dug deep for both snacks and strength. The roadside restaurant an hour up the road couldn't appear fast enough.

Welcoming the warm food and break from travel, the pilgrims gobbled up the generous buffet. Allie's challenged body, however, was craving anything BUT Nepali food. Her vegetarian mouth watered for childhood cravings; a Taylor porkroll sandwich with spicy mustard on buttery, toasted rye bread, Vic's pepperoni pizza, a monstrous salad with fresh avocado and broccoli, and her mother's chocolate mousse. Instead, her protein desperate vegetarian-self powered through the lovingly prepared chicken curry.

"It seems that looking death in the eye of a flood might've softened our angry friends," said Pearl, flashing her eyes toward Doug and Gloria who were seated at the end of the long family-style table with Jane and John and appeared to be listening intently to Jane. They were making eye contact, and their aggressive posturing had softened. Doug actually looked humbled.

"Agreed," Marianna confided. "I ran into Gloria at the restroom, and she actually asked how I was! I think they realize that if they'd gone ahead without us as they had demanded, they most likely wouldn't have made it. They probably would've died that first night in the floods."

"Probably so." Something caught Allie's eye. She thought she saw a familiar motion in the long, shadowed hallway that led to the bathroom. "I'll be right back." Standing, rather shakily, she tried to rush in that direction but only managed the now-familiar pace of a sloth. As she impatiently rounded the corner, she came face to face with her petite crone messenger.

"It IS you! How? Who are you?" Allie blurted.

"You've had quite a journey, haven't you?" The voice was sweetly clear and strong.

"How are you following me? Why?" Allie's voice was barely audible.

Warm and buttery, she replied, "Always the curious, thinking one." Her smile was spellbinding, and a soft glow surrounded her. "I am not following you, sweet friend." She paused as if she were trying to communicate without words. Allie forgot everything and stood, mesmerized.

"I am always with you. You can sense me as the water, the wind, the birdsong, the rush of the current. I am within and through you." Allie's eyes teared up, overcome with the resonance of truth.

"How?" Allie stammered.

"You've been searching for answers but are learning that

you cannot think yourself to them." The crone looked deep into Allie's eyes. Allie couldn't help but fix on her gaze. It was captivating and vulnerable. She felt the crone look into the very core of her being, and in that gaze, Allie connected with sensations of kindness, love, and acceptance unlike anything she'd ever experienced. Two tears trickled down her cheeks.

The crone continued, "This trip was important for your healing."

Allie found soft, honest words. "This trip has all but destroyed me."

"Yes, it feels that way. But what has it destroyed?" The wise one paused. "It has shattered the story that you hold on to. It has forced you to face the darkness within yourself." Her physical body reflected decrepit age, wrinkled by time, but Allie only stared into the shining, clear, golden eyes that were as fresh and sweet as the crone's ageless voice.

Pure exhaustion gripped every cell of her being. *If it's destroyed my story, what's left?*

The crone heard her thoughts. "What you have known is now destroyed. You can try to put back the pieces of your old life, but should you? This is a precious question and one that many don't take the time to ask."

Allie's stressed body struggled to breathe, but she stood, rapt with attention, waiting for answers. The crone continued, "You have the opportunity to build new; to explore, like the adventurer you have become and . . . to share this with others. You've experienced timelessness frequently on this trip . . . and this drew you into the present moment. This is the touch of sunyata. But there is more."

The crone touched two wrinkled fingers to Allie's sternum. "Do not hold onto the pain. It does not serve you. What you hold onto, you become. What you focus on, you become." Her fingers were warm and electric. Allie closed her eyes, took an easy breath, and reveled in the safe essence of love that she was feeling.

She heard the lullaby, "Om Bhur Bhuvaha Svaha Tat Savitur Varenyam Bhargo Devasya Dhimahi Dhiyo Yo Nah Prachodayat," and her breath deepened.

"Your group. . ." the crone continued as she slowly removed her fingers, and Allie opened her eyes, "and your teacher focused on an Indiana Jones adventure, and see what you have created? Your story is what you make it to be. Never forget that. The floods represent something for you and everyone. You were nothing to the water. It could have swallowed you up easily. And yet, you collectively wanted to live. Why? That is for each of you to learn."

"Is there a line?" Kate asked innocently, startling Allie from behind. She obviously didn't see the old woman.

"Um." Allie hesitated, flustered to be caught with her crone. "Do . . . you . . . not . . . see?

"See . . . ?" Kate looked down the empty hallway. "I see that you are a little pale. Are you okay? You look like you just saw a ghost."

"Uh." Allie looked down the empty hallway feeling like she

was now fully hallucinating her own personal Yoda. Shaking her head to bring herself back to "reality," she found her words. "It's been a trip. I'm just exhausted. You go ahead to the bathroom. I'm good, really."

"Maybe we need another one of those massages to end the trip!" Kate winked as she shut the bathroom door.

Allie stood in the "empty" hallway. *How's this possible? Kurt saw and heard her. Why not Kate?* She leaned into the wall and closed her eyes, willing the crone back. *I know I'm not crazy. These feelings are real.* Her hand flew to her chest, longing to hold the crone's frail fingers. She could still feel the lightning warmth that was embracing her from the inside out, filling a void with something long forgotten . . . Unconditional love.

I've never seen such peace in someone's eyes, Allie heard. *Thank you!*

CHAPTER 30

The Last Leg

They left the restaurant only to hear Babaji, Rajesh, and Sunita embroiled in another heated conversation with the drivers. It was becoming more normal to hear weight in their teacher's voice, strong and firm, as well as the word "asshole."

"Assholes want even more money to continue journey!" Babaji exclaimed to the group. Apparently, now that the sitting ducks were in the middle of the country, and with no other drivers to be found, their "asshole" drivers were taking full advantage of the situation. Rajesh and Sunita had no choice but to cough up the extra rupees.

CULTURAL LESSON #24
Enlightenment doesn't mean being walked all over by others but sometimes standing up firmly for what's needed. And sometimes what's needed is the word "asshole."

> CULTURAL LESSON #25
> A deal isn't a deal until it's complete. The
> constant renegotiation can cost you a pretty
> penny or rupee before you're done.
> Particularly in the middle of a monsoon.

As they piled into the vans yet again, Allie hoped that this would be the last leg of the never-ending journey to Kathmandu. Everyone fell into silence as they moved from the flatlands into the mighty mountains. The curving, mostly paved roads were becoming a challenge for Allie, and she was feeling uncomfortably hungry, nauseated, and weary.

"Rest here." Babaji sat next to her and patted his shoulder.

Really? This was a tender act, and Allie didn't know if it was appropriate for her to remain in close contact with him.

"Is okay. Rest." He patted his shoulder again.

"Thank you," she whispered. She rested her head on his shoulder. Feeling his warmth, she sensed a luminous energy that was subtle, yet strong, comforting, and full of love. She was being fed strength by his very presence, similar to that of the crone. Her stomach settled, and her stressed body began to relax. She fell asleep.

THE CARAVAN CONTINUED TO weave along the steep mountain roads, honking their horns and hugging the tree lines. Evening had settled over the Nepali mountains, and it was beyond time for a meal. Rajesh and Sunita were now in familiar territory and had arranged in advance for a special pizza dinner the Nepali way at a restaurant tucked into the side of the mountain.

Normally Allie would have been mortified to show her fragile state to others, but she was too weak to care. Kurt had to help her up the moss-covered stone stairs that led to the restaurant. It was ironic that she had finally manifested the pizza she'd so craved but now couldn't eat a bite. Instead, she sipped turmeric tea and lay on a couch in the far corner, lulled to a shallow sleep by her companions' distant voices.

"Is two more hours and we will rest at hotel." Babaji touched her shoulder to wake her and helped her back to the van after the group had finished their meal.

As they neared the outskirts of the city, Allie's van slowed to a halt in the middle of the main six-lane highway. The uninvited hitchhikers silently hopped out of the van onto the side of the road to continue on their mysterious journey. They had never said a word to anyone, not a mumble or grunt. Who they were or what they carried with them remains a mystery to this day. If Babaji knew, he kept it to himself.

CULTURAL LESSON #26

Some secrets are not meant to be revealed.
Not all silent parasites are harmful.

The group arrived in Kathmandu just after eleven p.m. It

had been a solid fifteen-hour day of unexpected challenges, and, even though they were simply seated in a van the entire time, they were exhausted. They had not climbed Mount Everest, nor had they swum across the Arun River, but they felt like they had. The stress of the trip was enough to impose weariness on the best of travelers.

Allie reveled in the steam of a hot shower with her mouth firmly closed. She let the warm water soak her hair and run down her unstable, stressed body. By now it was a habit to keep her mouth shut in the shower and to brush her teeth with bottled water so as not to pick up a parasite or yet another unwelcome hitchhiker.

Journal

Just when I tried not to think that it couldn't get worse, it did. The crone was right–we manifested a true Indiana Jones adventure. We shouldn't have survived driving through the flood waters, but we did. It was almost as if the van were lifted up just enough to move us forward to safety. After we got into some cell signal,

Babaji heard the driver call his boss to say that the roads were too dangerous and discouraged others from trying it. The invincible driver had his reckoning as well. We also learned that he DID understand English and the word "asshole."

I'm so happy to have access to my stored luggage again. I'd run out of my supplements and was desperate for clean, dry clothes. In addition to the best pee ever, fresh underwear is at the top of the list as a highlight of the day! Not to mention survival. Ha! Minor detail. Also, instant oatmeal has never been more delicious; familiar and soothing, and, I must say, I am craving familiar.

Crone message:

I don't need to go back to old ways—create new.

Be careful what you focus on; it just might come true.

It's okay to let go of the pain and my "story." But who am I without that?

CHAPTER 31

The Last Day

It was their final day in Nepal. Even as the rains continued to batter much of the country, the sun shined brightly in Kathmandu, and the clear glistening swimming pool beckoned to Allie. How others had the energy to go sightseeing was beyond her. She felt beat up inside-out and outside-in and happily lounged by the pool, staring at the clear, still water in wide-eyed nothingness. She had begun the journey immersed in her own muddy waters, carrying stress, worry, and constant mental chatter. And now her mind was a calm, clear lake. Not a thought could form, nor could an emotion arise. No desire to travel to the past and too exhausted to envision the future. It was interesting to experience—this nothingness. Was this the precious Sunyata?

"How are you, Allieji?' Babaji appeared and sat in the lounge chair next to her.

She sighed. "It's been a journey, Babaji. I feel all torn

up, weak, and I don't even know. I'm embarrassed at how challenging this has been for me."

"Is okay, Allieji. Nothing to be embarrassed for. Is hard for everyone. Doug and Gloria are now quiet. They see something in this, too."

"Babaji, please tell me what happened in your village? What did you do to help me?"

"Is darkness in all of us, Allieji. You fight that in yourself here. Was very strong. Was not sickness, no? But instead finding freedom for you."

"I saw a skull and a swirling blackness that was choking the light, choking me."

"Skull, I don't know, but light, even a smallest light, is stronger than dark. Tiny light fills a dark room. You always remember that."

"And the master teacher, he . . ."

"Master, ha, yes. Master has only power that you give him. He is not nice person, but he helps others in his way. He is threatened by your light, maybe, but cannot harm you."

"The choke, Babaji . . ."

"The choke." He closed his eyes and paused. "Yes. Fear can choke. Fear can quiet your voice." He gazed knowingly into her eyes. "Your fear is very strong . . . Many levels of fear . . . You are holding on really strong, but trying to let go. It was a great battle! You want to purify, so you learn to empty. Sunyata. Once empty, then what? You always have a choice."

288 | Denise Mihalik

Clutching her hands, he continued. "You have right to **live**. Remember, Allieji, you grieve, but you don't BE grief. You experience grief but still must love. You remember memories, but you don't grip memories." He took a long breath. "You have more to do. Much more, and you have right to live a happy life. Full life. Your loved ones, yes, they appear to suffer. Die." Allie felt an all-too-familiar pain of shifting shards in her heart. "But they are part of you, always. And you are here, now. You have breath and they live IN you." He smiled as if he could see Allie's future. The moving shards fell away. "You have right to smile, love, and be happy." Allie's eyes filled with tears as he continued, radiant in his smile. "Magic. Life is magic. Breath is miracle. We are surrounded by magic and miracles every day." A crow cawed and flapped its wings. They both watched it land in a nearby tree.

He continued, "Doug may yell. Master may try to choke. But yelling is not focus. Sunyata is focus. Choke is not focus. Love is focus. The Light is focus. Remember, little light makes dark room shine. Dark will try to put it out, but it cannot. Ever. Sing Gayatri, sing OM, sing and remember Light." Babaji touched two fingers to Allie's forehead. "Breathe, Allieji. Close your eyes. See. You are strong. You are loved."

Allie felt an electricity travel through her, as if she had chugged a power drink. Her toes and fingers tingled, and she felt a warm circulation of energy through every cell of her being.

Babaji removed his fingers and smiled his wide smile.

"We are okay. We survive great adventure! More Indiana Jones than we want!"

"I'll say."

"Now, I will get you food. I order you what?" Her mouth watered for vegetable Lo Mein and a cold ginger ale. Babaji rushed off to the restaurant to place the order.

Allie sat back in her lounge chair and closed her eyes. Babaji's talk merged with the crone's wise words to help her find some peace with her experience. *Maybe I didn't get hit with black magic after all. Maybe it really was my own doubts and fears that rose within me. Whatever it was, it kicked my ass.* She couldn't imagine anything like that happening at home. Or could she? *Was my grief and pain so suppressed that it almost destroyed me?*

Allie closed her eyes and thought of their first day at the Pashupatinath temple city. She was struck by the balance of the wailing grief of the cremation ceremony, where they sat and observed death, and the loving sharing of their welcome ceremony, where they celebrated life. Her group so innocently looked forward to their journey.

"What does your heart desire?" Allie was with her crone again, but this time they were both formless. "You can hold onto your experiences and your memories, or you can write a new story. One that is informed by your experiences. Not controlled by them."

They were standing on a peak overlooking the vast unending evening sky that shimmered with stars, a perfect balance of never-ending darkness with radiant light. "What does your heart desire? You long for love. Feel it. Love is in you now and always with you. It is unending and exists beyond anything you have experienced so far." The crone took her formless hand. "Step with me now into this luminous void."

They flew.

Allie awoke with a start. She must have fallen asleep poolside. There were two children taking swimming lessons in the glimmering, refreshing pool. Holding on to their floaty, they laughed and splashed as their instructor encouraged them to kick their legs to move forward. They were so alive and in the moment that Allie was inspired to jump into the fresh, clear water and splash alongside them.

CHAPTER 32

The Airport

It was time to leave Nepal. Allie anticipated the next two days of travel while moving through the motions of packing. Her depleted snack bag had served its purpose, and with minimal appetite, she shockingly filled the extra space with her new clothing rather than stocking up on more food. Her morning was blessed with the news that Kurt shared a similar flight time with Kate and her, so they traveled together to the airport.

"See you on the other side of the gate!" Allie yelled to her friends as they parted ways. They couldn't lose each other in the small airport and trusted they'd be able to say goodbye later.

Allie lugged her two suitcases up to the counter of the unfamiliar airline that would take her to Switzerland for the first leg of the trip.

"You have an extra bag, and it's over-weight," the young male attendant told her in good English.

"I know." Allie was prepared to pay the extra one hundred dollar penalty.

"Two hundred dollars for the bag," he said.

"Two hundred?" she gasped. By now, she knew the art of the deal but didn't expect a negotiation at the ticket counter. Playing the game, she stated, "No, that's too much. I won't pay two hundred."

"I'm sorry, ma'am, it is two hundred dollars," he repeated.

Just then, she felt a brush on her jacket. An old, tiny, male baggage attendant whispered broken English in her ear, "You pay me, I take care."

"Who are *you*?" She was startled.

"I help. Pay me extra, I take care." Looking official enough in a simple uniform, he held out his hand. The other attendant didn't bat an eye.

Flustered, Allie sputtered to the young man behind the counter, "Why's he asking for money?"

"It is okay."

"You pay me." The tiny man's whisper warmed Allie's left ear. "I take care." She could smell his stale breath.

She pushed away and searched for Kurt. This style of negotiation worried her, and she was afraid that, if she didn't do the right thing, her luggage would get lost or disappear.

Too tired to mince words, she declared. "This is ridiculous. I want to see a manager."

"Okay, your bag will cost one hundred dollars."

"You pay me, I take care."

She was an unwilling participant in this improvisational trio, awkwardly staged, disjointed, and negotiable. "What if I don't pay him?" Allie referred to the baggage beggar, "Will my bags still arrive?"

"They will ma'am. Pay me, and I will give you a receipt and get a manager," said the man behind the counter.

"You pay me," repeated the tiny man. His spit showered her.

"Please," she lost her temper on the persistent man. "Give me space!" He backed away and hovered in the far corner. *Lord, make this easy. Make something easy.*

"I assure you, ma'am, I will get you a manager. Your bag will cost one hundred dollars."

"I'll pay one hundred dollars but will need written proof that my bags will get onto the flight and land in New Jersey." She felt like Gloria needing written proof but, found clear words and paid with her credit card, fully expecting the number to get stolen. She searched for the tiny man, who had disappeared into thin air. He must have been an anti-crone apparition intended to test her strength and patience.

As she waited for the receipt, a content and calm Kate passed by. "How's it going?"

"Don't ask. How about I meet you in the waiting area?"

"Sure. You'll be all right?"

"Yes. If I'm not there for boarding though, please come look for me!"

"Gotcha. I won't board without you!"

Allie stood in her new-found power and held her ground for over thirty minutes.

"Here is your receipt," said a uniformed man who finally approached her, "I assure you, ma'am, your baggage will arrive in Newark, New Jersey, USA."

Surprised and grateful that she actually held the paper in her hand, she geared up for a scrutinous security check but thankfully passed through unscathed and greeted her friends in the waiting area.

"Kurt, I could have used your bravado. They gave me a hard time about my extra bag. But I stood up for myself quite well!"

"Funny, they didn't care about mine, and, get this . . . they saw my height and upgraded me to first class," Kurt chirped in surprised delight, almost clicking his heels.

"Well, aren't you the lucky one! My height just made them try to charge me double. It's just not fair! I'll bet that if you had been with me, they wouldn't have given me a problem."

"Sorry to say, but that's probably true." He paused and heard his flight announced. "Well, friends, this is the end of our journey, and it's, indeed, been quite an adventure!"

Allie smiled, trying to cover her tears. "I can't thank you enough. Really, I owe you my life."

"We supported each other on this trip. And I dare say, we all have a lot to process."

Allie was tempted to share her crone experiences with the two of them but decided to wait until later. She needed time.

"Soul brother, have a safe trip back. I'll see you again sometime." Allie stood on her tippy toes and gave Kurt a huge hug.

"Back at you, sister-Indiana-Jones-adventurer. Oh . . . Big news. I'm going to donate my hat. This was enough adventure for a lifetime. May it bring someone else courage and safety." He left it on one of the seats and without looking back, got in line to board his flight.

CULTURAL LESSON #27
Refer to Cultural Lesson #22:
You still have too much stuff.

CULTURAL LESSON #28
Be firm and confident in negotiations,
particularly if you are a woman traveling alone.
Use your height to your advantage—you just
might get an upgrade, particularly if you are a
large male wearing a high-crowned fedora.

CHAPTER 33

Home

Thirty-five hours later, including a long, smooth, and calm layover in Switzerland, Allie and Kate landed in Newark, New Jersey.

"Let's be extra good to ourselves as we step back into this time zone. Maybe a massage or two?" Kate smiled and glanced toward the baggage carousel, silently pleading with it to spit out their luggage.

"What choice do we have, really? We need a two week vacation to recover. But I think I'll pass on the massages for now." Allie spotted her suitcases and rushed to grab them. "I guess this is it. May the holy grail of Sunyata bless us as we step back into the rush of life. Not to mention Jersey traffic."

"Amen!"

After a forty-minute Uber ride, Allie arrived home to a stocked refrigerator and a pizza, a generous surprise from her aunt, who was thrilled to have Allie back on this side of the world. She had lost ten pounds from her already thin frame, and, once her body relaxed into the comfort of her own bed, she slept for more than twenty-four hours.

The pilgrims all processed their journey in different ways. The older couple, John and Jane, knew this was their first and last trip to Nepal. It had taken a toll on their strength, and they needed a long rest. Doug and Gloria were temporarily humbled; they had actually gained an ounce of gratitude for life itself. Pearl was unfazed and jumped immediately back into her full schedule. Kate fell ill with pneumonia but recovered after a month. Kurt returned to his teaching, gentler and filled with a renewed appreciation for life. Marianna hugged her mother and kept the challenges of her experience secret.

Allie had no choice but to take the next week off as she tried to restore her strength. After days of sleep, hot baths, and comfort food, she was still not ready to step into her normal routine. Instead, she spent time on her back deck, sitting in silent reflection. Sunyata. The neighborhood was quiet. The familiar maple extended its full branches over the deck, providing a comfortable shade during the early September heat. The birds welcomed the fresh seed at the feeder, and the squirrels puttered around the yard as if Allie had never left. The traffic on the major highway two blocks away hummed through the trees. Allie imagined the constant noise as ocean waves, until the fumes pervaded the air. Was this any different from Kathmandu? Perhaps not.

Life around her continued to move forward just like the raging flood waters. Like the van, she could resist and force against the push of life trying to drown her. Or she could go with the flow and find unique ways to ride the sea of life. As she slowly stepped back into her routine, Allie now knew that she had choices. Perhaps amidst the floods and rapids, she could find ways to float in clear reflection and rise above the choking "story" of life, honoring the wisdom of Sunyata and the touch of unconditional love.

EVEN THOUGH A FULL week had passed, Allie's mind was still unable to form conversations or thoughts. She had been hit hard and was enjoying the reprieve from the mental characters, who for years had dominated her mind. Contentment had evaded her all her life . . . until now. She sat, empty and content, doing nothing—according to society's standards. And she noticed that this "nothing" was very much "something."

Within this "something" a natural symphony surrounded her . . . The trees rustled in the light breeze, and the flutter of the birds' wings signaled their arrival at the feeder. A butterfly glided toward the blooming butterfly bush, silent and stunning. A bumble bee buzzed past in search of pollen. She heard it before she saw it. The squirrels' claws drummed as they scuttered around the tree trunk. Nature's symphony called her home.

She had not noticed these details four weeks ago but, today, this was all that was. Pure. Transporting. Her gaze softened, and she felt her heart beat . . . or was it her heart? She closed her eyes and easily began to drift into a timeless, liminal space. A subtle pulsing resonated from a distance, heightening the sounds around her. It was indeed a heartbeat, but it wasn't hers. Her body was heavy on her chair, but at the same time she felt translucent, like a hologram. Around her, or maybe within her, she became this heartbeat and the orchestra of sounds simplified into one all-pervasive, endless "whoosh." All was still but for the womb of this sound. And yet it wasn't a sound. It was nowhere and it was everywhere. It was safe, so safe, and resonated a feeling of love beyond anything she'd ever experienced. She reveled in the comfort of it. It was the "Om." The unstruck sound. She knew it with every bit of her being. It was timeless and then . . . too short.

Pop! She was back. *Wait, I need to get back there! I was IN the Om. Or I* **was** *the Om. Or . . . Wow. I think I was in the womb of the universe!* Allie kept her eyes closed, and her hologram self could feel every cell of her Being vibrate. She tingled with lightness and excitement. *And it's right here, just across some veil. I have to go back. Please take me back!* Allie took a long, focused breath. *Please.* She listened to the sounds around her and tried to listen beyond them. She waited to hear the "whoosh." The birds sang, and the squirrels bounced around the yard. The traffic continued to flow. *Bring it back.* She breathed slowly and did all that she knew to do, or not-do, and yet, she couldn't get back there . . . it was gone. Or was it?

Abruptly, she felt something cool, thin, and hard in her

hand. She opened her fingers to see that she now held a key. It was a large, rusty old skeleton key.

"Oh, my God, Dad, the key!" She looked at the very real key in disbelief.

Glancing around the yard, she thought she might see the crone, but even more so, hoped beyond hope to see her dad. No one. Allie couldn't begin to understand how the old key appeared in her hand. *A real key?* She laughed out loud. *What's a little magic at this point? The crone, then Om, and now the key. I'm either losing my mind or gaining a totally different perspective on reality—and how to live my life.*

Allie closed her eyes and held the key to her heart. *Thank you.*

"I've never seen such peace in someone's eyes," Allie felt the crone's sweet voice from the ether and heard, *"Om Bhur Bhuvah Swaha . . ."*

The timeless melody ran through Allie's being like ancient medicine, and she felt stronger and more alive than she had since she was a young, dreaming child. She was the phoenix rising from the ashes. This moment of wholeness was her greatest gift. The gift of living. The gift of unconditional love. She relaxed into a long, peaceful nap.

Upon waking, she suddenly yearned to know the translation of the Gayatri mantra and dared to start up her laptop. A quick search revealed:

One translation is Ga—"to sing" Yatri—"protection."

The essence is beyond translation but represents
a connection to Divine Light.
Through sincere repetition, the vibrations
shift consciousness.

"*Protection*" . . . *I was certainly protected during this trip, even in the darkest of times.* Allie stopped there. She didn't want to engage her mind any more than that.

Five hundred eighty emails called her attention just as she started to closed her laptop. *Should I? Can I do a quick scan?* Holding her new skeleton key as her life raft, she stepped as lightly as she could into the flood of messages.

One subject line caught her eye. Pilgrimage to India with Mukunda! She read the description and was immediately tempted to go. *How can I want to travel east again? Am I out of my mind?*

Just then her cell phone rang. It was her friend Mukunda.

"Hey Allie," the familiar voice greeted her. Hearing his warm, friendly baritone made her smile. "We just announced the itinerary for our January pilgrimage. Please, please, please join us? You spoke about wanting to go."

"Talk about synchronicity! I just saw your email." She took a full breath and exhaled steady and long. "I don't know. I just got back from Nepal. I'm exhausted. I almost died. Although my spirit is willing, I'm not sure my body can handle going halfway across the world again so soon."

"You almost died?"

Allie relayed a small part of the story. She didn't mention the crone. Not yet.

Mukunda was sympathetic. "From what you just told me, I think your innocent goodness was taken for granted on that trip. I promise you, if you come, you'll be respected and well-cared for. You have a full four months to gain your strength. That should be plenty of time. We're going to an area where local legend says that Jesus passed through during his 'lost years' and learned the Gayatri Mantra at a Ghat in Puri."

Jesus and the Gayatri?

"There'll be no monsoons," he continued his sales pitch, "and the weather will be perfect. It always is at this time. You'll be well cared for. You'll be safe," he repeated.

Allie paused for a moment as she rolled the key around her palm. Her mind whispered, *no way.* Her body pleaded, *please give me rest,* but her heart screamed a resounding, *YES!!* The OM rose within her and the Gayatri called out to her.

"Am I crazy to consider this?" She trusted Mukunda implicitly.

"You just might be . . . ," he laughed.

"You're sure it's NOT going to be an Indiana Jones adventure? Will it be restful and nourishing?"

"I'm not sure about restful, but it'll definitely be nourishing! You'll be well cared for, I promise."

"Okay . . . okay." *I'm an adventurer now, right?* "Sign me up." *Did I just say that?*

A crow landed in the maple and let out a loud "caw." The

squirrels dashed around the tree trunk, and the cardinals and sparrows sang at the feeder. A soft breeze kicked up, rustling the leaves. Allie's senses absorbed the moment as if it were her last. Drinking in the colors and sounds of her ordinary home in the familiar neighborhood, she was truly seeing it for the first time.

You can sense me as the water, the wind, the birdsong, the rush of the current. I am within and through you.

Allie took a deep breath inside the living OM. Amid the sounds, a silent peace rose within her. *My Journey to Sunyata is only beginning.*

Acknowledgments

As a child, I spent summers at the Jersey shore wandering along the water's edge at sunset and belting *The Sound of Music* to my first audience, the ocean. By no means a prodigy, I began voice lessons in 7th grade and quickly learned that progress required strict discipline and regular practice. In the process, I brought to life many characters from works others had written.

Writing *Journey* introduced me to a more refined discipline, one that wrestled with inner resistance, vulnerability, and the sweat and tears of creation. My own characters were calling out to be voiced, and I could no longer hide behind someone else's expression.

Journey is based on a true story. Even so, the characters of Babaji and the Crone rose out of the ether to share wisdom and offer answers when there were none. They've brought me healing and closure in unexpected and unanticipated ways, and for that, I bow down to their loving messages. Babaji and the Crone reminded me that I am worth it, and so are you.

I am eternally grateful to my team of friends, family, teachers, and mentors who have supported both the birth of *Journey* and also the journey of my own personal healing.

My deepest gratitude to:

My friend and writing mentor, Melodie Somers, who literally pulled *Journey's* details out of me, often with me kicking and screaming in resistance. With her encouragement, my writing transformed from memoir to novel, fear to honesty, and vague to vulnerable.

My editor, Betsy Robinson, who has been my life raft on this transformative journey. Her endless patience, expertise, and guidance kept me grounded, encouraged, and empowered. Her support rooted *Journey* so it could blossom.

Billy, who is not only the love of my life, my ice dancing partner, and best critic, but also my maddening grammar snob, who read *Journey* more times than he wanted to. He was also my lifeline from the States during my darkest hour in Nepal, but I chose not to write about that. Some details remain tucked away.

My friends, June, Pam, Auntie, Stephanie, Matt, and Mark, who lovingly read my first, second, third, and/or fourth drafts. It takes a true friend to survive the early drafts of a debut novel.

My many teachers, past and present whose divine wisdom continues to inform my path.

Adam Vaccarelli, sound engineer extraordinaire. His gentle guidance drew out the soundtrack of this novel and the audio book.

Becky Neiman's detailed audio book post-production genius.

Shakti from Bodhisattva Trading Company, who matched me with the magical antique singing bowl that drew out the melody associated with the Crone and inspired *Light of Compassion*, the soundtrack to *Journey*.

My amazing cover artist and book designer, Christine Horner who is truly the book cover whisperer.

And last, Nepal. The beauty, the challenges, and the healing. You stole my breath. But you also gave me back my breath.

About the Author

DENISE MIHALIK is an educator and performer whose life work has been to study the effects of vibration on the body, mind, and spirit. She began on the opera stage, moved to the yoga mat, into the world of singing bowls, and now onto the page with her debut novel. Her recently released album, *Light of Compassion*, accompanies the novel and is intended to invite listeners and readers into a moment of quiet reflection. Mihalik is the founder of Sound Awakenings and lives at the Jersey shore.

This book is based on a true story.

What do you think was fiction?

What do you think was real?

What do you hope was real?

—

Which cultural lesson(s) surprised you the most?

Which ones did you relate to?

—

Is there a scene that has stuck with you?

If yes, why?

—

Did you reread any passages?

If so, which ones and why?

—

Have you ever experienced a spiritual guide of your own?

What was that like?

How old were you when you had the experience?

Did it happen more than once?

—

Sunyata is a term used in this book.

What do you think it is?

Do you feel you've experienced Sunyata?

—

Do you take time each day to notice your breath?

Did any part of this story make you more aware of
your breath?

—

We all have a story we hold onto, like Allie.

What part of your story would you like to release,
but don't?

—

**What practices help you rise above the flood waters in
your life?**

—

Did this book encourage or inspire you?

If yes, how so?

—

**Are there lingering questions from the book you're still
thinking about?**

—

If you could ask the author anything, what would it be?

—

ALLIE'S POST-PILGRIMAGE BREATH PRACTICE

Sit comfortably. Feel your feet on the floor and support your back with pillows if needed. (This practice can also be done lying down.)

Eyes soft and unfocused or gently closed. Hands resting comfortably.

1. **Observation:**

   Observe the breath as it is without adjustment or judgment.

   Notice the quality of the breath:
   > Is it fast or slow?
   > Long or short?
   > Free or stressed?
   > Gripped or flowing?
   > Deep or shallow?

   Observe the mind-stuff:
   > Is it impatient?
   > Stressed?
   > Exhausted?
   > Inspired?
   > Bored?
   > Craving distraction?

Relax obvious tensions. Smile at rattling thoughts.

Repeat silently 5-20 times:

> Breathing in, I am calm.
> Breathing out, I am steady.

Magical Moment:

Breath informs and supports our life. We can choose breath awareness or we can ignore it and let it remain in the background. Oftentimes, when we begin a breath practice, the mind quickly becomes bored, leading us anywhere but with our breath. When the mind draws you away, simply come back to the feel of your breath and the words "calm" and "steady."

2. **Focus:**

Begin to deepen the breath:

> Slow, comfortable inhales
> Long, steady exhales
> Focus your awareness on this moment, that is unique only to you.

Repeat silently 5-20 times:

> Breathing in deeply, I am calm
> Breathing out deeply, I am steady
> Breathing in, allow the past to fall away
> Breathing out, allow the anticipation of the future to fade away.

Inhale presence

Exhale presence

Magical Moment:

Notice where the inhale shifts to the exhale and where the exhale shifts to the inhale. This is a magical space. In this fleeting transition, there is no thought. Listen into this space for a blessed moment of sunyata.

3. **Equalization:**

When the breath feels steady, begin to equalize the breath.

Inhale for a slow, personal count of 4

Exhale for a slow, personal count of 4

With each inhale, receive peace, and with each exhale shed stress

Inhale Peace

Exhale Stress

Inhale This moment

Exhale Deepen into this moment

Repeat for several minutes

Magical Moment:

Through repetition, the body is given the opportunity to shift from held stress to rejuvenating rest. In this resting space, the mind refreshes and sunyata blesses.

4. **Gratitude:**

After some time, return to your natural rhythm. Observe.

Offer gratitude.